BORROWING BLUE

A MADE MARIAN NOVEL

LUCY LENNOX

KEEP IN TOUCH WITH LUCY!

Join Lucy's Lair
Get Lucy's New Release Alerts
Like Lucy on Facebook
Follow Lucy on BookBub
Follow Lucy on Amazon
Follow Lucy on Instagram
Follow Lucy on Pinterest

Other books by Lucy:
Made Marian Series
Forever Wilde Series
Aster Valley Series
Twist of Fate Series with Sloane Kennedy
After Oscar Series with Molly Maddox
Licking Thicket Series with May Archer
Virgin Flyer
Say You'll Be Nine

Visit Lucy's website at www.LucyLennox.com for a comprehensive list of titles, audio samples, freebies, suggested reading order, and more!

My first book is dedicated to the baby sister who followed me, surpassed me and then took the lead and showed me the way. She inspires me, educates me, humors me, and trades ridiculous cat photos with me. Thank you, Bear. For all of it.

ABOUT BORROWING BLUE

Blue: *When my ex walks into the resort bar with his new husband on his arm, I want nothing more than to prove to him that I've moved on. Thankfully, the sexy stranger sitting next to me is more than willing to share a few kisses in the name of revenge. It gets even better when those scorching kisses turn into a night of fiery passion. The only problem? Turns out the stranger's brother is marrying my sister later this week.*

Tristan: *I have one rule: no messing with the guests at my vineyard resort. Of course the one exception I make turns out to be my future brother-in-law. Now we're stuck together for a week of wedding activities, and there's no avoiding the heat burning between us. So fine, we make a deal: one week. One week to enjoy each other's bodies and get it out of our system. Once the bride and groom say I do and we become family, it'll all be over between us. Right?*

1
———

BLUE

I didn't sit down at that bar intending to tell a perfect stranger my sorry-ass breakup story, and I sure as hell didn't expect to tongue-fuck said stranger before the night was over. But when my ex came into the bar all lovey-dovey with a damned twink, I couldn't help it. Three beers already sloshed in my empty stomach and I was feeling maudlin. There Jeremy sat, holding hands and staring moon-eyed at a young man who can only be described as a Gap model. One of those exotic red-haired ones with freckles that demanded to be high-lighted in black-and-white photography. Jeremy himself was as hand-some as ever and had a definite sparkle in his eye for the kid who was practically sitting on his lap. Fuck it. Whatever.

I had just arrived at the Alexander Vineyard for my sister's wedding. A full week of activities that seemed hell-bent on torturing my still-tender heart with romancey shit. After getting my room key, I had made a beeline to the bar to get a buzz on. It was no secret Jeremy would be there since he had been family friends of ours for years even before we started dating. I hadn't been prepared for him to bring a plus-one though, and when I saw them enter the bar two hours later, I was caught off guard.

Shortly after finishing my first beer, a man sat next to me and ordered a glass of wine. Caught up in my own pity party, I didn't notice him at first. But when I heard him call the bartender by name, I was intrigued. Who knows a bartender by his first name out here in the middle of the California wine country where the only thing for miles is the winery and attached lodge?

The man next to me was stunning. Probably in his early thirties like I was, maybe a few years older. He had dark hair and a dark shadow of a beard. He had almond-shaped eyes that were a striking light gray, contrasting against his dark coloring in a way that made him look otherworldly. My heart skipped a beat when he turned those eyes on me and raised an eyebrow.

When he opened his mouth to speak, a husky tone came out. "Enjoying yourself?" he asked.

It was so strange to have those light gray laser beams pointed at me that I almost, for a brief moment, turned to see if he could be talking to someone behind me.

"Not really," I answered, surprising myself with rude honesty.

The man barked out a laugh and the smoky sound surrounded me, plucking at all my tender spots and leaving them vibrating with a feeling I couldn't quite describe. I looked at my beer glass as if maybe it contained a stimulant instead of the local IPA I'd ordered.

"If you keep frowning like that, beer is going to start dribbling out of your mouth. Want to talk about it?" the stranger asked in a low voice. He looked a little bit like Stuart Reardon, an English fitness model I knew from work.

I sighed. "I just spotted my ex in the parking lot, so I came in here to drown my sorrows. Typical, pathetic, crying-into-my-beer scenario."

"Ah. I see. Sorry, man. That sucks."

"Yes, well, I'm mostly over it, but I just wish we didn't have to be under the same roof."

"That makes sense. I've been divorced for a few years but any time I run into my ex-wife around my family, I feel everyone's eyes on us. Even when you're over it, there are still plenty of shared memories that will always have a hold on you. How long were you together?"

"Three years. Been apart for six months now. I think it'll be fine, but who knows, really? We haven't seen each other since the breakup." I shrugged. "The stupid, immature side of me wishes I'd brought someone so I didn't feel so lame. I've dated a little but haven't met anyone I liked enough to bring around family." *And now I'm even more depressed because the sexy man at the bar is straight. It figures.*

"You wish you could make her squirm a little then? See what she's been missing?" he said.

"He's a he, not a she. And I don't know about squirming. I guess maybe a little. But it's more I want him to know I'm okay without him. That I'm not pining away and crying in my soup, you know? I get it. My family worries about me being alone. They want me to be happy. But it's not like I can just produce a life partner out of thin air to make them feel better. I need to get through this week and then I'll be out of the country for a while with a new job." I had been given a huge promotion at work that necessitated me moving to London for a few years. My flight was scheduled to leave San Francisco the following Monday.

"I know exactly what you mean. After Sheila and I divorced, my family looked at me for a long time with those pity eyes. Can't fucking stand that. My brother is the worst. He still keeps trying to set me up on dates. As if I won't be happy or complete until I find someone like he has."

I widened my eyes at him. "Exactly. God, your brother and my sister sound like the same person."

He laughed that smoky laugh. "And my mother still actually tries to get me to reconcile with my ex-wife. As if that would ever happen. No matter how many times I explain to her things were never that great with Sheila to begin with, my mom just tsks and tells me there's no such thing as a perfect woman. At this point, I really think she'd be happy to see me settle down with anyone. Just so she can stop thinking about it."

We smiled at each other in understanding.

The stranger reached out a hand to shake mine. "I'm Tristan."

"Blue. It's nice to meet you, Tristan," I said, shaking his hand. At the touch of his rough palm against mine, I felt that crazy fictional zing that people describe in novels. Was that shit for real? Nope, I'd probably been reading too much lately. Clearly it didn't work since it happened to me with a straight guy.

"Blue? That's an interesting name. Mind me asking how you came by it?" Tristan asked.

"Well, my name is Bartholomew but my oldest brother couldn't pronounce it properly when he was little. He ended up calling me Blue. It stuck."

"I like it. This sounds crazy, but it seems to fit you. Maybe it's your eyes," he said, studying my face. He shook his head and smiled. "Anyway, it's nice to meet you, Blue. Can I get you another beer?"

"Sure. I should probably eat something though. I came straight here from a crazy day at work in the city and haven't eaten yet," I said.

Tristan turned to the bartender. "Hey, Frank, would you get my friend here another beer and order us a couple of burgers with some of those homemade potato chips I like? Thanks," he said before turning his attention back to me.

"You work in San Francisco?" he asked.

"Yes, I'm in charge of graphic design for some fitness magazines."

"That sounds interesting. Do you like it?" he asked, looking interested in what I had to say.

"It's okay. I've been feeling a little jaded about it lately, so my boss gave me a huge promotion. I move to London in a week. Not sure if it will get my creative juices flowing again, but I appreciate the fresh start." Man, that sounded depressing. I tried to mitigate it with a smile, but it didn't seem to work.

Tristan's eyebrows came together in apparent interest. "What usually gets your creative juices flowing?"

I knew the answer immediately but I hadn't spoken the words out loud in years. Why not tell this guy? He was a stranger in a bar for god's sake.

"Sculpture," I said. One word. One word that might as well have been "heart."

Tristan's eyes turned warm and the sides of his lips began to turn up. "Tell me more. What kind of sculpture?"

"Metal mostly. But I like all of it. Wood carving, glassblowing, stone chiseling. I'd probably try ice sculpture if I wasn't deathly afraid of chainsaws."

"Are you able to sculpt in the city?" he asked.

"Not really. I sculpted in high school and college but gave it up after Jeremy and I got together. I've been thinking about picking it back up and trying again. Not sure there will be space enough when I move to London though," I confessed.

"Why did you give it up?"

I blew out a breath. "I listened to discouraging words from others. Unfortunately, I was young enough to take them to heart. It's only been in recent weeks that I've looked at the situation through an adult lens. Why in the hell did I let anyone discourage me from expressing a passion?" I shook my head in frustration at the kid I had been ten years earlier.

"We all do that at some point, don't we?" Tristan supplied, sounding as if he had specific knowledge. I wanted to ask him what passion he had that someone had tried to snuff out in him. Before I had a chance to get the words out, though, I saw Jeremy enter the bar with the twink on his arm.

Jeremy smiled and leaned over to kiss the young man on the mouth. After the kiss, the kid reached up to wipe Jeremy's lips, and that was when I noticed the wedding ring on his finger. My entire body went cold.

2

———

TRISTAN

I knew something was wrong. Even though we weren't touching, I felt Blue's body go rigid. He was looking past my shoulder, so without thinking, I turned to see what it was.

Two men walked into the bar, kissing and flirting. As they took a seat at a nearby table, they seemed to have eyes only for each other.

"You know those guys?" I asked. I almost used the word "men," but for some reason that would imply they both were old enough to be considered men. The redhead was young and good looking while the other looked more my age and could pass for the kid's soccer coach. I hoped they weren't soccer coach and student, though, because their body language oozed sexual attraction to each other.

"The one who is old enough to vote is my ex, Jeremy. The kid is…" He trailed off.

"The kid is a fucking gorgeous redhead like you are. That's gotta make you feel good." I laughed. "He's obviously trying to replace you."

Blue blushed at my words, and I realized I'd called him gorgeous. Well, he was. I mean, anyone could see he was an attractive human being. Still, best to change the subject before I came up with a word to describe how blue his eyes were.

"Are they married? That kid has a ring on," I asked distractedly.

"Don't know," Blue breathed. "Looks like it."

He looked like he'd been sucker-punched. I tried to imagine how I would feel seeing Sheila remarried without knowing about it ahead of time. It wouldn't be easy. No matter what, it would hurt even if only a little bit. I reached out and squeezed his shoulder.

"I'm sorry, Blue," I said.

"Thanks." He took another sip of his beer. Frank came with our dinner, but I could tell it was going to be a struggle to get Blue to eat anything. I put my hand on the back of his barstool and leaned closer to him.

"You need to eat something. At least try the potato chips. They're my favorite. If you get some food in your stomach, I'll help you get shitfaced after."

He laughed. "It's a deal."

We ate, and I tried to make Blue laugh as much as I could. I told him about finding out that my grandmother was gay when she stood up in the middle of Thanksgiving dinner and declared herself as "queer as a two-dollar bill" and told us she was "banging Irene like a teenager." By the time I was finished telling him about their raunchy bachelorette party that started at a sex-toy store and ended at a club called Cockblock, he was rolling with laughter. Tears streamed down my face when I finished a detailed description of Granny and Irene dirty dancing.

"The best part was when Irene kept yelling at Granny to go easy on her bad hip." I laughed so hard my voice went up a few octaves. I couldn't help it. The more Blue laughed, the more he set me off.

"My brother is still in denial. He calls Irene 'Granny's roommate.' So every time I get a chance, I describe dirty-granny-lesbian scenes to him. You should see him lose his homophobic shit." I laughed again.

Blue looked into my eyes, his own shone with mirth. "Poor guy can't be happy Granny's eating out more often?" He snorted when I gagged.

After his giggles died down, he spoke again. "Thanks, Tristan, for making me laugh tonight."

Something about the man made me want to take him away from the feelings he had about his ex. No one deserved to feel inadequate, and seeing your ex walk in married to a young model would never be easy for anyone.

After we finished eating, Blue turned to face me. "Did I eat enough to qualify for your offer to get shitfaced?" He smirked.

"Abso-fucking-lutely." I laughed. "Frank?" I called to the bartender. I asked him to pour us a couple of lemon drops. We downed the shots together, and I continued my parade of stupid stories.

"When my brother went to the prom, my mom begged him to escort our cousin Sarah. She was an introvert and really unpopular. My brother was very popular, so my mom thought him escorting her would be like our very own family Cinderella story. My brother is a selfish ass, so he refused. He started off telling Mom that it was inappropriate since it was practically a requirement to bang your prom date. After my mother understandably freaked, she still insisted. He ended up agreeing. Rather, he told Mom he would, but then he convinced Sarah to lie to our families and act like they were going together when really they weren't."

I gestured to Frank for another round of shots. "I was so pissed at my brother that I convinced Sarah to go in on a revenge plan with me. We snuck her into my brother's room after he passed out in bed. She stripped down to a strapless bikini bathing suit and wrapped a sheet around herself so it looked like she was naked underneath. Then we messed up her hair and smeared her lipstick over her face and the sheet. At just the right time that morning, she stumbled out of my brother's bedroom right in front of my parents. Oh my god, I thought my mom was going to have a heart attack."

Blue snorted. "You're kidding me."

"Nope. My mother pounced on my brother like a rabid dog, waking him from what had to have been a godawful hangover. He was so confused that we had him convinced he had fucked his own cousin. Priceless." I wiped the tears from my cheeks as I encouraged Blue to take the next shot with me.

After our next round of shots, our laughing began to sound a little more like tipsy giggling.

We heard another pair laughing and turned to look for its source. There were probably twenty people in the bar, but the laughing was coming from the direction of Blue's ex. Sure enough, those two were guffawing over something and drawing attention to themselves. In addition to the noise, they were hanging all over each other. Even though he quickly looked away, I could tell it made Blue uncomfortable.

"You know," I began, "we should come up with a revenge plan for you." Maybe it was the alcohol speaking, but it sounded even better when I said it out loud.

"Right? That's what I was thinking. Lay it on me. Ideas?" Blue leaned an elbow on the bar and rested his chin on his hand, facing me. He had a sneaky grin on his face that was magnetic.

"I could pretend to be your boyfriend," I suggested, surprising myself with the idea. *Where the hell had that come from?*

Blue scoffed. "Yeah, right."

"What? What do you mean? Why not?" I asked. "Am I not good enough for you?" I feigned righteous indignation with a fluttering hand to my chest.

He smiled. "Don't get me wrong, Tristan. You're smoking hot. But you seem to have forgotten you're straight. Not sure you could convince people you're gay, let alone into *me*."

"Dude, I can be gay. I can be SO gay," I explained.

"No." He laughed. "You SO can't. It's okay, sweetie. Cocksucking isn't for everyone. Don't feel bad."

I couldn't help but laugh at that. "Okay, so maybe I'd have to start with something a little lighter than cocksucking, but that doesn't mean I can't be convincing as your boyfriend. It's not like I'm a virgin."

Blue looked unconvinced, cocking an eyebrow in my direction as if to say, *Aren't you, though?*

All I could think about was how I wanted to find a way to wipe that smug smirk off his face and prove him wrong.

3

———

BLUE

Before I could tease him further, Tristan reached his hand out to grab the back of my neck and yank my face toward his. His mouth came down on mine in a possessive crush of a kiss. All lips and tongue and teeth. It was aggressive, erotic, and carnal. It was hot as mother-fucking shit.

I should probably stop this. This isn't right. Is it? We're kinda drunk. This isn't rational.

My brain didn't stand a chance because my mouth was all in. Whatever the hell was happening here in this bar with this stranger, it didn't matter. All that mattered was the taste of lemon drop shots on his tongue, the feel of his large callused palm gripping the back of my neck. Tristan's earthy smell of soil and... was that grapes?

His mouth was like a snake charmer, circling and humming in a way that made you sit there, transfixed. Like you were caught under a spell and would do anything the magician commanded.

My fingers grasped at the shirt on his chest and balled up the fabric in an attempt to give me something, anything, to hold on to before I floated away.

The steel pipe in my jeans began throbbing in time with my pounding heart, and I was pretty sure I heard myself whimper a little bit. When he heard the sound I made, Tristan moaned into my mouth and I drank it in.

Just when I decided I wouldn't stop the most incredible kiss of my life, even if it meant fatal asphyxiation, Tristan pulled back. He settled back on his barstool as if nothing had happened while I remained leaning halfway out of my seat, hanging in midair between our stools, panting and gasping like a waterless fish.

The entire bar was silent, but I didn't dare look around. Instead, I begged my composure to come out, come out wherever it was. I slowly brought myself back up straight in my seat and reached for my beer glass, hoping like hell no one noticed my shaking hands.

I spoke in a low voice so that no one would overhear us. "You're a damned fine kisser for a straight guy."

Tristan barked out a laugh, and just like that, we were giggling again. I ordered another IPA, and Tristan got a refill of the red wine he had been drinking.

I felt like a grinning fool. Tristan was funny and confident. He was the kind of person who made you feel like you were the only person in the room. I envied that confidence.

And the kiss. Motherfucker, the kiss. Why did he have to be straight? That was like a crime against gay humanity. But how sweet was he to take one for the team and kiss me like that to make Jeremy jealous? So sweet.

Gah, the man was all that and a bag of the best kind of chips.

Fuck.

I was grateful I hadn't been eating dinner alone in a hotel bar when I saw Jeremy walk in. That was something at least. And meeting a nice man like Tristan, even if he was straight, was nice.

Screw nice.

My cheeks felt warm and I tried to chalk it up to the alcohol instead of arousal and a smidge of beard burn.

When I reached out for my beer glass, Tristan turned to me and smiled, all teeth and even a goddamned adorable dimple. I was so fucked. So very, very fucked.

I couldn't remember the last time I'd gotten a crush on a straight guy. That was like day one in the Intro to Gay class. Never fucking fall for your fucking straight friends unless you want your heart ripped out of your goddamned chest and chucked into a meat grinder. *But maybe this time is different,* you think, like the asshole you are. *No, idiot self. This time is not different.*

A deep sigh escaped me and Tristan's smile faltered a little. "You okay?" he asked. *No, dude. Not okay. I want your dick inside my ass, and I want to suck you off right fucking now. Except that you like pussy. Not okay.*

"Yep. Totally fine," I lied.

"Good." He beamed. "Now tell me why the hell you'd order beer when you're at a winery?"

I laughed. "Good question. I love wine, but I don't know much about it. Never know which one to order. Or maybe you just can't teach an old dog new tricks."

"Fair enough," Tristan said. "As far as beer goes, that's a good choice. Knee Deep Brewing Company is from Auburn, northeast of Sacramento. Do you know it?"

I looked at the glass of draft beer as if it could remind me of what it was. No dice. I shrugged and blushed. "Okay, so maybe I don't know much about craft beer either."

"Ah. A neophyte as it were. Allow me to educate you." Tristan clapped me on the shoulder before speaking slowly and deliberately in a caveman tone while gesturing to my glass.

"Dis. Is. Beer." Then he delicately picked up his wineglass stem between his thumb and middle finger, allowing his pinky finger to stick out like a princess at a tea party.

"This, my good fellow," he continued in a posh English accent. "This is ambrosia, the divine nectar of gods and goddesses throughout the millennia. The solution to all that ails human kind. The sweet, sweet elixir of love, peace, and happiness."

When he was done pontificating, he sipped as if from the Holy Grail and replaced the glass down on the bar with a flourish before slipping into the low sexy purr of French.

"*Le vin... est l'orgasme.*"

My eyebrows must have risen into my hairline. Tall, dark, handsome and a French speaker? Motherfucking jackpot. I blinked before raising my hand to get Frank's attention. When the older man turned to me with a questioning glance, I pointed to the Holy Grail and said with a grin, "I'll have what he's having."

Tristan looked at me with humor in his eyes. "Ah, a man willing to experiment. Maybe they're wrong about old dogs and new tricks after all."

I replied in the same smooth fluency he had used on me. "*Mieux vaut tard que jamais.*" *Better late than never.*

4

TRISTAN

Holy mother of god, that kiss. I tried to hide my reaction to Blue, but inside I was a lump of quivering jelly. Taking that man's mouth with mine was the single most sensual experience of my life.

It wasn't the soft, dainty kiss of a woman, demure and unsure, and... polite. It was strength and prickly scruff and naked, lusty want.

And fuck, did I want. I wanted him so much it took my breath away. Had we been in a private space instead of the bar of a winery I owned, I would have pounced on him like a cat on a ball of string. I wanted to unravel him.

Blue felt amazing under my hands, and he somehow tasted of indulgence. Sliding my tongue into his hot mouth felt like sliding a key into the door of a home I'd been looking for my whole life. The feelings that came over me should have scared me to death, but for some reason they calmed me.

Once I felt that calm come over me, I ended the kiss and pulled away. Even though I was still trembling on the inside, it was a good feeling. Like the nervous fluttering of anticipation instead of shaky fear. I wanted to kiss him again, and somehow I knew I would find a way back to that mouth.

We were laughing again, which was probably the bubbling of relief that things weren't awkward after my oral assault.

After ordering a glass of my favorite red wine, Blue told me about the time he had his wisdom teeth removed when he was eighteen years old and was so high on pain meds that he was seeing double.

"I could have sworn I saw my dad kissing a dude in the kitchen. I kept insisting that Mom go in there and stop Dad from being gay. My entire family thought it was the funniest thing ever. They made up a story about Dad's special friend Kevin. That it was okay when Kevin and Daddy shared secret kisses. Then as we got older, the stories got wilder. Mom admitted she and Dad had three-ways with Kevin. And every once in a while they'll put on an exaggerated voice and whine, 'Blue, stop being gay like Dad,' as if it's the most original joke in the fucking world." Blue rolled his eyes. "My family is crazy, by the way. In case you couldn't tell because I'm so normal."

Then it was my turn to laugh, which just made him laugh harder and swallow beer down the wrong pipe until I had to smack him on the back.

"Tristan, thanks for the laughs, man. I truly can't thank you enough. I really needed this tonight," Blue said. His smile was thanks enough.

I squeezed his shoulder again to assure him it was my pleasure, and I took another sip of wine with my hand still resting on his shoulder. A voice came from behind us. Turning around on my stool, I saw two men had approached us.

"Blue?" the older man asked. I didn't know Blue's ex yet, but I already hated him. Obviously.

The man looked from Blue to me.

"Hi, Jeremy," Blue said in a neutral voice.

Our stools had swiveled around toward each other and I took the opportunity to lean a little closer to Blue, settling my hand lightly on his knee. I felt his body tense for a brief moment before relaxing. Our jean-clad knees brushed together and I pressed mine against his.

Jeremy leaned toward Blue and hugged him awkwardly. I felt my body tense and my jaw clench. What the hell? He was just going to manhandle my fucking boyfriend right in front of me? *Jesus, Tristan. Get a grip. This stranger isn't your boyfriend. But still. Rude.*

When Jeremy stood back, I reached my arm over and placed my hand on Blue's upper back. I just... I don't know. I guess I didn't want him to feel alone. The guy needed to know someone had his back.

Blue's body seemed to relax again at my touch, and I felt relieved he wasn't mad at me for touching him. Jeremy introduced his little sidekick to Blue.

"Blue, this is Brad. Brad, this is Blue."

Brad reached out a hand to shake Blue's. "Nice to meet you. Blue, was it? Like the color? How do you know Jeremy?"

The question was said with honest curiosity and politeness, but I winced anyway. Clearly, Jeremy hadn't told his husband about a previous three-year relationship he'd gotten out of only six months before. That didn't even make sense. How could that be?

Blue sat there, stunned into silence. I began speaking to cover the awkward moment. "Blue is short for Bartholomew. He and Jeremy were together for three years until just a few months ago."

There was venom in my words. I felt its sour taste as the words came out of my mouth. Brad's eyes widened as he looked in astonishment to Jeremy. For a split second, I regretted getting involved. But then I felt Blue lean the slightest bit closer to me and noticed he was shaking. It was so subtle I almost missed it. My thumb idly traced circles into the spot below his nape in an effort to calm him.

"I'm Tristan," I volunteered, reaching out my hand to shake. Brad took it first and shook, even as my words about Jeremy and Blue were still sinking in. Then it was Jeremy's turn and he shook my hand with a little too much muscle. I met its strength with my own.

After shaking his hand, I put my arm back around Blue, and Jeremy's eyes couldn't help but watch every move I made. When his eyes flashed over to mine, I grinned a knowing grin. *That's right, buddy. He's with me.*

Jeremy looked back to Blue. "So, I heard you're being promoted and moving overseas."

"It hasn't been announced publicly yet, but I guess the editor was impressed with my willingness to speak truth to power," Blue said with a pointed look at Jeremy.

Jeremy looked away, nostrils flaring.

Brad seemed to get his thoughts together and decided it was time for him to have a private conversation with his husband.

"Will you excuse us, please? Jeremy and I need to get back to our table," Brad said, pulling Jeremy's hand. I wondered idly if he had the legendary red-headed temper. "Nice to meet you both."

Blue and I swiveled our stools back around to face the bar. We sipped our wine in silence for a few minutes and then Blue did something completely unexpected.

He turned and leaned into me, burying his face in my neck. I brought my arms around him immediately and held him tight.

"It's okay. I promise," I whispered into his ear. "You're going to be all right. One more week and you'll get your fresh start." I rubbed his back in slow strokes and rested my face against the top of his head. God, how I wished it could be different for him. If only he'd gone straight to his room instead of coming to the bar. But then I wouldn't have met him. I wasn't sure if I was selfless enough to wish for that.

5
____

BLUE

I wished there was a way to tell Tristan how much it meant to me to have him there when Jeremy approached with Brad. Tristan seemed like a good man. Maybe because he knew what it was like to break up and still be faced with the memories of someone, or maybe it was just that he was a sympathetic person in general. But feeling his reassuring touch and knowing I didn't look like a pathetic loser eating alone at the bar made me feel a profound sense of relief and comfort.

After I pulled back from the hug and took a deep breath, I sent him a smile of gratitude. His face was so open and genuine that I didn't feel any discomfort with him. With any other strange guy I might have been embarrassed or afraid of coming off as needy, but this was someone I probably wouldn't see again and he seemed genuinely okay with my brand of crazy.

Tristan gestured to Frank and the bartender walked over. "Two red-headed sluts, please," he ordered in a strong, confident voice.

My jaw dropped open at his order and I gaped at him. He looked over and raised a brow at me. "What? They're good," he said. "I can't help it if the drink I like also happens to be extremely appropriate."

And just like that, I was back to laughing. How did the Tristan do that? In one of my most dreaded situations in months, this man had the ability to make me laugh.

The shots went down too easily and he ordered a second round. While we were waiting for Frank to fix the drinks, Tristan told me another story from his past to distract me.

We each downed our second shot before Tristan asked Frank for two glasses of ice water. I looked over my shoulder and saw Jeremy sitting close to Brad, both men leaning their foreheads together. A sigh inadvertently came out of my mouth.

"Forget about those two, Blue. You deserve better than that guy," Tristan said in a low voice only I could hear.

"I know that in my head," I admitted. "But it's still hard to see. And it's not that I want him. I just want that. Intimacy, you know? Physical touch. I miss being with someone."

"You said you'd dated since the breakup?" he asked me.

"Yes, but it sucks getting back out there. Once you're in your thirties it seems like people are either already in a relationship or they just want the meaningless club hookup. What about you? Have you dated other women since the divorce?" I asked.

"Not really. I've been out on some dates but... I don't know. Something's always missing. I've kind of given up on trying. And I agree that at our age it's harder than it was years ago."

I watched his lips as he spoke. Those full, red lips framed by dark, shiny stubble. Whiskers that had felt scratchy against my skin but might feel softer by morning. His lips were perfect. Red like punch and still wet from a sip of his water glass. As I stared at them, his tongue snuck out to run along his lower lip. My eyes jumped up to his in embarrassment, and I noticed a look in his eyes I was not expecting. Desire.

Surely I was wrong. This guy was straight. I needed to stop drinking. Quickly grabbing my water glass, I chugged it down. Was I trying to put the buzz out like it was some kind of fire? It sure was hot like a fire. Was it a buzz from the drinks or a heat of attraction to the straight man sitting next to me? What the fuck was I thinking? Run into Jeremy and then pick the closest guy to latch on to? I needed to get out of there.

"Uh," I stammered. "Frank, I think I'm ready for my check, please."

"No, no," Tristan said. "I've got this. Frank, it's on me."

"I can't let you do that," I said, pulling out my wallet. Tristan's hand came down on top of mine.

"Please let me just cover your dinner, Blue. I enjoyed your company and otherwise I would have eaten alone. I won't take no for an answer." He smiled a smile I couldn't help but return.

"Thanks, Tristan. I appreciate it."

As I slipped my wallet into the back pocket of my jeans, I noticed Jeremy staring at me. Tristan turned to see what I was looking at and must have seen it too.

Just then I saw Tristan look from Jeremy to me and back again before he cupped my face in both of his hands and leaned forward to kiss me full on the lips. And it wasn't just a peck. The kiss happened in a tender kind of slow motion. Lips ghosting, tongues caressing. It all came together in a burst of fucking stars and took my breath away.

Tristan's mouth was warm and tasted like a red-headed slut. I drank him in and wanted more. My hands ended up on his hips even while my brain was trying to flash a red alert flag that screamed, *He's straight, he's straight.*

My dick flashed a different flag. This one was black-and-white checkered and screamed, *Ready, set, go!*

Tristan's fingers threaded into my hair and held on, dragging my head even closer to his. My own fingers found belt loops in his jeans to hook into and pull his hips closer. His tongue swirled and explored inside my mouth. I felt his stiff length against my abdomen and shuddered at the realization he was as hard as I was.

Wait. *WAIT*. What the fuck was happening? This didn't feel like a fake kiss any more than the first one had. I felt the long, stiff evidence that not all was as straight as it seemed. And there had been a look of desire in his eyes earlier.

I wrenched myself away with a small step backward, panting, bringing my hand up to my mouth, and staring at him in surprise.

Tristan's eyes darted to where Jeremy and Brad sat staring at us. Both of them sat openmouthed after witnessing our full-frontal assault. I felt blood rush to my face as I remembered what Tristan was doing. He had felt so sorry for me that he kissed me to help make Jeremy jealous. Again.

While unbelievably sweet of him, especially considering he was straight, it made me feel like a goddamned charity case. Like the recipient of the Most Pathetic Man Alive award. I had come to a pity party and been voted its queen. It wasn't real. Maybe he had a physical reaction to his little sexual experimentation, but that didn't mean he was interested in fucking men.

I turned and bolted out of the restaurant, hearing Tristan's voice behind me. "Wait, Blue. Hang on."

Nope. Not hanging on. Running away.

I blindly followed signs to the guest room hallway. With shaking hands, I dug the room key out of my pocket and matched the room number on the key envelope to a door halfway down the hall.

I couldn't get the key card to go into the slot, and it finally dropped onto the carpet. I blew out a frustrated breath and rested my forehead on the door to calm down a second.

"Blue." It was Tristan's deep, comforting voice, only this time it sounded like it had a note of pleading in it. I was too tired for this. The long day hit me suddenly and I just wanted to fall asleep between crisp, cool sheets. I tried so damned hard not to imagine Tristan right there next to me in the bed. Fuck.

6

TRISTAN

Thankfully, I didn't have to wait to pay the bill. I owned the damned place so Frank knew to comp it all under my name in the system. While following Blue down the hall toward the guest rooms I couldn't help but notice how his ass looked in his suit pants. His button-down shirt was wrinkled from his workday and the sport coat he'd worn into the bar earlier was slung over one arm while he fumbled with his room key.

I hadn't realized how tall he was until I was standing behind him in the hallway. He was probably only an inch or two shorter than my six two, but he was trimmer than I was. While I had the dense build of a rugby player, Blue had the frame of a downhill skier, long, slender muscles hidden by graceful movement. I had no idea what made me look at him that way. I hadn't looked at another man like that since college, and it took me by surprise.

He fumbled with his room key and dropped it, leaning against the door as though he'd had enough.

"Blue," I called out. "I'm sorry. Please let me apologize."

Without lifting it from the door, he swiveled his head to look at me. "It's fine, Tristan. I'm just tired. Listen, I appreciate what you were trying to do back there. I really do."

I crouched down to retrieve his key card, stepping close to him to get the door open.

When the door opened, Blue walked in and sat down on the end of the queen-sized four-poster bed before taking off his shoes. I wanted to say something but I felt I'd already bothered him enough for one day. As I began to back out of the doorway I heard him call out.

"Do you want to come in for a minute?" Blue asked in a tired voice.

I really did.

After making sure the door closed behind me, I walked in and sat down on the only chair in the room. I hadn't done much to the lodge rooms since I bought the vineyard three years before. They had been recently remodeled and I was satisfied with the clean, airy look the decorator had chosen for them. This room was painted in a neutral beige but the bedding was a luxurious white puffy duvet topped with navy, beige, and white accent pillows. The glass lamps on the maple bedside tables sported fat rounded shades that softened the light to provide an intimate feel to the room at night.

The only other furniture in the room were a maple dresser opposite the bed and the antique French corner chair I remembered being unique to this room. Blue looked over at me, obviously waiting to hear what I had to say.

"I don't know what came over me," I began. "I saw Jeremy staring at you and then I saw the look on your face and I ... I guess I just wanted to help you show him that you were going to be okay."

Blue's lips tightened. "But instead you showed him I'm so pathetic a straight guy pity-kissed me to make me feel a little less like an absolute loser?"

What? My eyes flashed at him as I realized why he was so angry. "Is that what you thought? That you were some kind of pathetic loser? That's not it, Blue. You're... wonderful," I finished lamely. *Wonderful?* God, why did I sound like a generic greeting card?

He looked at me, confusion etched on his face. "I just don't understand, Tristan. Did you kiss me because of Jeremy, or did you kiss me for some other reason?"

"I... because..." I stammered. How the hell was I supposed to know? It wasn't as if I'd stood there planning some big gesture before I launched myself at him. "Honestly? I'm not sure. I just wanted to kiss you."

More confusion from Blue. "But you're straight." Statement, not question.

"Well, maybe," I said hesitantly.

"Maybe? What the hell does that mean? You're either straight or not straight. Which is it?" he demanded.

"If you'd asked me earlier today I would have said I was straight. But then you walked into the bar and I... was really attracted to you. Maybe if Jeremy hadn't been there I wouldn't have kissed you, but I'm pretty sure I still would have wanted to."

"Just like that? You go from being married to a woman to kissing a dude? You don't seem to be freaking out right now, Tristan. Why aren't you freaking out?"

"It's not the first time I've kissed a man. I was attracted to guys in school, but just haven't acted on it since then. Haven't wanted to. Until now," I admitted.

Blue studied me for a minute with his head tilted. Like I was a zoo exhibit he was trying to figure out. "Why not?" he asked.

"Why not what?"

"Why haven't you been attracted to men since then? You're suggesting you're bisexual, but you haven't considered men since college? Seems unlikely. I'm guessing there's a story there." Blue hit the nail on the head, but I wasn't sure I was ready to peel my heart open like a banana and present it to him on a tray.

"The short version is that my last experience put me off men pretty badly. I thought it would be safer to stick with women, so I did," I said.

Blue slid back to rest his back against the headboard, long legs extended straight out in front of him crossing at the ankles. His feet were bare and they kept drawing my eyes. What was it about some-one's bare feet that made them look both homey and vulnerable?

He was still studying me, but this time there was something else behind his eyes. "Tristan, did someone hurt you?" he asked quietly.

My throat felt tight at the sound of his concern. "No, not like that. Not really."

He must have sensed I didn't want to talk about it because he changed the subject slightly.

"Is it just me or does that guy Brad look like he's twelve?" he asked with a wicked gleam in his eyes. "My mom is going to lose her shit when she sees him with that kid."

"Definitely a preteen." I laughed agreeably. "Wonder if he had to get parental permission to leave town."

"And how the hell does someone find a life partner and get married in a matter of months? I mean, Jesus Christ. Rush much? Fuck. Why not just sleep with him? Why marriage? What's the hurry?" Blue seemed to be picking up speed.

"Don't know. I have good friends who met and got married that fast and have been together for years. I asked them once. They told me that when you know, you just know. I disagree."

Blue asked, "It wasn't like that with Sheila?"

"No. But then again, nothing was spontaneous with Sheila. Marrying her was a little bit like negotiating a business deal. She wanted to wait until it made sense financially, logistically, etc. When the time was right, we got married at the courthouse. No fanfare, no family. No romance at all. I hated it," I remembered.

"Then why did you do it?" Blue asked.

I shrugged and he laughed. "Seemed like a good idea at the time."

"That sounds awful. No wonder the marriage didn't last."

"No shit. It was never good. I don't know what I was thinking. Maybe it was one of those situations where our body clocks told us it was time to settle down so we went with who was right now instead of who was right," I explained.

7

BLUE

I could have listened to Tristan talk all night long. Just the deep reverberations of his voice lulled me like a siren song. The news that he was probably bi sent shivers of excitement through me, and I had to tamp down my excitement. I had to remind myself he probably saw me as the pathetic loser I still felt like, despite his reassuring words. And even if he didn't, it wasn't as though a guy experimenting in college with a friendly roommate blow job was the same thing as being prepared to live as a fully out gay man. Life didn't work like that. And I was moving to London.

Tristan stood up to grab the two complimentary water bottles that sat on a tray on top of the dresser. He handed me one and cracked the other one open for himself. I patted the bed next to me.

"Sit here. That chair looks like an antique torture device," I told him.

"Right? And it looks better than it feels. Christ, my ass is unhappy." He laughed.

He sat next to me on the bed after kicking off his shoes. Leaning back against the headboard, he took several sips from the bottle.

I thought of something. "Do you have children? With Sheila?"

"No. She didn't want kids. We both had jobs that kept us too busy, but I think it was more than that for her. She's a doctor, and I always thought if given the chance, she'd choose medicine over her family. I'm not sure she ever realized she could have had both. And I was an attorney practicing international law for a large company at the time, so I was flying all over the world. With neither of us at home, our kids would have been raised by nannies. Not great."

It surprised me Tristan was an attorney. He didn't seem like the jet-set type, although he did seem worldly. For some reason I could see him enjoying a slower-paced life or something wilder, outdoorsy. What the hell did I know, though? It wasn't like I really knew him.

The alcohol buzz was turning more and more into a liquid exhaustion. I felt my body weight sinking farther into the pillows as Tristan talked. We ended up lying on our sides, facing each other with heads on separate pillows. When I realized we were basically experiencing pillow talk without the benefit of sex beforehand, I chuckled.

"What?" Tristan smirked at me.

"I guess since you bought me dinner I felt like I needed to invite you into my bed," I joked.

He chuckled too. "Sorry. I should go. You look really sleepy."

"I am," I admitted. "But I don't want you to go. You're very easy to talk to. I've had a great time tonight despite the bozos at the bar."

"Blue?" he asked me, and his gray eyes looked right into me.

"Yeah?" I replied.

"I want to kiss you again," he whispered.

"Fuck, yes," I breathed, but before I finished speaking, his lips were on mine.

For the second time in a row he kissed me with a slow tenderness that nearly broke my heart. His lips were soft and warm. They caressed mine and skimmed across them like a slow dance. I felt the stubble of his jaw, but it wasn't rough on my face because he was being so incredibly gentle with me.

I brought a hand up to his cheek, and one of his hands landed on my side just above the waistband of my jeans. His earthy smell surrounded me, and I wondered if he'd been here longer than I had and somehow picked up the smell of the vineyard around us. There was a faint trace of a soapy smell too, but I couldn't define it that late in the evening. His voice hummed with pleasure and I felt the sound on my tongue.

My body rolled closer to his and he mirrored me, bringing a leg up to push its way between my own. I felt his bare foot brush against mine and a voice inside of me chanted, *More, god, please more.*

I moved my hands down over his back to his ass as he kept rolling over until he was on top of me. My hands cupped his tight ass and pulled him against me. His erection pressed against mine and I stopped kissing long enough to moan as pleasure shivered through me from my groin to my fingertips. Feeling his hard length straining against mine was enough to make me want to come in my pants like a teenager. Luckily I held on and avoided embarrassing myself.

Tristan's hands moved down to fumble with the button of my fly, and I suddenly felt like I was suffocating in my clothes. Naked. I needed to be naked. I heard Tristan's voice mumbling but couldn't make out every word.

"Off... damned things...fucking...dammit... off," he muttered.

I felt a laugh burble up through my chest and spill out. He looked down at me, frustration creasing his brow.

"What are you laughing at?" he grumbled. "Is this fashion's version of a chastity belt?"

I laughed harder. "Yes, Tristan. It's called an actual belt. I think you're just not used to opening it backwards."

He looked down at my belt. "Oh... Right."

Then he glanced up at me with the cutest puppy-dog look ever. I reached out to cup his face with both hands and kissed him.

"Why don't we slow down a little? It's late; we've been drinking. You're kind of straight. I'm afraid if we get naked we might do something one of us will regret."

He looked disappointed but agreed. "I guess you're right, but shit. You're so sexy, Blue. Jeremy is an idiot." He rolled off me, landing on his back. He brought one hand to his face to cover his eyes and the other he used to press against his cock through his jeans.

I did the same.

Tristan turned and looked at me. "You did the right thing, stopping us. I don't want you to regret it later."

I stared back at him. "Me? I was talking about you. No fucking way I'd regret it."

He frowned. "Then what the hell did you stop us for? I'm not going to regret it either. Jesus, Blue. I'm thirty-four years old. I can handle sleeping with someone without crying about it the next day." He took a deep breath and reached a hand out to cup the fly of my jeans. "I want. Your dick. In my mouth."

My own mouth went bone dry at his words. Well, hell. He had a point, but I didn't think it was smart to start off with him doing something that might make him uncomfortable. Before I had a chance to overthink it, I was on top of him, unfastening his fly and pulling his jeans down his legs before throwing them onto the floor. Trying to temporarily ignore the impressive bulge pushing out of his boxer briefs, I moved up to pull his shirt off, dropping it at the foot of the bed.

Tristan's eyes were wide and disbelieving that I had turned my no into a yes in mere seconds. Before he knew it, he was completely naked underneath me and my mouth was dragging kisses down his bare chest to his navel. He had a smattering of dark chest hair and the sexiest damned happy trail that snaked from his navel to his cock, like a giant arrow pointing me to my happy place.

I ran my tongue down that trail while running one hand up from his tight abs to one of his nipples. His breath was coming fast and shallow now that he knew what I was doing. My name came out of him in moans and whimpers as my tongue found the tip of his cock and I felt it jump under my touch.

He threw his head back when I slid my tongue along his slit, dipping the point of it to enjoy his salty precum. I grasped the root of his erection and slid my mouth up and down the outside of his shaft before taking him all the way into my throat in one big gulp.

"*Fuck!*" he cried. His hips tried to buck off the bed but I anticipated the reaction, using my free hand to hold one hip down with a strong grip.

"God, so good, Blue. God." He writhed beneath me as I swirled my mouth around the head of his thick cock. He was losing his shit. I loved making him crazy. Seeing him naked and on the verge of spilling into my mouth was like taking a hit off a magical happy pipe. I felt my own cock straining inside my pants, so I reached down to free it with one hand while I continued stroking Tristan with the other. I pushed my pants down just far enough and had never been so grateful in my life for going commando.

I cupped his balls and he sucked in a breath. My mouth moved over his sac until I used my tongue to draw a wet trail between his balls and his tight hole. Moving my lips back to tease his cock, I began stroking myself to the same rhythm. I thought about what my dick would feel like inside his tight channel and felt my orgasm start to build. I squeezed the base of my erection to hold off coming until I was sure Tristan had the best experience ever. Part of me felt like a used *gay* salesman. If I could just convince him how good this was, he'd never look at another kind of sexuality again.

I quickly sucked on the tip of my thumb before using it to trace light circles around his tight pink hole. I didn't stroke over it, just kept the touches light and teasing, leaving him begging for more. No need in scaring the guy with a true threat (or promise) of Big Scary Anus Sex. He'd already dealt with quite a bit of gay tonight, thank you very much.

Tristan's words were no longer actual words, just mewling sounds of lust and desperation and need. I could feel my own release building back even stronger than before and took pity on him.

"Look at me, Tristan," I encouraged. "Watch your cock slide down my throat. I want to swallow you all the way down."

Before I even had a chance to deep throat him, he was shooting hot jets of come into my mouth. My words had pushed him over the edge, and he cried out my name as his hands gripped my hair. His immediate fevered reaction to me and the taste of him on my tongue slammed together causing my own orgasm to rocket through me. I spilled onto Tristan's shirt lying on the duvet. Wave after wave of pleasure crested through me and I realized I had dropped my head onto Tristan's stomach while I came.

He lay back gasping, trying to catch his breath as I settled down and willed my heart not to beat out of my chest.

Tristan's chest heaved with labored breaths. "I'm dead. Did I die? Am I lying here dead?" Tristan gasped.

I smiled at him and lay back down beside him on the bed. "From the number of times you called his name, I think you might have at least met god at some point."

"Thought so."

When his breath slowed to a more normal level, he turned his head to look at me. A relaxed grin spread across his gorgeous face. "God, you're good at that. I might need to take lessons."

"Nah. Just takes practice. I'm happy to be your test subject."

He looked down at my open fly and worn-out cock. "Looks like someone cheated me out of my first attempt."

8

———

TRISTAN

"Fuck you. Couldn't help it. You're not the only one who met Jesus just now." Blue laughed.

I stretched out and felt my foot land in cold, wet sludge. I yelped and winced. Blue sat up to see what had happened.

"Wet spot," I said before realizing that the wet spot was actually the shirt I'd been wearing. I looked at Blue with a raised brow. He blushed all the way to the tips of his ears.

"Oops." He grinned. "I'll have to loan you one of mine for your walk of shame."

He was so damned cute. His wavy, strawberry-blond hair was messy and his blue eyes shone with a clarity I hadn't seen in them before. I wanted so badly to wrap him up in my arms and hold him while he slept. But maybe he was trying to tell me something.

"I should get out of your hair then," I began. Blue's face turned cloudy.

"What? No, that's not what I meant," he said.

I looked at him to try to gauge his thoughts. "It's okay if you'd like for me to go. I know this isn't exactly how you planned your evening."

"You're right. It's not how I planned my evening. I planned to host a massive solo pity party at the bar and fall into a strange hotel bed alone. Instead, I met a sumptuous piece of man candy and got to lick it," he finished with a tease.

I smacked his chest. "Be serious, you ass."

"Okay. Instead, I met an interesting, kind man who actually cared and listened. We had a wonderful dinner together despite me finding out that my ex had possibly married a newborn baby. This mysterious stranger then kissed the hell out of me to make said ex jealous. He let me use his exquisite body to have a star-spangled orgasm and, god willing, will warm this beautiful bed with me tonight." He looked into my eyes with complete focus and sincerity. "There, how was that?"

What I wanted to say was that it took my breath away. *He* took my breath away. But what I said was, "Meh."

Now it was his turn to smack me, but he kissed me instead. "Stay," he said in a quiet voice. "Please stay."

At that point, the voice of doubt floated through my brain. *Don't sleep with a guest. Don't start something the week of your brother's wedding. This guy is just passing through and will be gone next week. Then what? Oh, and he's a guy.*

But by the time my brain demanded answers, my body was naked under the big duvet, wrapped around the warm, sensual man beside me and sliding into delicious sleep. Blue's body smelled faintly of lemons and the distinctly male scent of his body after a long day. I inhaled it like it was laughing gas at the dentist, desperate to draw it into my body in search of sweet surrender.

I woke up a few hours later needing to take a piss. When I came awake, I felt coarse chest hair under my hand and was startled for a nanosecond before remembering it was Blue. As soon as I remembered, I sank back down into him just wanting to stay fully connected to him for a moment before getting up for the bathroom.

My lips found his shoulder blade and I softly kissed it, sliding the tip of my tongue out to taste his delicious skin. I had been wrong when I described wine as ambrosia. The true nectar of the gods was this man's skin.

Finally I forced myself up and to the bathroom, cursing the drinks I'd had that led to my bladder's insistence. I kept the lights out and did my best to stay quiet, but when I slid back against Blue's warm body, I could tell he was awake.

"Sorry," I whispered. "Didn't mean to wake you."

"S'okay," he mumbled sleepily. "Gotta pee too."

When he got back to bed he grinned at me. "Didn't cut and run, I see."

"Nope. I ain't skeered," I joked. "Plus, you're all warm and snuggly. And furry. Like curling up with a puppy or some shit."

"Is that a fancy way of calling me your bitch?" he asked.

"I'd never call you that. Unless we were in prison. In which case, yes. I'd be happy to claim you as my bitch. I'd consider it an honor if you'd be my prison bitch. In fact, now that I think of it, since I've discovered that I'm attracted to you, we should go on a crime spree and get caught. Think of all the sex we could have while we did our time. People would even cook for us. It's worth considering."

"Sounds delightful. Tell you what, you try it first and let me know how it goes." He chuckled, burrowing into my chest. I lifted my arm up so he could slide closer and rest his head on my shoulder. It felt good. It felt right. I kissed the top of his head, inhaling the scent of his shampoo.

I slid my toes under one of his calves to pull his leg between mine. Better. He tilted his head to look up at me, but I couldn't make out his expression in the mostly dark room.

"What is it?" I asked and almost, *almost* called him "baby." *What the hell?* Maybe I had taken a fall and was now in a strange drug-induced coma. I woke up that morning a regular straight guy going to work. And now here I was, naked in bed with a strange man who I wanted to lavish with affection.

"Nothing," Blue said.

"Liar."

"Fuck, Tristan. It's too late for deep thoughts. Let's just go back to sleep."

Part of me wanted to push. Wanted to know what deep thoughts were grinding around in that head of his. But he was right. It was really late and I had to work the following day. I also had to make it out of that room without my employees seeing me do the unthinkable: a walk of shame out of a guest's room.

I should go now, but I just can't bring myself to leave him yet. Just a little longer. Just a couple more hours of my skin against his and the feel of his warm breaths on my chest.

My phone alarm went off at 6 a.m. and I turned it off within seconds. Luckily it started off at a lower volume and I was so attuned to it I could react before it woke Blue. Peeling myself away from him was disheartening, because I didn't know when I would see him again. I took a quick shower and then pulled on my jeans, remembering my ruined shirt.

After finding the notepad and pen I knew would be in the bedside table drawer, I scribbled a note and left the pad propped in front of the bathroom sink.

Blue had just arrived, so I had to assume he was staying for more than one night. That meant I would probably see him, but would he want to be with me? Would he let me into his bed again? Or would he wake up this morning regretting what we did?

I leaned over and kissed his forehead. He looked so peaceful in the full relaxation of sleep. The man was stunning. Not perfect, but so gloriously imperfect in all the right ways. A golden boy. I had to remind myself that if I never got another chance to touch him, I would still be one lucky asshole for having had one night with him.

I grabbed a gray T-shirt from Blue's suitcase and slipped it on before I snuck out into the quiet hallway and made my way out a back door and to my parked vehicle.

I drove the short quarter mile to my cabin and saw Piper leaning against the fence, watching me from the backyard. She looked pissed, her blue eyes boring holes through me. Great. Just what I needed. A guilt trip. It was well deserved. I had left the night before, promising her I'd be back an hour later. She wasn't happy about it, but I left anyway. And then everything happened with Blue and I hadn't thought about her at all.

Okay, maybe I deserved the guilt trip. After all, I had let down the love of my life again, but I knew full well she would forgive me the way she always did.

9

BLUE

When I woke up, I wasn't really surprised to find myself alone. It had been too good to be true. But I was still disappointed. No, that was too weak of a word. Heavy hearted. Yes, that was better. I was fucking heavy hearted. I'd gone to sleep wrapped around a magnificent naked man whose mere voice made my insides play a thousand tiny bells. But I woke up alone. Wrapped around nothing that made my insides play nothing. God, I couldn't stand myself.

I would have to pull a Taylor Swift and shake it off. Was I really turning into such a pathetic lovesick preteen that I was now quoting Taylor Swift? *Fuck.*

When I stepped into the hot shower I was feeling more pitiful than I had been before even meeting Tristan. And I thought I'd been pathetic then... haha.

I poured some shampoo into my hand and remembered a song I'd heard in an old movie once. It said something about washing that man right outta your hair. *Yeah, that. That's what I'll do. When I get out of the shower, I'll be over it. Over him.*

As I turned around to rinse off my head, I glanced through the glass shower door and noticed something.

Hold up. Is that a note?

After quickly finishing my shower routine, I scrambled to dry myself enough to reach for the note without getting the paper wet. I'd seen movies. I knew getting the paper wet before reading the message spelled certain doom. The ink would smear until it was unreadable, the mystery would then become ten times harder to solve, and someone would end up shot in a Russian snowbank. No, thanks.

The note was written in a strong masculine hand.

BLUE,

You have no idea how hard it is for me to leave you here, all naked, sleepy and hot as fuck. But I have to work and didn't want to wake you. Below is my cell number. I'm around so text me if you want to get together or need anything. I'd love to see you again. And if you ever want me to be your plus-one, whether it's for Jeremy reasons or family reasons, just say the word. I'd be proud to claim you as mine.

- T

OH HELL NO. Now I was in some major trouble. So much for shaking it off. That note had just changed my shake-it-off plans into stroke-it-off plans. I grabbed the mini bottle of hotel lotion from the bathroom counter and invited it to join me for an intimate interlude on the bed. It didn't protest.

When I was done fantasizing about Tristan's thick cock in my tight ass, I was sporting a limp dick that smelled delightfully like honeysuckle. I tucked it into a clean pair of underwear and worn blue jeans before pulling on a soft black T-shirt. After programming Tristan's number into my phone, I slipped into some flip-flops before leaving my room in search of breakfast.

There was a complimentary continental breakfast set up in the back of the main lobby of the lodge. I hadn't seen much in the dark the night before, but the building was beautiful.

A large log-type structure from the outside gave visitors a false sense that it would be dark and primitive inside. Instead, the lobby was vaulted and airy with large windows spanning the back wall showcasing a view of a green manicured lawn stretching to a small lake and the rows and rows of grapevines beyond.

I stopped to take in the magnificent view from those windows. The property was sensational. The morning sun was sparkling off the lake water, and dew on the lawn winked here and there in the light. The blue of the sky was clear and rich with just a few high scattered clouds.

There were open French doors leading out onto a stone patio, and I felt drawn through them to the fresh morning air outside. It was unlike me to walk in the opposite direction of the smell of coffee, but that's what I did. I sank down on the wide stone steps leading down to the grass of the yard beyond.

No wonder Simone had chosen this place for her wedding.

Off to each side of the lawn were clusters of trees with carpets of pine needles underneath. Everything except the trimmed grass of the sloping lawn was left in a natural but tidy state. Beyond the lake the vines were stretched out on their trellises, laid out in rows upon endless rows, reminding me of the battle scene from Lord of the Rings.

There was life and energy in those vines. Everything the vineyard needed to be successful came down to what this land produced on those vines. What a different kind of life than the office life I led in the city. I couldn't remember the last time I had spent any amount of quality time outside just enjoying sunshine and fresh air unless it was sunbathing by a pool or on a beach during a vacation.

It was strange to realize that. I'd been outdoorsy in high school but after starting to work full-time I'd let it dwindle. Once I was with Jeremy, my outdoor time almost vanished completely. He didn't like being outside, so we did things in the city. I'd forgotten what I'd been missing.

After a while I could no longer ignore my rumbling stomach. I returned inside to the breakfast tables and gathered a cup of coffee along with a muffin, apple, and banana. I juggled my items as I returned to my step on the patio.

After eating the banana and half of the pumpkin muffin I heard someone calling my name in an excited squeal.

"Bluuuuuueeeee!" Simone cried. "You're heeeeere!"

I stood and turned before she launched herself at me. Her arms went around my neck and I knew her legs would have gone around my waist had she not been wearing a sundress. My arms held her tight and I smelled the vanilla scent of the body lotion she'd used for years. I loved this woman. She was six years younger than I was and the youngest biological sibling of the six of us. Below her we had three adopted brothers. Considering she was the only girl in a family of nine kids, this wedding week was going to be over the top.

My mother had always wanted a daughter. Not that she didn't love her boys, but she doted on Simone. We didn't mind though, because we all doted on Simone. She was all of five foot nothing and had brown curly hair and brown eyes like all my brothers. In addition to being adorable, Simone was also kind and tender hearted. We were all named after Jesus's apostles but I'd always thought it would have suited Simone better to be named after Saint Francis. My sister was a gentle caregiver and she had grown up to become a veterinarian just like she had always said she would.

"Hey, baby girl," I said into her mass of curls. "I missed you so much."

"God, Blue, where the hell have you been lately?" she asked, even though she probably knew the answer to that.

"I was whooping it up at the world's lamest pity party, but don't worry. I shut the place down and am finding my way again," I assured her.

"Good, because Jeremy's going to be here, you know that." She pulled back to study me with concern.

"Been there, done that, sister. Saw him and his new bride last night in fact. Hell of a thing."

Her eyes widened at the information. "What the fuck? Jeremy married a woman? Jeremy is married?"

"Yes, I think he's married, but no, it's not to a woman. Just the prettiest little twinkie you ever did see. Either that or he kidnapped some poor kid and is parading him around as his husband. Take your pick. You'll see him eventually." I tried being flip about it but I knew if anyone would know how I really felt, it would be Simone.

"Shit, Blue. Did you know?" she asked.

"Nope. Not until he walked into the hotel bar and saw that kid with a ring," I admitted with a wry grin.

"Did Jeremy have a ring on?" she asked.

"No, but he's an asshole like that. I'm sure he wouldn't wear one anyway."

"Fuck," she muttered. "I'm so sorry."

She gave me the sad pity eyes that made my skin itch. If Simone was giving me that look, that meant every person coming to the damned wedding would give me that look. Ugh, I hated that.

Her face perked up with a thought. "Ooo! My coworker Zane is coming and he's gay and single. Cute too. I'm totally going to hook you guys up."

"Oh, hell no, baby girl. You can forget it. I don't need a pity setup. I'm fine."

"You say that with your mouth, but your forehead lines tell a different story," she said.

"Enough about sad me. Tell me all about our new brother. I heard he has a biblical name so we're good to go," I joked. It was funny because our parents were atheists.

My parents had both been raised by strict Catholic families and when they began to have children, the pressure to choose wholesome names came at them from both sides. They compromised by selecting the apostle names but then immediately shortening them to sound more modern. We ended up with Pete, Jamie, me, Thad, Jude, and Simone. And while I wasn't religious by any stretch of the imagination, a part of me thanked god every day for sparing me from the nickname Bart.

"John is around here somewhere. He went looking for his brother, Alex. Their parents are arriving soon. Is your room okay?" she asked.

"Yep, no problem. This is a gorgeous place. Who did you say owns it? Someone in John's family?"

"Alex. He bought it a few years ago from a great uncle, I think. John didn't remember the place, but Alex remembers visiting here as a little boy. It wasn't much back then. But Alex has worked hard to make something of it.

"Smaller specialty vineyards are being recognized as unique and valuable again like craft beers are in the beer industry. He's been featured in plenty of wine magazines. I don't know much about the industry, but I've talked to him about it several times at their parents' house. Nice guy. You'll meet him. Isn't it pretty though?"

"Beautiful. And so peaceful. Made me realize it's been too long since I've had a break from the city." I looped my arm through Simone's. "Where are Mom and Dad and the guys?"

She laughed. "Inside. You walked right past all of us twice. We waved and called for you but you were oblivious. I figured you needed a chance for the coffee to kick in."

"So true. It's hard enough to handle the Marian family fully caffeinated, much less with an empty tank. Lead on, Bridezilla," I teased.

10
___

TRISTAN

After I spent twenty minutes loving on Piper, I gave her some break-fast and told her she could come with me to the lodge. She spent the entire twenty minutes reacquainting her nose with my scent. It was a little strange, but I chalked it up to her missing me or the fact I was wearing a shirt with someone else's laundry detergent smell.

As soon as I cracked open the cabin door, she bolted outside and leaped onto the bed of the electric utility vehicle I drove on the property.

On the quarter-mile drive to the lodge, I could see her in the side mirror. Her black-and-white muzzle pointed directly into the wind and her ears flapped happily. Border collies were smart as hell, and she was no exception. She knew something was up at the vineyard, and I wondered if she was keen enough to smell my family members from this far away.

When I parked, she jumped over the side of the vehicle and made a beeline for the front door of the lodge. It was propped open to take advantage of the cool morning cross breeze, and she disappeared inside in a flash. I was curious to see which of my family members or friends she would scope out first.

I stopped by the front desk to make sure there weren't any issues that needed my attention before wandering toward the guests lingering over coffee in the lobby breakfast area.

Before I had a chance to scope out familiar faces in the groupings of people having breakfast, I followed Piper out the French doors to the stone patio beyond. I saw Blue sitting on the stone steps to the lawn and damned if my slut of a dog wasn't sitting in his lap with her head resting on his shoulder. His arms wrapped around the dog, running hands up and down her sides and over her back while her tongue lolled out and she made noises of ecstasy. Lucky bitch.

"Jesus, Piper. Have a little self-respect, will ya?" I called out.

Blue turned and saw me striding toward him. His face cracked into a beautiful smile and his deep blue eyes drew me to him like tractor beams.

"You know this whore?" Blue laughed, wrapping his arms farther around Piper in a bear hug.

"She's the one I was cheating on last night," I confessed in stage whisper. "And she was none too happy with me this morning, I can assure you."

"Oh no. Was she stuck inside that whole time?" he asked with genuine concern.

"No, she has a dog door into a fenced yard. She was just bored. I told her I was leaving for an hour and then… well… you know. I got a little sidetracked." I felt my face flush.

"So, you live close to the winery?" he asked.

"My cabin is about a quarter mile from here," I said, sitting next to him on the steps.

"This place is incredible. You're lucky to live so close. It's like heaven out here. Every time I walk back inside, I find myself back out here again."

A kind of warmth spread through my chest. No one in my family had understood my attraction to the vineyard. They all thought it was a stupid folly or an early midlife crisis. John and my father both scoffed at the idiocy of walking away from a lucrative legal partnership. My mother just didn't understand why anyone would trade a large paycheck for a smaller paycheck. None of them saw this place as anything more than a financial spreadsheet.

"I feel the exact same way, Blue." I smiled at him.

Just then, my brother and his fiancé walked out onto the patio and called to me.

"There they are," Simone said. "I see you two already met."

I looked at her in confusion. "Uh, yeah," I began.

"Good, because we've decided to set our single brothers both up on blind dates with our friends this week. It'll be fun," Simone said with a smirk.

"What the fuck are you talking about?" I asked before I could rein in my frustration. "John?"

"Don't look at me, it was her idea. I think Mom was upset at you still being single and the Marians felt the same way about Blue. He just went through a terrible breakup," John said.

Surely this wasn't happening.

Blue looked between Simone and me. "How do you know my sister?"

My brother spoke up next. "Because Tristan's my brother," he said.

Blue and I just stared at each other as the realization set in. Oh fuck.

Simone and John stared at us, waiting for someone to say something. Blue's face flushed and I thought he was going to explode.

"Can you give us a second?" I asked Simone and John before pulling Blue down into the yard by his elbow.

"Your sister is marrying my brother," I said quietly when I pulled him around to face me. Blue stared at me with his gorgeous eyes. "John is my brother," I clarified.

He still stared. I put my hands on either side of his face and brought it close to mine. "You okay in there? Say something."

"But... how... why didn't you say something sooner?" His voice started off perplexed but built to a tentative anger. "Jesus, Tristan, John is your brother? We're going to be *related*?"

"Blue, hang on," I began, wanting to cut off his freak-out at the pass.

"John's brother's name is Alex. He has more than one brother?"

"My name is Tristan Alexander. John calls me Alex because he doesn't like the name Tristan. Don't ask. It's a stupid and shitty story," I explained.

"You're Alex. Alexander Vineyards. John's brother owns the vineyard," he mumbled to himself before looking back up at me with startled eyes. "You own this vineyard?"

"I do."

"But... you're an attorney. Why do I feel like you've been lying to me?" he asked me, pain visible in his face.

"What? No! I haven't lied to you at all. Damn it. I used to be an attorney. I didn't know about any of this either. And why would I have mentioned I owned the vineyard?" I countered. "'Oh hi, beautiful stranger, look at what I own, let me flash around my possessions to impress you.' Bullshit. How do you think that would have gone down, Blue?"

I could tell he understood what I was saying but he was still annoyed. His jaw clenched and I could see his gears turning as he continued to build up steam.

"Blue, stop freaking out and just relax," I started, feeling the need to calm him and somehow get us back to it being about us without the issue of our families in the mix.

"*Relax?* You're telling me I sucked off my future brother-in-law, my *straight* future brother-in-law, and I'm supposed to chill out?" he growled in a low voice growing in strength.

He kicked up the volume several notches as the steam finally blew the top off the whole thing. "*I fucking slept with you,*" he shouted at the exact same time I lost my own shit and yelled, "*Clearly I'm not straight.*"

Startled gasps came from behind us and we both snapped our heads around. A healthy handful of sexagenarians stood with Simone in the doorway, gaping at us. John must have disappeared inside.

I wanted to burst out laughing at the absurdity of the moment. For some reason I expected Blue to lose his shit, but he surprised me. He shrugged and leaned over to whisper in my ear.

"You still want to do the pretend boyfriend thing? Because right now, I could fucking stand to shake some shit up. If they think they're going to spend the week setting me up with strangers, they are sorely mistaken."

"Bring it on," I responded with a wink.

"By the way, you're wearing my family reunion T-shirt. Welcome to the Marian family; be careful what you wish for."

And then he grabbed my hand and pulled me toward the door.

"Mom, Dad," Blue said cheerfully. "This is Tristan, John's brother. And... my boyfriend."

My parents gasped again and my mother stumbled back a few steps before my father's arm instinctively reached out to steady her. For that moment alone, I was going to give Blue the blow job of his life later.

I joined the fray and addressed my own parents. "And this is Blue, one of Simone's brothers and my partner." I felt more than heard him snort beside me. I looked over at him see him rolling his eyes. What, was "partner" the wrong word? What the hell did I know? It wasn't as though I was that gay yet. I hadn't had time to pick up the lingo.

I reached out to shake Blue's father's outstretched hand. He had a familiar grin on his face and looked to be as friendly as Blue was. "Thomas Marian, nice to meet you, Tristan."

"You too, sir."

Then Blue introduced his mother as Rebecca Marian. I kissed her on the cheek. "Nice to meet you, Mrs. Marian."

"Oh, please call me Rebecca. It's a pleasure, Tristan. Nice shirt, by the way," she said with a wink.

It wasn't until then that I chanced a closer look at the shirt I was wearing. For some reason I had thought it said something about Robin Hood. But when I looked down at my chest I realized my mistake. There in navy block letters on a gray background it said: MADE MARIAN.

11
____

BLUE

I thought Tristan's face was going to turn so red that he'd stroke out.

"Right, well, yes. Thank you," Tristan stammered to my mom. Aww, poor little fucker had some chickens coming home to roost. I couldn't help but laugh, which earned me a look of complete annoyance from his narrowed gray eyes. I snorted again, and he rolled his own eyes before looking back at our families.

"So, what's everyone up to this morning?" he asked, obviously attempting to return to his lord-of-the-manor persona.

All six people in front of us began shuffling feet and muttering about this and that. *Awkward.*

Tristan piped up again. "Well, I'm giving a vineyard tour at three o'clock for anyone who's interested. There will be heavy hors d'oeuvres and a wine tasting at the end of the tour. Don't know about the rest of you, but I sure could use a little alcohol right about now."

Energetic agreement tittered out of all of us, and I knew right then that Tristan's vineyard tour was going to be the most popular event of the day. I certainly recognized I wasn't about to miss a chance to watch and listen to him while wandering through this beautiful property. For all I knew, I'd fallen through some kind of space and time continuum and was now residing in one of the novels I'd been reading recently.

I mean, come on. Who really got to spend a week at a vineyard in Napa with their entire family and the most beautiful man to ever walk the earth? No one. And clearly this novel was fiction because there was even a villain. Jeremy. And the villain had a sidekick like Dr. Evil's Mini-Me. Brad. God, didn't you just want to say the name Brad with a preppy singsong voice? I knew I did.

As our little patio party began to break up, Tristan's parents clearly wanted to have words with him. His father gave him a stern look and flicked his head in the direction of the interior of the lodge. I felt Tristan stiffen beside me and I squeezed his hand.

"Want me to come with you?" I asked in a low voice.

"Nah. It'll be fine. I'm just glad John's not here. Wait for me though?" Then he leaned over and kissed me right on the lips for the whole world to see. It wasn't a quick peck either. The kiss had legs. And tongue. And penises that wanted to wake up and find out what the hell they'd been missing since earlier that morning. I ripped myself away from his face before things got indecent.

Too late. I heard a wolf whistle from inside the building and recognized it as coming from my brother Jamie.

Tristan grinned like the Cheshire cat as he backed away.

That fucker.

I gripped the tip of my tongue between my teeth to keep from calling out to Tristan's retreating form that payback was going to be hell.

Beside me Simone was laughing and my mother was swooning. My dad was just looking at me with twinkling eyes of merriment.

"Oh my god, Blue. Why didn't you tell me? I didn't even know John's brother was gay," Simone said. Well, that made two of us. Scratch that. That made all of us, including Tristan himself.

"He didn't either," I admitted. "And we didn't realize the family connection at first," I hedged. At least that much was true.

My mom sniffed. "Aww, sweetheart, it's so good to see you happy again. He's obviously smitten."

"I don't know about smitten, Mom, this is all very new." That was an understatement if ever there was one.

Simone snorted. "Blue, that man looked at you like he wanted to lay you down on a pedestal and feed you grapes one at a time."

My face flushed as I imagined taking a grape from Tristan's long fingers and then sucking his fingers into my mouth. *Get a grip, Marian.*

"Stop being weird. You're making Dad blush," I chastised.

My dad was definitely blushing. He spoke up. "I'm happy for you, Bee. Hate to say it but I never really liked Jeremy." That was not news.

"Well, then you're going to get a chuckle when you see who he brought to the wedding," I promised.

We wandered back into the lodge and saw my brother Jamie standing with my oldest brother, Pete. I gave them hugs and asked Pete where his family was. He was married to one of my favorite people. Ginger and I had been close friends in high school. When I had found out she was dating my brother in college I almost puked. Things were strained between us for a while, but eventually we found a new normal and returned to being close. The two of them had twin girls who were six years old and adored their Uncle Blue. The feeling was mutual.

"The ladies saw a barn on the drive in and insisted I drop them off so they could flirt with the horses. They'll be along at some point," he said, pulling Simone into a giant hug. "Baby girl, you are going to make one beautiful bride."

"Thanks, Petey. Sorry you missed the show outside. It was glorious." She laughed. Ha-fucking-ha. Glad I could make everyone's day.

"We didn't miss the raunchy stuff," Jamie said. "Pete and I looked out in time to see some guy's tongue down Blue's throat. I could have lived without that. Even though the guy is totally hot. Come to think of it," Jamie grinned his trademark dimple parade, "do they have any other hot brothers?"

Pete elbowed him. "This is all starting to feel incestuous somehow. And have you forgotten your decision to be temporarily celibate?"

Jamie balked. "Haven't forgotten, but Blue's new man might have just reawakened my libido." He winked at me and I shot him evil eyes.

"I thought you were being hit on by that guy at work," Pete said to Jamie. "Whatever happened to him?"

"Don't ask," Jamie warned. I shot Pete a look that said, *No, really, don't ask.* He nodded in acknowledgement.

"Who wants another cup of coffee?" Simone asked. "I know I could use one. John went to pick up Aunt Tilly. Maybe we should switch to mimosas instead."

Tilly was our father's aunt who held the role of family matriarch. She was 100 percent the cause of our particular brand of crazy. Her attendance this week would have the same effect as having a comedy troupe on site. I couldn't wait to see her.

We made fresh cups and chatted about the usual stuff. I asked where Thad was, and Mom told me he'd missed his flight and wasn't going to arrive until the following day. He worked on international aid projects and had been in Kenya for two weeks. The poor guy was going to be dead on his feet when he finally arrived.

The final missing brother was Jude. *The* Jude. As in, Jude and the Saints. Three-time Grammy-winning country music star and all-around American heartthrob. The guy who had women's underwear thrown at him and needed huge bodyguards to accompany him everywhere. He was finishing up a domestic tour and would be arriving tomorrow morning after performing the final concert in Los Angeles later that day.

My brother Jude and I were in sync with each other as if we had been twins. Even though we were four years apart in age with Thad between us, Jude and I were bosom buddies. He was my very best friend and one of the finest human beings I knew. We told each other everything and texted multiple times a day. Standing there in the vineyard lodge, Tristan's vineyard lodge, I was struck by a desperate need to talk to Jude.

I excused myself from my family and walked back out onto the patio. Piper stuck to me like glue, and she trailed along with me out into the sun. I pulled out my phone as I sat down on the patio step.

Piper sat down right next to me and leaned against my side. I reached out an arm to pull her in close, enjoying the warmth of her shiny black-and-white coat. Her tongue found my ear as I dialed Jude's number with my free hand.

It was fairly early in the morning and I hoped I wasn't waking him.

"Hullo?" his sleep-slurred voice answered.

"Hey, it's me," I said. "Sorry to wake you. Want to go back to sleep?"

"No. S'fine. What's up, Bee?"

"I met someone," I blurted. I could hear sheets rumpling in the background as I imagined him rolling over or sitting up in bed.

"Tell me."

So I did. I told him everything. As usual, he listened without interrupting. Until I told him about the family reunion shirt, that is. Then he burst out laughing.

"He sounds nice," Jude said. "But you're saying he's sort of straight? That's a problem."

"No shit, it's a problem. Tell me something I don't know. But he said he hooked up with guys in college, and it sounds like something happened to scare him off."

The sound of water running came through the phone and I heard him brushing his teeth.

"Gotta ask him," he mumbled around the toothbrush.

"I know. But is this crazy? I mean, am I crazy to go along with this ridiculous lark?"

I heard the water turn off and Jude smacking his lips. "It depends on how much you give a shit. Part of me says just to relax and enjoy yourself. Why not? If this guy wants to experiment for a week, let him. He's a big boy. Plus, it will help you deal with the Jeremy shit at the same time. I'd love nothing more than to see that fucker squirm."

No kidding. So would I.

Jude continued, "But if you think there's a chance you could really fall for this guy, like it's more than sex, then be careful. I'd hate to see you spend a week falling head over heels for a guy who is going to go back to the softer side after a week of experimentation. Trust me, I've been there. It ain't pretty."

I was the only person in our family who knew Jude's secret. The whole world assumed he was straight, and because of the country music industry, I understood why he had to remain so deeply closeted. There was no doubt how much the deception bothered him, and I knew he'd do about anything to come clean at least to our family.

But Jude had been burned before. He had trusted our family with confidential information in the past that had somehow still found its way out and to the media. It was one thing for that to happen when you were hiding inured vocal cords from the public eye and quite another when you were hiding your homosexuality from millions of potentially homophobic country music fans.

"I'm not in a position to fall for him, Jude. I'm leaving in a week for London, remember?"

His soft chuckle reached me through the phone. "Right, like it's a choice when you fall for someone. But if the London thing is really happening then, yeah. Enjoy the dude in the short term and make Jeremy squirm. You deserve it."

"Thanks. I think I just needed to talk it through with someone. How's LA?"

"Fine, but I'm fucking exhausted. Can't wait to get there and try to unwind. I hope Mom doesn't nag me about being antisocial, but I've got to spend some time catching up on sleep."

"She'll understand. No one wants you to get sick, and we have all week. Enjoy the Hollywood Bowl show tonight. I really wish I could be there."

"Me too. See you tomorrow, Bee."

I felt a warm hand land in my hair and turned to see Tristan standing behind me.

"Sing 'Bluebells' for me," I said into the phone.

"Always do." He laughed before disconnecting.

12

TRISTAN

Seeing Blue and Piper sitting together on the patio gave me a strange feeling. Like deja vu but in reverse. He looked so at home here, and I wondered if he enjoyed the outdoors as much as I did. I assumed he didn't, but maybe that was my own stupid stereotyping. An urban guy who spent the day in an office seemed more like the type of person who would rather be in an art gallery or movie theater than wandering through a forest. But maybe I was wrong.

As I approached him, I noticed he was on the phone so I didn't say anything. Just put my fingers into his hair to let him know I was there. I reached my other hand over to rub Piper's ears.

When Blue's call ended, I said, "'Bluebells'… Jude and the Saints? Love that song."

He smiled up at me. "It's my favorite."

"Because of your name?" I asked.

"Because he wrote it for me," he said, and I felt my eyes widen in surprise. But then my gut soured as I realized if a man had written Blue a song, it meant they had probably been lovers. Fuck, why did that burn me up so much?

"Oh," I said. "You know Jude?" I sounded like an idiot.

"He's my baby brother," he said. I couldn't help it. A nervous exhale of relief whooshed out of me and I collapsed next to him on the step.

"What was that about?" Blue laughed.

"Never mind," I said. "Jude's your brother? Really? Holy shit."

"Yep. He'll be here in the morning, so you can meet him tomorrow. Just don't go all weak-in-the-knees fangirl when you do. Don't forget you're *my* pretend boyfriend. You'll have to show some restraint," he joked.

"I'll try hard to keep from jumping his bones. How 'bout that?"

"See that you do." He chuckled, bumping my shoulder with his own.

"I have some time before the vineyard tour. Do you want to do something?" I asked.

"Like what?" He grinned. *Like me*, I thought.

"Come on, I'll show you my place. Maybe I can change shirts while I'm there," I teased, standing up and offering Blue my hand.

"No way, dude. That shit was priceless. You're wearing my name all day like a hickey."

I groaned. "You know I'm going to get you back, right? I don't know how yet, but it won't be pleasant."

We walked through the lodge and out to the utility vehicle. Piper trotted along in front of us, knowing where we were headed.

"Tris, nothing you could possibly do would be better than our families seeing you wearing my clothes this morning. I'm hoping to god you have some kind of surveillance system that caught it all on tape. I'd give anything to watch a replay of your mom's face. Her face went from full grape to shriveled raisin in a matter of nanoseconds."

I groaned again. "Don't remind me. She wasn't nearly as impressed with you as your family seemed to be with me."

"Braggart," Blue griped. "Apparently you're hot enough to make one of my brothers break his vow of celibacy. And before you ask, I'm not telling you which one."

"Oooh, like some kind of gay brother threesome," I said, deliberately making it sound dirty.

"Dude, shut the fuck up. We're changing the subject now. Tell me how you went from lawyer to grape-er, or whatever."

We got into the vehicle and I saw that Piper was already loaded up.

"Vintner." I laughed. "And I'm not sure I'd call myself a vintner as much as an owner. It's a long story, but basically I hated the law. My great uncle had been managing this family vineyard for years, and I remembered playing here as a child. I loved it. Always felt more at home here than anywhere else. I don't really know why."

"I can take a guess. It's nirvana. And would be especially for a little boy," Blue explained.

"I guess. Uncle Henry ran the place with his best friend, Art. They both lived on site and worked their asses off at it. But when the big wine labels all joined together in the 1980s, Art and Henry were too old to keep fighting. The place floundered and they barely kept it going through the 1990s and early 2000s. Henry and Art told me they were going to have to sell it. At that point, I'd made plenty of money in my legal practice already and decided to go for it."

I pulled down the long dirt lane toward my cabin. "I bought it about three years ago. For the first year, I kept practicing law so I had some cash to pour into the vineyard to implement some of the changes I wanted to make. Part of me expected to have to remain in the city practicing law for years before the vineyard could support me, but the second year I was already seeing results. Mostly it came from a lucky turn in the industry.

"For the past two years, I've worked it full-time. Obviously I have plenty of good help. Art's grandson, Keller, is the operations manager on the estate. He's been invaluable in providing consistency to get us through the transition. Art and Henry retired to Florida."

We parked and walked to the front door of my cabin. I watched Blue's face to see what he thought about my home. He seemed to be taking it all in, the small structure, the surrounding trees, the view beyond to the rows and rows of red grapes growing plump in the late summer sun.

Finally he turned to look at me. "It's really amazing, Tristan," he said sincerely. "This place is beautiful, and I'm so glad it makes you happy."

A feeling of well-being burbled through me as I reached out to open the front door. Before I had a chance to close it behind us, Blue launched himself at me. Our mouths collided in a bruising kiss and I grabbed his arms to keep from stumbling back onto my ass. He tasted like sweet coffee and smelled like... honeysuckle?

Once I gained my footing, I moved my hands around to grab his ass. God, he had a nice ass. Firm rounded muscles that filled out his jeans in a way that made my dick hard when I had seen him walk in front of me to the cabin door.

His hands were everywhere. In my hair, on my face, my neck, sneaking up underneath my shirt to skim across my abdomen. I felt my skin prickle and knew there were goose bumps popping up in the wake of his touch.

"*Blue*," I gasped between kisses. It was the only word that came out when what I really wanted to say was, *Please, make me come, fuck me, take me, I want you, how the hell do you make me feel this way? Don't stop. Don't ever fucking stop.*

"*Yes*," he whispered with lips pressed against my ear. Had I said those things out loud? We both heaved labored breaths as we stood by my open front door. My heart pounded in my ears, but I still felt every tiny vibration from his breath against my face as I tried to slow my breathing.

I pulled my head back and looked at him. Those blue eyes were dark azure, boring a hole right through me. If it was possible, more blood raced to my cock, and I began breathing rapidly again.

"Tristan," he said in the voice of the hypnotist. "Tell me what you want. Tell me what will make you lose your fucking mind."

My eyes slammed closed and my hand went straight to my crotch, pressing hard. "Jesus, fuck, you're going to make me come in my pants like an idiot," I muttered.

Blue chuckled as he stepped away from me, closing the door after making sure Piper was inside. "You're not coming until your dick is buried so deep in my ass that it's pushing my eyeballs out. Bedroom. Where is it?"

After a full body shiver, I led him to my room, closing Piper out. I was nervous enough as it was without an audience.

13

____

BLUE

All right, now here was where I may have been putting on a front. Don't get me wrong, I was excited and horny as all hell. But I'd never planned on being someone's first. That was more responsibility than I knew what to do with. What if he didn't like it? What if I let him down?

Oh, who was I kidding? What man wouldn't want to sink his throbbing cock into a hot, tight channel? Relax, Marian. How hard could it be?

Don't make a pun, don't make a pun...

Pretty damned hard.

Dammit.

I looked around his bedroom and noticed he had a king-sized bed in the same style as the antique maple one in my room at the lodge. A simple pencil-post in a honey-brown satin finish. Instead of a crisp white duvet cover, his duvet was topped with a faded antique quilt with a pattern of patches forming interlocking rings. It made the room look homey and lived in.

I glanced back up at the man standing next to me. His dark hair and beard growth looked different to me now that I knew him a little better. No longer did I see him as the dark, somewhat intimidating stranger I'd met at the bar. Now he seemed more real. A mix of humor, magnetism, vulnerability, and kindness. Sensuality and mischief. And hot. Don't forget the hot. *Sigh.*

His cock was straining against his fly as was mine. I stepped toward him and began unfastening his jeans, leaning forward to trail kisses down the side of his neck. He hummed his pleasure and ran fingers through my hair. I noticed he did that a lot. He must like the shaggy 'do.

When I unfastened his pants, I pushed them down, bending at the knees to rake both jeans and underwear all the way down to his feet. I stood up slowly, running my hands lightly up the back of his ankles to his calves, then the sensitive skin at the back of his knees, his hamstrings that were quivering under my feathered touches. Finally, to his bare, beautiful ass. God, that ass.

I squeezed the globes and pulled them slightly apart, moving my hands to dip one finger lightly down the top of his crease just to tease. His breath hitched and his ass cheeks bunched under my touch.

"Relax, Tris. Tell me to stop if I do anything that makes you feel uncomfortable," I reminded him in a low voice.

His voice came out like a rake across gravel. "Are you fucking kidding me? It's taking all the self-control I have not to bend you over the foot of my bed and shove myself right into you. Just say the word, Blue."

Holy mother of god, I may have misinterpreted his lack of experience.

What happened next went so fast it made my head spin.

"The word," I hissed in answer to his declaration.

His hands were all over me, shucking off shirt, pants, boxer briefs and flinging them god knows where.

Condoms appeared from somewhere and I was coherent enough to direct him to the packet of lube in my wallet. Before I knew it, I was completely naked, sprawled out on my back in the center of his bed. His duvet and quilt were nowhere to be found, on the floor maybe, and I writhed underneath his exploring mouth.

His warm wet tongue was all over me, tracing lines of abdominal muscles, drawing nipples in with hard, painful sucks, running kisses along my inner arm, and licking the trail of precum that had fallen onto my abdomen from my leaking cock. My mind was blank and desperate at the same time under the sensual assault.

I was moaning and calling his name. Begging and arching underneath him. I realized I had been a fool to think I was ever in charge of any of this simply because I was the one with the most experience with other men. I may have been more experienced on paper, but damn if he wasn't more adventurous, aggressive, and all-around sexual. The man had moves. Even his moves had moves.

His nose was buried in my sac and I felt his tongue paint a stripe between my balls and my hole. "*Fuck, Tris, fuck,*" I gasped. "You're a goddamned liar if you say you've never been with a man." I threw back my head and grasped the headboard behind me.

"I never said I hadn't been with a man," he said as he brought a finger up to tease my crease while he spoke, tracing circles around my entrance and tapping it lightly. "I said I hadn't been with a man since college. But, for the record, I haven't had sex with a man. Just messed around. It never went that far."

"Liar," I gasped as his finger pressed in just the barest amount, making me buck.

"Nope. What can I say, baby, you inspire me," he said before putting his tongue to work again.

"Stop, *stop,* or I'm going to come in your mouth and I'd much rather wait until you're buried in my ass," I panted, trying desperately to hold out.

He sat back on his heels and grinned, his dark hair sticking out in wild spikes.

"Blue," he said, turning my earlier words against me with a devious grin. "Tell me what you want. Tell me what will make you lose your fucking mind."

Goddamn it all to hell.

"*Your,*" gasp, "*dick,*" pant, "*my,*" hiss, "*ass,*" moan, "*rightfuckingnow.*"

That's all it took. He was up like a shot, scrambling for the lube and condom that had gone missing somewhere under my ass. Fingers dug under me, searching, and I couldn't help but yelp when he accidentally hit a ticklish spot. Tristan found the missing items, raising his booty triumphantly.

He sheathed himself and opened the lube packet, drizzling some onto his cock and some onto his fingers, letting a few drips land straight on the crack of my ass. I felt the cold slick dripping down and his fingers slide across my skin to press it against the circle begging for him. One of his fingers breached me and I sucked in a breath as it passed the ring of muscle. *Finally. Thank you.*

He seemed less sure of himself, forehead creasing with intense focus as he worked to stretch me. His finger moved in and out, hesitantly at first. That wouldn't do. "Dude, I'm not a delicate flower. You're not going to hurt me," I ground out.

A second finger joined the first as his mouth crushed against mine. "Shut up," he said against my lips. "Your mouth has better things to do than sass me." He nipped my lower lip with his teeth and I hissed. Just then, his fingers twisted inside of me and I saw stars.

"Holyfuckingshit you hit it. Yes, god, right there," I cried. "Just like that, Tris, please." I pushed back against his fingers, chasing the pleasure pushing power of those long digits.

He chuckled, deep vibrations rattling from his chest into mine. "Good, huh?"

I tilted my chin up and drew my top lip between my teeth, begging my balls to shut the fuck up until I was ready. They were pulled up tight as acorns against my body and I knew it wasn't going to take much to make them shoot.

After a few more scissoring motions, he withdrew his fingers and began teasing my hole with the fat head of his cock. He squeezed more lube on the tip and I heard a slight smacking sound as his head toyed with my entrance. Finally I felt the sweet, sweet push of him breaching me. A ragged breath came out of me with a groan as his thick, hard cock slid into me, inch by slow, slick inch.

14

TRISTAN

Sliding into Blue's body was unlike any feeling I'd ever imagined. He was tight and hot, responsive and vibrating with need. His pupils were blown and his glassy eyes stared into me like I was his entire world. And hell if I didn't want to be. I made myself stop when I was completely inside him. I assumed he'd need a minute to adjust, and I definitely didn't want to hurt him.

In that moment of connection, I felt complete ownership of his body and his pleasure. I wanted to make him feel sexual gratification on a level he'd never dreamed of. His body was like a playground and I wanted to be the only kid allowed on it. I felt sweat drip down my face and saw a single drop fall from my nose onto his mouth as I hovered above him, trying desperately to control myself. He slowly poked his tongue out to lick the bead of sweat. I felt my balls tighten.

"Fuck, baby, tell me I can move already," I begged.

"Move, dammit," Blue growled. "God, what the hell are you wait —?" A loud cry replaced his words as I pulled back and slammed into him. Hard. I crushed my lips down on his and branded a deep kiss inside his mouth while I repeated the process once, twice. On the third slam of my body against his, I twisted and came in at a different angle.

"*Fucckkkk,*" he gasped.

I froze, words coming out between my own gasping breaths. "Are you okay? Jesus, am I hurting you?"

His eyes were frantic. "No, god, prostate. Fuck, *don't stop,*" he begged.

I felt like an idiot, but I tried to shake it off, returning to the rhythm that was driving us both wild. With every roll of my hips, I felt his hand stroking his hard cock between our bodies and I reached down to take over. I didn't know how much longer I could last, and I didn't want to take my pleasure without giving his. I stroked him in time with my thrusts as I felt the spine-tingling warning of my pending climax.

I moved my mouth to his ear and sucked his lobe into my mouth, holding it between my teeth as I breathed low and desperate against his ear. "Let go, baby."

His body squeezed my dick like a vise and I cried out, tilting my head back as he shouted my name and shot into my hand. It was the hottest fucking thing I'd ever imagined, and my orgasm hit me like an NFL linebacker tackling a Pop Warner rookie. Stars exploded in my skull as my vision darkened. I was down for the count and could honestly say had I been one of those guys who died of a heart attack during sex, it would have all been worth it.

After removing the condom and stashing it in a ball of tissues from my bedside table, I collapsed back down on top of Blue.

I felt his arms and legs come around me. I was lying on his chest, making a feeble attempt to keep some of my weight off him by propping my elbows under me. There was a sticky mixture of sweat and semen and body hair between us, but I couldn't have cared less.

Blue's lips landed softly on the top of my head.

"I think I'm being punked," he said quietly.

I lifted my head up to look at him in confusion. "How so?"

"You're a sandbagger. Probably have an entire Boy Scout uniform's worth of gay sex badges. After claiming not to know how to shoot pool, you ran the table on me. Where's the hidden camera? Don't get me wrong. Still totally worth it."

I laughed and dropped my forehead back town to his chest. "No, I just have twenty years' worth of repressed sexual fantasies that all decided to come out at once. Plus, I have a very vivid imagination. And I wanted try out all of the playground equipment at once."

He laughed too, shifting me onto my side so we could face each other. "What playground equipment?"

"Partway through I realized your body was like a playground. And I swear to god if any other kid comes around, I'm crackin' skulls," I growled.

He snorted. "Feel free to slide down my pole any time, Tris. Seriously, I won't protest."

I groaned. "Never mind. Forget I said anything. That orgasm loosened my tongue too much. I'm getting all schmoopy now."

He kissed the corner of my mouth softly. "I like you all schmoopy. It's cute."

"Arghhh, not cute. Jesus, I've been gay for five minutes and now I'm acting cute. Next thing you know, I'm going to be bringing you flowers or some shit."

Blue laughed. "Could be worse. Had I packed my suitcase any differently, you'd have been wearing a T-shirt that says 'Is it gay in here or is it just me?'"

I barked out a laugh. "Oh god, my poor mother. I guess I should be grateful I was wearing the one that practically announced our impending wedding instead of one that just outed me in general."

Blue grinned. "Dude, when we do get pretend married, that shit is going to rock. I'm having T-shirts made for us that say something totally cheesy. Yours will say, 'This Wedding Is So Gay.' And mine will say, 'He Said He Was Straight Until He Came In My Ass.' You know, something like that."

I snorted. "Oh my god, shut up. You're awful."

"At least now I know pretend boyfriends don't have pretend orgasms," he said with a cocky eyebrow.

"Says who? I totally faked it." *Totally didn't fake it.*

Blue snorted. "Dude, ain't nobody that good at faking."

"Right? That shit was intense," I agreed with a grin. "Is it always like that for you?" *Because that was the hottest sex of my fucking life.*

Blue's laughter faltered as his eyes grew serious. "No. It's definitely not always like that for me. It's never been like that for me, Tris. I'm assuming it was maybe because that was your first time or something."

I studied him for a moment, feeling something stir in my chest. Clearing my throat, I shrugged. "Meh, beginner's luck then. I'll take it."

"Right," Blue said, looking away from me. "Ah, we should probably get cleaned up before we're glued together permanently."

And just like that, things got weird. I mean, this whole thing was weird. What were we even doing? I needed to get my head out of my ass and remember this was just for fun. Make Jeremy jealous, keep nosy family members off our backs, and if we could have some white-hot orgasms in the process, more's the better.

I stood up and hustled to the shower before I did something stupid, like invite Blue to join me or ask him when we could do all of that again. We needed a little distance to put things between us back into perspective. I was suddenly grateful for the vineyard tour and wine tasting that afternoon.

Because lord knew nothing quenched a blazing lust fire quicker than spending the afternoon with William and Elizabeth Alexander.

15

BLUE

What. The. *Fuck.*

I was in soo much trouble with this guy. Like serious trouble. The kind of trouble that walks in all tall, dark, and handsome. The kind of trouble that makes you wish the word "pretend" had never been invented and there was no such place as London.

Trying to ignore the slight sting of not being invited into Tristan's shower, I lay back on his bed, covering my face with an arm. *Give him a break, Marian. He probably needs a little space to freak out.*

I wondered what he was thinking in there. Was he upset? He hadn't seemed upset, but then again, I didn't know him that well. Maybe he was good at putting on a front. Maybe he hated it and was cursing me for pressuring him into something he didn't want to do. Because I was the one who attacked him the minute we got into the cabin. I shouldn't have done that.

I rolled over and pulled a pillow over my head.

Don't be an idiot. He was the one who fucked me, not the other way around. No one forced his dick in my ass. That was all him. And, quite frankly, he didn't seem all that upset about it. He seemed... awestruck.

Right. Because my magical asshole was something special. *Jesus,*

Marian. Reality check. He was horny and you had a place for him to stick it.

I groaned at the rude thought. No, that wasn't fair. While I may not have known Tristan that well, I didn't think he was the type to use me for sex without giving a shit about me. He was a nice guy.

Even if I was boring in bed like Jeremy said, Tristan had a great orgasm. Probably the excitement of fucking a man for the first time. That's bound to have made him more excited than normal.

The reminder of Jeremy's words to me the night we broke up hit me like a bowling ball to the gut and I groaned again.

Piper must have heard my distress because she came bounding through the door Tristan had left open. After leaping onto the bed, she nosed under the pillow and licked my cheek. I rolled over to pet her, allowing her attention and enjoying the soft silk of her shiny coat while I returned to my self-doubt.

Stop overthinking this and just enjoy yourself. Why do you have to do this whole post-sex evaluation thing? Since when are you so hard on yourself?

I thought about how sexually confident I was until six months ago.

Did Tristan think I was boring in bed? I didn't think so, but then again, I hadn't thought Jeremy did either.

I considered dressing and walking back to the lodge. It was close enough, but ultimately, I didn't want to be rude to Tristan. And I didn't want to walk back toward my entire family coated in dried spunk.

I heard the shower turn off and Tristan returned to the bedroom looking as though he stepped off the poster every gay teenage boy wishes hung above his bed. His chiseled body still dripped, hair spiky and messy. A small blue towel fought to stay together where it was wrapped low around his hips and those hips... I wasn't sure I'd seen him clearly enough to appreciate just how fucking exquisite his body was before. The first time I'd seen him naked it had been dark in my room. Then, earlier in the cabin, I had been out of my mind with lust and unable to form a coherent thought. But now, in the daylight of his bedroom, what I saw nearly caused me to choke on my tongue.

Be cool, Marian.

"Holyfuckingshit you're hot as hell," I stammered.

Atta boy. Way to stay cool, jackass.

"I mean," I tried to correct. "Sorry, I mean, you're like... hot. Really fucking hot."

Better. So much better.

"Fuck, don't listen to me. I'm drunk," I said.

His eyebrows raised in amusement and his lip lifted in a bemused grin. "You are not."

"Sure I am. I downed half a bottle of Jack while you were in the shower. Dude. I am sooo drunk," I singsonged, sitting up and dangling my legs off the side of the bed.

He laughed and walked toward where I was sitting, pushing my legs open to stand between my thighs. His steely eyes were locked on mine as he slowly lowered his mouth to mine. The kiss was slow and light. Sweet as a goddamned newborn kitten. His tongue traced my lips like he was savoring every millimeter of them. When my mouth opened for him, he brought his hands up to cup my face and slowly slid his tongue over mine, tasting and drinking me in until my head spun.

When he pulled back from the kiss, he smiled a sultry grin. "See? No Jack. I only tasted Blue."

I rolled my eyes and stood up, pushing him gently back so I could move around him toward the bathroom. "Okay, well, I may not be drunk now, but promise me you'll help me change that during the wine tour when we're surrounded by all of the crazy related people."

He slapped my bare ass as I walked past him. "I promise."

I lingered under the hot spray, enjoying the scent of his soap as I scrubbed with it a second time. I couldn't get enough of that smell, reminding me of pressing my nose into Tristan's neck and inhaling.

Walking back into his room, I saw that Tristan was dressed in dark jeans and a burgundy button-down shirt sporting the vineyard logo on the pocket.

"It's still strange to me that you own this vineyard," I said.

"Yeah, well, it's still strange to me that your sister is marrying my brother," he replied.

"That too," I agreed, pulling on my jeans before remembering something. "Wait, didn't you say your brother was homophobic?"

He looked up at me, the smile fading from his lips. Just then we heard a pounding on the cabin door.

"Open up this goddamned door, motherfucker!" John shouted through the wood.

Tristan shot me an apologetic look. "Stay here. And try not to listen to his bullshit, okay? I apologize in advance."

I stood there unable to formulate a response while he left the bedroom, closing the door firmly behind him. He had tried calling Piper out with him, but she refused to leave my side.

The sounds of the front door banging open were followed by John's angry voice. "You're *gay*? What the fuck is going on? I leave the place for an hour and come back to hear that my brother is a queer, and he's fucking Simone's brother? Jesus Christ, Alex. What the hell are you playing at?"

I could hear Tristan's low voice respond, but it was quieter and harder to make out the words. From the tone of it, he sounded like he was trying to calm John.

It wasn't working. "None of my business? How can you stand there and say it's none of my business when my brother decides to fuck up my wedding by making up some bullshit about being gay? What, are you just trying to give Mom and Dad a heart attack?"

More low mumbles from Tristan but this time I heard the tone begin to change from placating to angry.

"You tell that fucker to stay the hell away from you. I don't give a shit who he is. Do you know how upset Mom is? She wants to call Sheila. Maybe your *wife* can talk some sense into you, because you've lost your damned mind."

Now I could hear Tristan's voice loud and clear. "Get the fuck out of my house."

A moment later, the cabin door slammed and I heard Tristan let out a deep sigh. This was all too much. What started out as a lark had just gotten real, and it hadn't been the sex that made it that way.

I had let him jeopardize his relationship with his entire family, and now I was screwing with my sister's wedding weekend. The immature part of me wanted to blame it on Jeremy, but the adult in me knew the blame rested solely on me and my lack of self-confidence. If only I could have been ballsy enough to meet Jeremy and Brad on my own two feet, this wouldn't have all gone down the way it had.

When Tristan opened the bedroom door, I was ready. I had gathered my wits about me and put on my neutral face, despite wanting to burst into frustrated tears.

"Can you give me a ride back to the lodge?" I asked him.

"Blue, I am so sorry about that. I knew he would be an ass, but I never wanted you to hear any of it. I tried to get him to step outside, but I couldn't get him to move."

"It's okay. Really. Can we go?" I tried to give him a reassuring smile.

He tilted his head to study me.

"No," he said.

16

TRISTAN

I wanted to punch my brother in his homophobic, selfish fucking face. He had been an asshole to me my entire life. Despite being four years younger, he had always tried being the dominant brother. He had an aggressive personality while I was more of a go-along, get-along kind of guy.

To look into Blue's eyes, knowing what he heard but not knowing what he was thinking, was heartbreaking. The only thing I could determine was that he was ready to bolt. Full-on, "get the hell away from here, never want to see you again" running away.

"We're not leaving until we talk about this, Blue," I said as gently as I could, pulling him over to the sofa and sitting us both down.

"There's nothing to talk about. He's right. This is fucked up. You *are* making up being gay. And it *is* messing with their wedding week. What did he say that wasn't true, Tristan?"

I ran my hands through my damp hair, unable to formulate an answer.

"See?" Blue said. "He's right."

"No, he's not right. The only people upset about this are my mom and my brother. Your family, including Simone, seemed thrilled," I pointed out.

"What about your dad?" he asked.

"My dad's mother is gay. He's come to terms with it since Granny came out, and he loves Irene. It's only my mom and John who are still assholes, and I refuse to stop being with you because of two ignorant throwbacks."

Blue opened his mouth to argue, but I cut him off.

"Look, Blue, I know this whole thing is a little weird. It started off as a kind of joke, but I really like you. And I like the way I feel when I'm around you. Can't we just keep hanging out and enjoy ourselves this week without worrying about what other people around us think?"

"I don't know, Tris."

"What if we had met this morning for the first time? Been introduced by our families as who we really are. And what if we'd been attracted to one another at that point? Would you refuse to flirt with me for fear it would fuck up our families? People meet and hook up at weddings all the time. Doesn't mean we're planning our own wedding. You're leaving in a week, remember?"

"Maybe I'd want to hook up with you, but I wouldn't make a big scene about it in front of everyone," Blue said.

"All right. So we don't make a big scene in front of anyone. I can handle that," I said.

He laughed. "Babe, I think it's a little too late for that. Have you forgotten your Big Gay Moment on the lawn?"

My heart squeezed at the return of his laughter. "I'm not sure I'll ever forget that. As far as coming out moments go, it was a doozie."

"Come on," Blue said, standing and reaching a hand out to pull me up. "I need to eat something before the tour this afternoon. Can't go into a wine tasting on an empty stomach."

We made our way out of the cabin, Piper running past us to load up in the bed of the utility vehicle.

"Are Granny and Irene coming this week? I'm dying to meet them," Blue said, obviously trying to change the topic.

"Yep. They actually got in last night. I'm sure they'll be at the wine tasting tonight. Granny's a wine slut."

I told him more about the people from my extended family who would be there that week. We talked about the events that were scheduled for each day. The tour with wine tasting was Tuesday's event. Wednesday night included a men's poker night and a ladies' spa night to mimic bachelor and bachelorette parties. Thursday there was a myriad of events offered to people from horse trail rides to balloon rides to tours of other local wineries.

My family had insisted I not be in charge of anything other than the tour because they wanted me to be free to spend time with friends and family. Keller was taking point on the rest of the events, including the wedding and reception on Saturday evening. Thankfully, the rehearsal dinner Friday night was being held in the cellars of a neighboring winery. Their barrel room was a perfect venue for it, and I was grateful to have one full day without the vineyard being responsible for any of the festivities.

When we parked in front of the lodge, I told Blue I had to head on over to my office in the estate house to do some work before the tour.

"Do you need help with anything?" he asked me as he stepped out of the vehicle.

"Don't think so. Go have fun with Simone and your folks." I noticed Piper had hopped out with Blue and I told her to load up. She just stood there by Blue's side.

He laughed, looking from my traitorous dog to me. "Guess she has a new bestie," he said with a smirk.

"She's the most obedient dog I've ever met. If she's ignoring my commands, she must be stupid in love. But I don't want you to have to worry about her," I said as I stood up to grab her.

"It's okay, Tris. I don't mind. She can keep me company and I'll bring her with me at three," he said, scratching her ears.

Something about the way Blue shortened my name made my insides warm. No one had ever called me that, and I'm not sure I'd have been okay with it if they had. But coming out of his mouth? Yes, please.

"You sure?" I asked, but I could tell he was fine with it.

"Absolutely. I'll take her on my run. Go, I'll see you in a couple of hours."

"Okay, thanks," I said with a smile before backing out and driving in the direction of my office.

When I pulled out of the parking lot, I took one last moment to look back and appreciate Blue's body as he walked into the lodge. Tall, lean frame, muscular back, trim waist, fucking stellar ass packaged to perfection in designer blue jeans. What the hell was happening to me?

In the main winery building, I spent a few minutes catching up with Keller and answering his questions about how everything was going so far with the family's arrival. After making my way to the privacy of my own office, I booted up my computer to get some work done.

After about fifteen minutes I realized my mind had wandered back to Blue and what a difference a day made. It hit me that I'd just had sex with a man. Correction: I'd just had amazing, earth-shattering, mind-blowing sex with a man. Finally. And it wasn't weird.

I thought back to high school and college. My senior year in high school I dated a girl named Amber Lombardi. The entire time I dated her, I tried desperately to ignore the fact I was ridiculously attracted to her twin brother, Adam. I finally broke it off with Amber because I realized I could no longer hide my feelings if I spent any more time around their family.

I wasn't about to try anything with him because I owed at least that much to Amber. But I knew Adam was gay, and I couldn't get him out of my mind. Finally at a huge graduation party, Adam came on to me. We were in the basement of a big house on a hill, and there were drunk kids everywhere. Music pounded and the smell of pot permeated the air. I was looking for the bathroom when an arm grabbed me and pulled me into a storage room.

It was Adam. Before the door to the storage room even finished closing behind us, he was kissing me and palming my dick through my shorts. And god was it hot. There was no way I was going to stop him when it felt that good.

My dick was screaming for more, and the alcohol I'd consumed made me braver than normal.

"Suck me off," I begged. He was on his knees in an instant and it took about two seconds of his hot, wet mouth on my cock before I spilled into him, thanking god for the most amazing feeling in the world in addition to the loud music covering my grunts and groans.

While I tried to recover and catch my breath, I saw Adam fumbling open his own shorts and jacking himself before spurting on the floor of the storage room.

"Fuck, that was hot as shit, Tristan," he gasped, stepping back from the wet ribbons he'd left on the floor and tucking himself back into his pants. "I've wanted to do that for years."

I looked up at him, wide-eyed. "Dude, why didn't you say anything?"

He shrugged. "Didn't think you were into it."

The kid had a point. "Me either, really. Until I started going out with Amber."

He nodded. "Yeah, that was fucked up."

I agreed. We had a few more stolen moments that summer before college. Jacking each other off in a bathroom somewhere or him going down on me in a bedroom at someone's house party. But I never went down on him and we didn't kiss much. And there sure as shit was no full-on sex. I was way too confused about how I felt, and I knew that, for me, sex was a big step. I didn't want to go all the way with someone I didn't have any feelings about. I'd slept with Amber, but that was it.

I had gone back to dating women in college but was never truly satisfied. It was like I had an itch that needed to be scratched, and I thought that when I did, I'd be over it and could go back to being "normal."

It wasn't until the end of my freshman year in college that I found a man I wanted to sleep with. And that man was the one who turned me against being with men for the next fifteen years.

It all started to make more sense to me. I truly was bisexual, but I had been denying myself something I'd wanted for a long time because of one bad experience. Fuck. I felt cheated. After my experience with Blue that morning, I realized I'd been cheated out of fifteen years of feeling that good.

For fifteen years, I hadn't let myself think about men. I hadn't let myself believe I could be with a man or be loved by a man. That a man wouldn't love me like a woman would. Wouldn't make me feel good. Would only use me, abuse me, and toss me aside like I was disposable.

But that wasn't at all the way I'd felt with Blue. How could I have been so stupid to think that way all these years? The truth was, I hadn't let myself think anything about it at all. I rushed into a relationship with Sheila and then used it as a protective shield. I'd put my true feelings in a closet and locked the fucking door.

I grabbed a cup of pens and pencils from my desk and flung it at the wall. The cup bounced off but remained intact as it fell to the ground. Pens and pencils scattered across the stone floor and rolled around everywhere.

A moment later, Keller poked his head in. "Everything all right in here?" he asked tentatively.

"Yes, sorry. Just frustrated about something. No worries."

He looked at me with concern in his face. "Something you want to talk about, Tristan?"

I appreciated his concern. Keller was a nice guy whom I'd known since we were little, but this was all too mixed up to discuss with someone else. Especially someone who worked for me.

"No, thanks. I'll be fine. Just letting family shit get to me," I lied. "Remind me it's only a week, okay?" I winked at him and he blushed.

"It's only a week. You can do it, Tristan. Want me to sing you an inspirational song from my favorite Disney movie?" he asked.

I laughed. "What's your favorite Disney movie?"

"Don't have one, was hoping you'd say no," he admitted with a grin.

"How about humming the tune to *Chariots of Fire*?" I suggested with a smile.

"Done," he said and turned around to walk out while blasting out the tune at the top of his lungs. I rolled my eyes and laughed.

"That's not humming!" I yelled over the racket his mouth was making.

"But it got you laughing," he called back.

True.

17

———

BLUE

When I entered the lobby of the lodge, I found a group of my siblings and parents hugging Aunt Tilly. As I got closer, I noticed Jeremy and Brad approaching the group from the guest room hallway.

Just as I was about to call out to Aunt Tilly, I heard her say, "Jeremy, what the hell are you doing here?"

I froze at her angry tone. *Oh shit*. Besides Jude, the only other person who knew the dirty details of my breakup with Jeremy was Tilly. This wasn't going to be pretty.

"And did you bring your baby brother with you? Who's this little boy?" she scoffed at Brad.

My feet began moving and I hustled over to where they all stood.

"Aunt Tilly, this is Brad. Brad, this is Tilly Marian, my great-aunt," I said, politely trying to keep my jaw from tightening.

"Uh," Brad stammered. "Nice to meet you, Mrs. Marian."

"Aunt Tilly," Jeremy said. "It's wonderful to see you," he said as he went in for a hug.

If my great-aunt had packed a taser in her handbag, 50,000 volts would have coursed through Jeremy's body. As it was, she endured the embrace with a stiff frame and bugged-out eyes pointed at me. I winced and shrugged, mouthing the word *sorry* at her. She rolled her eyes.

After he hugged her, Jeremy greeted the rest of my family as if he was still one of us. Jackass.

I hugged Tilly, trying desperately not to smell Jeremy's cologne on her. She whispered into my ear, "What's the story on the twink?"

"Tell you later. Let's avoid a scene, old lady," I warned.

"That's no fun," she chastised.

"Do it for Simone," I reminded her.

"Fuck," she muttered.

I loved that woman so very much.

After the awkward moments of Jeremy hugging my family members and Brad standing horrified on the edges of the group, they raced off to attend some very important thing. I assumed that thing was wildly adventurous sex somewhere outdoors. Because Jeremy had three fucking years of vanilla sex to make up for.

Not that I was sulking.

I noticed Ginger and my two nieces were with the group and I gave them all big hugs. The girls were talking over each other to tell me all about the horses they saw.

Tilly announced her plans to lie down in her room for a little while, and I asked if there was anyone who wanted to go for a run with me. Ginger said she did, so we agreed to change and meet back in the lobby after grabbing a bite to eat.

We ran along a trail through trees and past some of the rows of trellises. Piper ran forward along the trail and then back to check on us before running forward again. The smell in the air reminded me of Tristan, and I realized why I'd smelled soil and grapes on him the night before.

When we slowed to a walk, Ginger broke the silence. "So, I hear you're sleeping with the enemy."

I looked at her in confusion. "What do you mean, the enemy?"

"John's brother. C'mon. Are we going to pretend we like John and his parents? They're assholes."

"They sure seem like it," I agreed. "But Tristan is different. He's a really nice guy."

She studied me and grinned. "Aww, you really like him, don't you?"

I felt myself blush and hoped it was covered up by the red face I usually got when running.

"Yes, I like him. Like I said, he's a really nice guy."

"How did you two meet?" she asked.

Uh-oh. We hadn't thought about how to answer detailed questions.

"We met at a bar one night and really hit it off." *True.*

"Well, he's a looker, that's for sure." *Also true.*

"Yup," I agreed, trying not to grin like a lovesick fool.

"Tall, dark, and handsome," she continued.

"Sure is." I swallowed.

"You're hiding something," she accused.

Fuck.

"Why do you think I'm hiding something?" I asked.

"Because you and I had lunch three days ago, remember? And you would have told me if you were dating someone seriously enough to introduce them to your parents. Spill it," she demanded.

"I'm not going to tell you all about this because then you'll tell Pete and he'll tell Mom and Dad and..."

"Fine, I won't tell Pete."

"That's not fair of me to ask you. Can't you just accept what I'm telling you?"

"Just tell me one thing. Are you really sleeping together, or is this all made up for some reason?"

I thought about what to say. "We had sex an hour and a half ago. Does that answer your question?"

She barked out a laugh. "TMI, Blue."

"Well, you fucking asked. Nosy bitch," I grumbled.

Her hand reached out to grab my arm. I stopped walking and turned toward her.

"Blue, I'm happy you're moving on. Jeremy was toxic. You deserve so much better. I can't wait to meet Tristan."

"Thanks, Ginger. You'll meet him this afternoon. He's a really nice guy," I said with a smile. "And that ass..."

She elbowed me with a laugh. "Better than Pete's ass? I don't think so."

"Ewww, gross." I pretended to gag. "That's disgusting."

I whistled for Piper to come back from exploring in the shrubbery, and we made our way back to the lodge for a shower and quick bite to eat before the vineyard tour.

When it was time for the tour, my family and I met in the lobby and walked over to the main winery building together. It was a beautiful two-story stone structure with vines growing over one of the walls and fronted by a matching stone courtyard edged with massive pots overflowing with colorful flowers.

As I entered the open double doors, I saw Tristan talking to a young woman behind a reception counter. Piper ran over to get his attention, causing Tristan to lift his head in search of me. When he saw me walking in, his entire face opened up into a smile that made my step falter.

Fuck if those weren't butterflies in my stomach like I was some kind of schoolgirl. *Act cool, Marian.*

"Hey there," I said, acting cool.

Tristan hustled out from behind the counter and strode toward me. "Hey back." He reached out to cup one side of my face and leaned his head in to whisper into my opposite ear. "Come to my office for a sec?"

I nodded dumbly. I'd follow that fucker off a cliff if he asked me in that smoky purr.

He grabbed my hand and led me down a hallway before the rest of my family entered the building. When Piper tried to join us, he commanded her to stay at the front desk. There was enough force behind his word to cause her to obey.

Dude meant business.

When the office door closed behind us. Tristan sat back on the edge of his desk with his arms crossed in front of his chest. I had hoped he wanted to screw around or something, but obviously I'd misread him. The thought sent a chill down my spine. Was he having second thoughts? Did he want to make sure I didn't embarrass him during the tour?

"What's up?" I asked nervously.

"My dick is what's up," Tristan confessed. "And I'm terrified of giving a tour to our friends and family when all I can think about is how badly I want to come inside of you again."

I felt my blood rush south as I gawked at him. He raised an eyebrow at me.

"What?" he asked. "You're looking at me like I've shocked you."

"Well," I began. "You kind of did. You're standing there with your arms crossed like you don't want me anywhere near you. I thought you were mad at me or something."

"Blue, that's because I'm afraid the minute I touch you I'm going to rip your fucking clothes off. It's all I can seem to do when I'm with you."

My jeans were feeling stupidly tight suddenly, and I wished he'd act on his temptation. The tour was in fifteen minutes, though, which meant there wasn't time for getting naked.

I stepped forward and grasped his belt buckle. He sucked in a breath.

"What are you doing? I just needed a minute to calm down, Blue."

"Yes, and I'm going to help with that." I smirked as I undid his belt and his fly. I pulled down his trousers and boxers, exposing his beautiful cut cock.

"Mmm," I hummed appreciatively. "This bad boy needs to be sucked into submission."

I dug the tip of my tongue into his slit, enjoying the taste.

"*Fuck,*" he hissed. My hand wrapped around the base of his cock while my mouth toyed around the head in light, teasing licks. His thighs began to quiver so I pushed him farther back to sit completely on the desk.

I nuzzled his warm sac and inhaled his musky scent. God, that was the best part. Smelling him and feeling his wrinkled skin against my lips. His large hand landed in my hair and I heard him making small noises of pleasure as I took one of his balls into my mouth and sucked it with my tongue.

"Blue, *god*," he gasped. "*Fuck* that feels incredible."

One of my fingers traced the seam of his balls while I licked up his shaft and then took his entire length in my mouth at once. He started to cry out, but I quickly reached a hand up to cover his mouth. His eyes closed and his breathing came fast and hot against my hand. He grasped my hand and moved it, sucking two of my fingers into his hot, wet mouth. I could feel my dick leaking, making me thankful I put on underwear earlier.

My fingers fucked his mouth as his cock fucked my swollen lips. I opened my jaw and pulled at his hips, encouraging his instinctive thrusting. His hips thrust upward and his head hit the back of my throat. Tristan's fingers gripped my hair and I brought my own hands down to cup his balls and stroke a finger over the tight pucker below.

"Shit, baby, I'm coming," he ground out. I held him to me and felt the warm jets hit the back of my throat as I brought my hand back over his mouth just in time to stifle his moans. I licked him clean, and we sat there gasping for a minute before I realized my hand was still over his mouth. As I pulled it away, he caught it with one of his and kissed it, looking over our hands to meet my eyes. His gray eyes were still sparkling with energy but this time is was less lust and more... intrigue. Or maybe... appreciation. It was hard to tell.

My dick was as hard as ever and I pushed a hand over it, standing up straight and trying to adjust. I caught Tristan staring and I shrugged.

His eyes came up to meet mine again. This time the lust was back and the gray eyes were stormy and fierce. I swallowed.

"Touch yourself. I want to watch you jack off while sitting in my office chair."

"I don't think so," I began.

"Please," he whispered.

I moved over to sit on the leather chair behind his desk, fumbling for my belt and fly before shucking everything down to my knees. I sat back, wondering idly what I was going to do if I made a mess on his chair or carpet. He must have seen me glancing around because he opened a cabinet, exposing a stack of vineyard T-shirts.

My hand was already stroking by the time he came to stand next to me, tossing a T-shirt onto my stomach before leaning back on the desk again, but this time he was facing me and his knee was brushing mine. His gray lasers were trained on my leaking cock and it was enough to start the tingle in my balls.

"You have no idea how sexy you are like that, Blue, stroking for me." He leaned over to slide his tongue into my mouth and grabbed my balls with a warm hand.

18

TRISTAN

Watching Blue come apart right in front of me was spectacular. His chest heaved with labored breaths, tendons stood out from his flushed neck, long fingers pulled his swollen cock out of a mass of red-gold curls. Sculpted abs contracted where he had rucked up his shirt to keep it clean. His hand pulled and twisted as he jacked himself. As his climax approached, I couldn't resist putting my mouth on him. I just wanted it.

Wanted to taste him and feel that smooth warm skin against my tongue. I leaned over and took him into my mouth, causing him to immediately come in a rush of heat against the back of my tongue. I never expected to swallow the first time I gave a guy head, but with Blue it was different. I wanted to take every single bit of him inside my body and not let it go. So I did.

The look on his face when I stood back up, licking my lips, was downright comical. I burst out laughing.

"Dude, the look on your face right now," I said.

"At the risk of sounding repetitive, you're a total sandbagger," Blue said with a sulk.

"I'm not, I swear. I told you already, you just inspire me. You're sexy as hell, Blue. I couldn't just stand there and watch. Now, come on. We have to go out there. Try not to look like you just swallowed my load."

He stood and fastened his jeans again, glaring at me. "Ditto. And you're going to have to shave that beard or we won't be able to kiss anymore. My skin shows fucking everything."

I leaned over toward him and kissed him so passionately that his tongue came out searching and his hands reached around to grab the back of my head as a moan escaped his lips. I pulled back just as quickly and smirked. "Still want to complain about my kisses?"

"Fuck you," he grumbled, rubbing his scratched cheeks.

I laughed and opened my office door to join the others while Blue detoured to the men's room to gather his composure.

We had about twenty people for the tour. Most of them were family members since many of Simone's and John's friends wouldn't arrive until Thursday or Friday.

After walking through the vineyard itself, explaining grapes and varietals, the growing season, and the harvesting process, we made our way into the winery, which took up the back half of the large estate house. Keller helped explain the science behind winemaking as well as the processes of crushing, pressing, fermentation and its various stages, cold stabilization and aging. He described the reasons for aging and how some wines needed aging more than others.

The stainless steel equipment sparkled in the sun coming through the windows around the vaulted room. I was always impressed by how clean the room was kept. We moved on to the bottling process and finished the tour in the cellars where the staff had set up the tasting and food.

The entire time I was conducting the tour, Jeremy was making a point to glare at me. Brad hadn't joined him for the tour and I wondered if it was because the kid had realized how uncomfortable the week was going to be surrounded by an ex and his entire family.

At one point I saw Jeremy sidle up next to Blue in an effort to get his attention. I felt my shoulders stiffen in response to seeing Jeremy lean in and whisper into Blue's ear. Blue shook his head and tried stepping away from Jeremy, but Jeremy grabbed Blue by the elbow. I started to take a step toward them when Blue caught my eye and shook his head subtly. He shook off Jeremy's grip and went to offer his Aunt Tilly an arm for the walk down to the cellars.

When everyone took a spot at the long tasting bar, Blue seemed to make sure he was sitting between Tilly and my cousin Sarah. Sarah had grown into a successful medical student who was just finishing up her residency on the East Coast. I didn't get to see her very often so we had to settle for catching up over Facebook when we got a chance. It would be fun to spend time with her while she was in town for John's wedding.

As I walked around to the serving side of the bar, I noticed Piper was staying by the base of Blue's barstool. She really was a nut for that man, but who could blame her? His hand snaked down to idly scratch her ears as if, even with out looking, he knew she'd be there. Something about that gesture made my throat feel thick.

When I stood opposite their place at the bar, I introduced Sarah to Blue and Tilly on one side of her, and Simone on the other side of her. Keller and three staff members helped facilitate the tasting. We offered each participant a five-glass tasting flight, explaining how to check the wine's appearance first.

After appearance, we went on to explain how to assess the wine in the glass, in mouth, and finally the finish, or aftertaste. We discussed complexity and character, and I enjoyed watching Blue's face as he tried to determine what flavor notes each wine had.

Finally, we discussed potential, which included aging. I gestured to the oaken barrels surrounding the room in built-in brick cubbies made especially for them.

By the time everyone had gone through their five flights and a full glass of their favorite, the room was buzzing with laughter and conversation. People milled around to sample the gourmet appetizers laid out on tables around the room and a jazz trio played music in a corner.

That cellar room was one of my favorite places for a gathering of friends. There were twinkle lights that made the space intimate and the shadows in the barrel nooks hovered mysteriously along the edges of the room. The long bar top was an old, seasoned butcher-block type with scars and red wine stains under a hand-rubbed finish to preserve its hundred-year-old history in that spot.

Old oversized barrels acted as bar-height tables around the room and stools had been carved by a neighbor of the vineyard twenty years before to mimic the twisted look of grapevines wrapped around the legs.

I stood talking to Blue, Tilly, and Sarah for quite a while, finally pulling a stool around to my side of the bar so I could sit.

When Blue had introduced me to Aunt Tilly at the start of the tour, I noticed she looked at me with a mischievous grin on her face. It reminded me of Granny, which scared the piss out of me.

After she'd loosened her lips during the wine tasting, Tilly went to town.

"So, young man, how long have you been fucking Big Blue here?" she asked at full volume. Red wine shot out of my nose and I began to choke. I looked around and noticed not one single member of Blue's family was taken aback by her words. My cousin Sarah gawped before howling with laughter.

Blue came around to my side of the bar while I scrambled to catch my breath. He found a bar towel and helped wipe off my face, my shirt, and the bar. I caught a glimpse of his smirk and narrowed my eyes at him.

"Aunt Tilly, Jesus. Remember what I said about not making a scene?" Blue chastised.

"I thought you just meant not to make a scene about Jeremy," she said, again at full voice. I looked around the room and spotted Jeremy talking to Brad, who had shown up for the alcoholic portion of the tour. Smart man. Luckily, he either didn't hear Tilly or he ignored her like all the other Marians. Not that he was a Marian. *Fuck*.

I decided to claim Blue publicly and give Aunt Tilly as good as I got. "How long? What do you think, Blue? This morning it took about an hour and then in my office right before the tour—" I was cut off by Blue slapping a hand over my mouth.

"Oh my god," he laughed, "I'm going to kick your ass. Shut the fuck up."

Aunt Tilly burst out laughing and Sarah did too, despite her face turning beet red. Blue was blushing to the tips of his ears, and it was adorable. I poked my tongue out to lick his palm and he pulled his hand away as if I'd stung it. I laughed.

"That old lady of yours is playing with fire. Wait till she meets my Granny and Irene," I warned. Tilly kept on laughing.

Sarah laughed even harder. "Oh god, Tristan's right. Granny and Tilly will be new best friends. Poor Irene will be jealous. Where are they anyway?"

"They should be here any minute. They ended up going out for nine holes of golf somewhere," I answered.

My dad came over and sat on Blue's abandoned stool. He greeted Sarah, and Blue introduced him to Aunt Tilly. Dad was very polite and kind to both of them but seemed to make a concerted effort to speak to Blue.

"So, Blue, tell me what you do in the city. Your mom says you're a graphic designer of some kind?" he asked. I stood there feeling a little surprised and a lot grateful. This was the first inkling of kindness from anyone in my immediate family toward Blue since I had told them we were together. Even if the relationship was pretend, they didn't know that.

"Yes, sir. I am the creative director for a trio of fitness magazines in San Francisco. My staff and I are in charge of everything visual in the magazines including layouts, photography manipulation, and graphic elements. Some of our advertisers also hire us to design their ads for the magazine so that we can incorporate elements specific to our content or target audience that month," Blue described.

"That sounds interesting. Have you been at it for long? You seem young to be a director. I know your parents are very proud of you," Dad said.

Blue smiled and glanced over at me before responding. "I'm thirty-two and have been the director for two years. I started at the magazine as a junior graphic designer straight out of CalArts and worked my way up. While I do like it, I'm feeling a little frustrated lately. The marketing and commercialism is making me a bit jaded, to be honest."

Dad leaned forward, interested in what Blue had to say. "How so?"

"Well, designing for a magazine is basically using visual means to manipulate the consumer into spending their money with advertisers. Two out of the three magazines I design for have a target demographic that's getting younger and younger. Those kids don't have that kind of disposable money.

"Not only that, but the use of Photoshop is turning realistic fit bodies into fake, unattainable bodies. It's creating a cultural crisis. Being a part of it is wearing on me," he said. I obviously hadn't known this about Blue, and hearing him tell it to my dad was eye opening.

"I agree with that, Blue. There are some magazines and catalogs that are trying to do away with Photoshop, but our society still has a long way to go. I presented the negative financial effects of Photoshop use in apparel advertising at a conference last month. I've been working on changing things as much as possible for a while now, but it's not easy."

Blue raised his eyebrows in surprise.

I piped up to tell Blue that my dad was the CFO for one of the largest apparel companies in the country, and then I turned to Dad.

"Dad, what's the financial argument?" I asked with genuine interest.

"Well, younger generations are activists. They know to put their money where their mouth is. When these smart, strong young people see articles and discussions online about the deadly impact negative self-image is having on our country's youth, they take a stand by preferring companies who don't contribute to the problem. It's similar to what happened with cosmetics when you were young, Tristan. The companies that tested on animals were boycotted until they changed their policies."

"Exactly," Blue said. "I've tried changing things from the inside by not ever using underweight models or over-sexualized models, but it's hard when corporate is breathing down your neck to conform to industry norms. I've been transferred to London to be the creative director for the parent company. It's an incredible opportunity, so hopefully I can have a better influence in that position."

Just then Granny and Irene burst on the scene and my dad shot me a smile before climbing off his stool to greet them.

Blue looked at me. "He seems cool."

"He is. I think he was just surprised earlier," I decided.

I felt Blue's hand come up to settle on my lower back and I leaned into him a little. God, he felt so good. Just a touch from him and I was a goner. Smelling my soap on him made me want to sniff him obsessively like Piper would. Instead, I took a step away from his hand and said, "Come on and meet the crazy ladies."

I offered my arm to Blue's great-aunt. "Tilly, will you allow me to introduce you to my granny and her wife, Irene?"

"The two hot chicks who just walked in?" Tilly asked with a wink.

"Yes, ma'am. Two craziest ladies I'd ever met until you." I winked back.

As we walked across the room, she leaned in so only I could hear her. "What the fuck is Jeremy doing staring at Blue all night? He had his damned chance. Don't you want to kick his ass or something?"

"Don't tempt me. But take a look at the kid's ring finger," I whispered back.

I heard Tilly make a sound that sounded like a growl.

19
____

BLUE

Tristan's granny was as nutty as Aunt Tilly even though she was half the size. The woman was teeny tiny and seeing Tristan lean down to hug her made me want to laugh. He could probably put her in his pocket. She had tight white curls that hugged her head, and her skin was a pale powdery grandma skin with blush circles over her cheeks.

Irene was clearly the demure sidekick to Granny's crazy. Irene was a tall, slender woman with salt-and-pepper hair. She looked like a retired librarian, and I almost felt compelled to whisper in her presence. It took all my self-control not to picture them naked together.

I might have thrown up a little in my mouth when I saw Granny pinch Irene's ass. Tristan noticed my distress and leaned in, lips brushing against my ear, sending shivers down my spine. "That's nothing. Wait until they take their teeth out and start kissing. I call it gumming."

I barked out a laugh so hard everyone's heads turned. My face turned bright red from the attention and when I got inquiring looks, I put my hands over my face. Tristan squeezed my shoulder with a laugh.

Gradually, everyone who was still in the cellar, including Jeremy and Brad, joined together in a group around Granny and Irene.

After a few minutes of small talk, Aunt Tilly piped up.

"Oh my gosh, Brad! Did Jeremy make an honest man of you?" she cried with fake excitement.

Jeremy looked caught like a deer in headlights. Brad looked down at his ring as if he'd never seen it before.

"Oh," Brad said with a laugh. "No. This is my father's wedding band. He passed away when I was in high school, and I've worn his ring ever since. I usually wear it on my middle finger but I broke my hand a month ago and the ring still only fits on my ring finger. I guess I never thought about how that looked." His eyes darted to me and I tried to hide the relief that washed over me.

Brad wasn't the only one studying me for a reaction. It seemed like everyone in the fucking room was. I felt Tristan tense up beside me, I saw Jeremy search my eyes with an apologetic look, and I saw my brother Pete roll his eyes in an effort to get me to laugh. I begged myself to project Switzerland. Not happy, not sad, not relieved, not disappointed. Just neutral.

Tilly couldn't stop there though. "Well, that makes sense. I just couldn't figure out why such a nice young man would want to rush into marriage when he was barely out of high school. Do you still live with your parents, honey?"

Brad's face bloomed pink, and I felt sorry for him.

"Aunt Tilly," I reprimanded. "Leave the poor guy alone." I turned to Brad with a sincere look of apology. "I'm so sorry. Ignore the old bat."

I noticed Tilly wink at Tristan out of the corner of my eye. What was that about?

Brad smiled appreciatively at me. "It's okay. I get that all the time. For the record, I'm twenty-six. I can only hope that when all you guys are old and gray, I'll still pass for ten years younger than I am."

Score one for the Bradster.

After the subject changed and the group began to break apart, I asked Tristan if he would mind getting me another glass of wine. When he walked over to the bar, I took the opportunity to approach Brad and apologize again. Jeremy had gone to find a bathroom or something so it was my chance to catch him on his own.

"Listen, I can't imagine how excruciating this week is going to be for you, so I just want to tell you I'm sorry in advance for anything and everything my family does to make you feel uncomfortable, okay?" I asked.

He smiled and nodded. "Blue, if I'd had any idea that Jeremy had an ex here, I would have never agreed to come. I'm sorry if I'm putting you or your family in an awkward position. If you want me to leave, please say the word."

"Not necessary. I just wanted you to know that we're good."

Brad let out a relieved sigh and reached out to shake my hand just as Jeremy returned. I shook it and walked away without acknowledging Jeremy's raised eyebrow aimed at me. It was no longer my job to explain anything to Jeremy.

I caught up with Tristan at the bar and he handed me the glass of wine without asking me about my conversation with Brad. His calm demeanor was contagious and I let it wash over me for a moment. I felt a hand clap on my shoulder and tensed, thinking it was Jeremy. But it was Tristan's father.

"Good night, gentlemen. We're heading back to the lodge," he said, squeezing my shoulder gently. The gesture was clearly meant to reassure me that he accepted what Tristan had told him about us. I was torn between appreciation and guilt. I noticed Mrs. Alexander standing stoically beside Mr. Alexander and I leaned over to kiss her cheek. She stiffened but didn't recoil from my touch. Baby steps.

I'd noticed John had avoided Tristan and me all afternoon and evening. The regret at messing with their relationship returned to gnaw at me. Tristan must have noticed John's coldness too, because he strode over to John to strike up a conversation with him a little while later.

Jeremy approached me without Brad in tow and asked if he could speak to me in private. I said no before walking out of the cellar to find a bathroom.

While I desperately wanted nothing more than to crawl into bed with Tristan that night, and every night for the foreseeable future, it was a bad idea. Maybe if I gave Tristan some space, he could spend some time patching things up with his brother. They could talk without John worrying about me interrupting or Tristan feeling like he had to hang out with me.

Instead of visiting the restroom, I took the opportunity to slip out and accompany Pete and Ginger back to the lodge. Their girls had been left in the hotel room for movies and board games with my brother Jamie.

Pete and Ginger were happily tipsy from the wine and their parentally small tolerance levels. I enjoyed watching them flirt with each other and giggle as we walked back through the cool night. I felt a nudge against my leg and noticed Piper walking beside me.

"Oh shit, guys. I have to take Piper back to Tristan so he doesn't wonder where she is," I said, kicking myself for not making sure she didn't follow me.

Ginger and Pete barely noticed me leave and I made my way back to the main winery building. Before I got to the courtyard, I saw Tristan come flying out the front doors, looking around for Piper.

"She's here, Tris. I have her," I called out.

He turned and looked into the darkness until he could make us out. Piper stayed by my leg, nudging.

As I approached Tristan, I could still see apprehension in his eyes. "It's okay," I repeated. "She's right here with me."

"Dammit, Blue," Tristan snapped. "I wasn't worried about Piper. It was *you* I couldn't find."

My stomach dropped. "What?" I asked.

"I saw you leave with Jeremy and I..." He looked down at the ground, curling fingers into fists beside his legs. "I wanted to make sure you were okay."

"What?" I repeated.

"I saw you leave with Jeremy." I saw the hurt and confusion on his face and I wondered what was behind it. This was sort of pretend, right?

"But I didn't leave with Jeremy," I explained. "He asked me to speak in private, and I said no."

Just then, the remaining partygoers came giggling out the front doors and spilled into the courtyard. Tristan and I faked smiles as they all bid us good night. When they were gone, I looked at him. God, he was beautiful. The gas lanterns by the front doors flickered against one side of his face and the moon gave off enough light to illuminate the other side.

"You said no?" he asked. "But he followed you out of the room."

"He did?" I asked in confusion. "I didn't see him. I was going to go to the bathroom, but I saw Ginger and Pete. They walked back to the lodge with me until I realized Piper had followed me."

"You were leaving for the night and didn't say goodbye or anything?" he asked with furrowed brows. "Was it me? Was it my parents? Did they say something?"

"No. They were great. Well, your dad was great and your mom wasn't terrible," I joked. "I saw you talk to John and just wanted to give you some space."

"Why?" Tristan asked.

"Why did I want to give you some space?"

"Yes," he said, sounding frustrated. "Quit fucking answering my questions with questions and talk to me."

I blew out a breath I'd been holding and threw up my arms. "Because I fucked things up for you and wanted you to have a chance to make it right with him."

He let out a sigh. "Can we talk about this back at my place? Preferably naked?" he suggested.

I felt my dick stir at the mere suggestion of a naked Tristan.

"You make a compelling argument," I said, walking closer and leaning my forehead against his chest. "But now you have me all worked up. So maybe less talking and more naked."

His hands came up to settle in my hair and I felt him drop a kiss on my head. "It's a deal. C'mon."

The walk back to his cabin didn't take very long. We held hands and when we entered his front door, he turned to me with a grin. "How did I get you all worked up earlier?"

"Uh," I said. "You looked right at me. You know, with those eyes and shit."

Tristan laughed. "And that's all it takes?"

"Apparently," I admitted with a sheepish grin.

"Good to know," he said, eyes boring into me. I blushed and looked away.

"Now get naked like you promised." Command, not question.

So I did.

20

———

TRISTAN

I quickly tossed food into Piper's bowl and made sure the cabin was locked up for the night. Blue was in the process of stripping and stumbling into my room at the same time, and the wine he'd consumed earlier didn't seem to be helping his equilibrium.

After a moment of enjoying the view, I finally had mercy on him and pushed him onto the bed to finish peeling off his jeans. His strawberry-blond hair was messy and curled up over his ears, and his cheeks were flushed from the alcohol. There was a silly grin on his face and cobalt eyes shined from under his light lashes.

"You are sexy as fuck," I told him as I stripped off my own clothes as fast as I could.

"I'll bet you say that to all the girls." He batted his eyelashes and I snorted.

"Just your Aunt Tilly," I joked, crawling on top of him and licking my way along his rib cage.

"Fuck, that's gross." He laughed. "Don't mention my Aunt Tilly if you want me to stay hard. Jesus, Tris."

"You think I can't get you hard again?" I teased, finding a nipple with my tongue and sucking it into my mouth.

He hissed and arched his back, bringing his hands up to grasp my head.

"What was up with you and Tilly tonight anyway? I saw you two in cahoots about poor Brad," Blue said as his fingers threaded into my hair, raising goose bumps along my neck.

I moved my mouth to his collarbone and slid my tongue along the bone until I found the dip.

"Just wanted to solve the mystery of the kid's wedding ring; that's all," I admitted.

His finger twirled a lock of my hair and tugged gently. I could feel his stiff cock against my thigh and it made my own throb harder. I was ready to get this show on the road and stop talking about old ladies and ex-boyfriends.

I reached down and grabbed a hold of Blue's erection. He sucked in a breath on the words, "Fucking *finally*."

I couldn't help but laugh. "Sir, if you have a complaint, kindly shove it up your ass."

Mischievous blue eyes met mine. "Just let me write it on your dick first."

"Touché." I smirked as I made my way down to replace my stroking hand with my watering mouth. Earlier in my office I had gotten a quick taste of Blue, but it wasn't enough.

My lips teased lightly down his shaft as I cupped his balls gently with one hand. I pushed his legs farther apart, giving me more room to explore. My free hand trailed along his inner thigh, feeling his course hair and long, lean muscles under the skin. My thumb brushed down the crevice where his thigh met his body and I stuck my tongue out to lick my way back up his cock.

Blue's hands returned to my hair and found a lock to twirl again. I loved that feeling for some reason.

When I got to his tip I pulled back, studying the throbbing purple head. It twitched under my gaze and a thick bead of precum began to drip toward his belly. I reached out a fingertip to swipe it up and then I met his eyes as I brought my finger to my lips to suck. Blue's pupils widened until they looked fully blown, and I could see his wild pulse jumping at the side of his neck. I had never felt so powerful and desired in my life.

I climbed back up his body to kiss him, sharing the taste of him between our tongues and worshipping his mouth with my own. He needed to feel how much I wanted him, so that he could experience the same heady sensations he was giving me.

As our tongues twisted together, our dicks ended up sliding along side each other. Holy fuck, did that feel amazing. I'd never felt anything like it my entire life.

I pulled back from the kiss, gasping. "God, that feels good. Why have I never done this before?"

Blue smiled and reached a hand down to grasp both of our cocks together, squeezing briefly before pulling away and asking me if I had any lube.

"Shit, no. Wait. I have lotion. Does that work?" I asked, reaching over to my nightstand to get the bottle of lotion I used to jack off.

"Lie on your right side," Blue said, reaching for the lotion. We lay side by side facing each other, cocks together as he pumped some lotion into his hands.

"Gonna be cold." He laughed, rubbing his palms together in an effort to warm the lotion as much as possible.

"My dick will run and hide if you put that cold shit on me," I warned.

He smirked up at me and repeated my words from earlier. "You think I can't get you hard again?"

When his slick hands came around both of our cocks again, I hissed. "Jesus, Blue."

"Give it a second," he said. "You'll thank me later, I promise."

As the heat from our erections warmed the lotion, Blue began moving his large hand. Fingers gripping, clasped fist sliding, my slick dick gliding smoothly along his hard shaft. It was amazing.

"*Fuck*," I cried, bucking into him.

Blue's eyes sparkled in triumph as his hand continued to jack us. I thrust rhythmically into his hand, leaning in to crush my mouth against his.

We kissed desperately while Blue worked his magic. I grabbed his ass to pull him even closer. My moans came out and were eaten up by the gorgeous man in my bed. He gasped my name and mumbled other broken words into my own mouth. My orgasm built and grew until my entire body felt electric.

He moved his mouth to my ear, our scruffy cheeks scratching together. Blue's tongue licked beneath my ear and then he breathed into my ear in a low, gasping voice.

"You drive me fucking crazy."

That's all it took to push me over the edge. I cried his name as hot ropes of come snaked out of me and landed on both of us. Blue climaxed as the wetness coated his fist. I landed my mouth on his to drink in his cries, desperate to gather up anything he gave to me.

When we finally collapsed onto our backs to catch our breath, I was overwhelmed by unexpected emotion. My eyes stung and I could feel them begin to fill. Jesus, what the hell was wrong with me? I put my arm over my face to keep Blue from seeing my reaction.

I heard him get up to go to the bathroom so I took the opportunity to calm down and pack the emotional shit away in a lockbox.

He returned with a warm, wet washcloth and gently wiped it across my chest and abdomen. It was such an attentive gesture, and I realized I had never been cared for like that. No one, including my mother, had ever touched me with such sweet tenderness. While it was thoughtful as hell, the timing was terrible. All my carefully packed emotion came tumbling back out, and I felt a tear slide down my face.

Blue's eyes widened when he saw it and I quickly brought my arm back over my face. "Ignore me," I warned. "Orgasms make me stupid."

Blue dropped the washcloth on the floor and climbed back into bed with me, wrestling the duvet out from under us to maneuver us under the covers. I turned away from him and squeezed my eyes closed, willing my shit to go back in the box.

His warm hand landed on my shoulder and began rubbing my back.

"Don't be nice to me, goddammit," I said gruffly. "That doesn't help."

Blue's hand froze on my back and I wanted to kick myself for being an ass. Then I felt the hand move to my shoulder and pull me down to lie on my back. He straddled me, leaning his face into mine until we were only inches apart.

"I'll never stop being nice to you, Tristan Alexander. So you might as well get used to it. Talk to me about what's going through your head."

More tears leaked out and I tried closing my eyes.

Blue's voice sounded smaller this time, less sure. "Are you having second thoughts about what we're doing?"

My eyes flew back open. "No! God no, baby. Never."

Relief flooded into Blue's eyes. "I like it when you call me baby." He smiled.

I reached out to cup the side of his face. Such a sweet man. The kind of person I knew wouldn't judge me. But did that mean I should dump my shit all over him? We barely knew each other. But then again, sometimes it was easier talking to someone you barely knew.

21

BLUE

I could see him struggling with something and I was desperate to know what it was.

His gray eyes searched mine. "Blue, I don't think I'm bisexual."

My heart dropped. This was it. I knew it. I knew he was regretting hooking up with me. It wasn't that I hadn't expected it, but I was still crushed. More than I thought I'd be.

I slid off him and lay on my back again. "That's okay, Tristan. I completely understand."

His head swiveled to look at me, gray eyes sparking with words still unsaid. Suddenly I saw a dawning realization hit him.

"Wait, you think I'm telling you I'm straight?" he asked incredulously. "Really? After the way I respond to you? How could you possibly think that? Jesus, Blue. I'm *gay*."

When the word came out of his mouth it seemed to shock him. And then a laugh bubbled out of him. And then damned if he didn't lose his shit and start laughing full out.

My eyes widened. Huh, that was unexpected.

"Can you repeat that, please?" I asked.

He leaned over and kissed me full on the mouth. "I'm gay, Blue.

Pretty sure I always have been. Either that or you have mad skills at turning people gay," he teased.

"I don't really understand. You remember you were married to a woman, right? That probably indicates you're bisexual," I corrected.

"Remember when you were talking about why you stopped pursuing your passion for sculpture? You said you listened to discouraging words from others, and you were young enough to take them to heart. That's what happened to me when I thought I was attracted to men. Maybe I am bisexual, but I truly think I prefer men."

I turned on my side to study his face. His eyes had changed from dark intensity to lighter excitement. He turned so we were on our sides facing each other. His hand came up to rest on my hip.

"Tristan, is this about the bad experience in college?" I asked.

He nodded. "I want to tell you about it. Can we go out to the kitchen and let me make a sandwich or something while we talk?"

"Of course. I could eat too. At the wine tasting I made a plate but your cousin Sarah ate everything off of it before I had a chance to."

We got up, Tristan grabbing some athletic shorts out of a drawer for both of us. After slipping them on, we made our way out to his kitchen, which was open to the main room. A big island sat in the middle of the kitchen and had a smooth stone top on it unlike anything I'd ever seen. The kitchen was modern and clean, but I could tell it was used often.

"You like to cook?" I asked him.

Tristan smiled. "Yep. The goat cheese ravioli at the party earlier was a recipe I came up with a few months ago. The catering chef is using it all the time now."

"No way." I snorted. "No offense, but you don't seem like the winery-owning, goat-cheese-ravioli-making kind of guy."

Tristan looked up at me from where he was bent over at the open door of the fridge. "Dare I ask what kind of guy I look like?"

"Dunno. International man of mystery? Corporate big wig who specializes in hostile takeovers? Asshole *attorney*?" I teased.

He swiped a dishtowel at me, barely catching me on the leg.

"Yeah? Well, you look like a spoiled Hollywood actor who demands Evian for his bathwater," Tristan retorted.

"Perrier, you ass. Evian is so… gauche."

"*A chacun son gout,*" he muttered. *To each his own.*

"*Ne pas casser du sucre sur le dos de quelqu'un,*" I threw back. *Don't talk about someone behind their back.*

"*Tu parle français?*" he asked.

"*Mais oui.*" I smirked.

Tristan blushed. "I remember now. When I was talking about wine at the bar. No one else I know speaks French."

I nodded. "Tell me about it. Seven years of French plus a semester in Paris and I never get to speak it anymore. None of my siblings took it. I wish I'd taken Spanish instead."

"Same here. God, what I wouldn't give to speak Spanish. But now that I'm in the wine business, it's finally earning its keep. I took it in school then did a year of college in Bordeaux et Anjou."

Tristan started pulling food out of the fridge and cabinets to cook something, asking if I had a preference. I told him I wasn't picky. When Piper nudged my leg, I stood up to take her outside. It was still fairly early, maybe around 9 p.m. It was clear to me Tristan was taking his time working up to telling me about his past, and that was okay.

I sipped on a bottle of water and stood on the porch of the cabin. It was so dark and quiet that far out of the city. Stars sparkled and the air was cool on my bare chest and arms. Piper sniffed around the bushes and I heard tires crunching on gravel.

A small SUV approached, headlights washing across the yard before it came to a stop beside Tristan's Tahoe. I made sure Piper was safe off to the side of the driveway and then saw Keller get out of the vehicle. I sent up a silent prayer of thanks I wasn't standing there in my underwear.

I'd met Keller briefly at the wine event and had felt his eyes on me several times during the evening. I wasn't quite sure what to make of him. My guess was he was my age. Good-looking guy, if a little quiet. Tristan had said he was Art's grandson and the operations manager for the winery. I wondered how he felt about Tristan owning the place now.

"Hey, Keller," I greeted. The man jumped a little and peered into the darkness of the porch where I was standing.

"Blue?" he asked tentatively. "What are you doing here?"

"Tristan's inside. Come on in." I held the door open and called Piper back.

She came right away and skittered past me into the cabin. Keller gave me an odd look and I decided maybe he was just an odd man.

Tristan was walking out of his bedroom, pulling a T-shirt on and tossing me a second one. He must have heard the car pull up. I caught it and slipped it over my head, realizing even if they'd known each other for years, Keller was a coworker and employee of Tristan's.

"Hi, Keller, what's up? Everything okay at the main house after we left?" Tristan asked.

"Yes, fine. Stacey stayed and cleaned up with me. That's not why I'm here." He glanced over at me, clearly bothered or surprised by my presence. "I, uh, wanted to talk to you about something private." He looked to me again, and I got the hint.

"I was just going to go check with a guy about a thing," I said, winking at Tristan before walking into his bedroom and closing the door. I found my phone and checked email, trying to stay as far away from the bedroom door as possible so as to avoid the temptation of eavesdropping.

I responded to a few work emails from the day and read the news from one of my apps. I texted Jude to break a leg, on the off chance he hadn't taken the stage yet, and then I texted Simone to tell her I wanted to find some time alone with her the next day to catch up.

I lay back on the bed to rest my eyes and wait for Keller to leave. The next thing I knew, I was woken by Tristan's soft lips against my ear.

"Wake up, baby," he whispered. The words went straight to my dick before I even had a chance to open my eyes.

"Shhhh," I scolded in a sleepy voice. "I'm having a wet dream about a corporate takeover and the handsome attorney who's getting ready to raid my assets."

His deep rumble of laughter vibrated into my ear. "Just say the word, Blue Marian, and I'll be happy to raid your assets."

He grabbed my hand and pulled me to a seated position. I yawned and tried to clear my head. "How long did Keller stay?"

"Thirty minutes maybe? Then I let you sleep another twenty while I made dinner."

I stood up and followed him back to the kitchen, eyes locked on his tight round ass in those shorts. My hard-on wasn't standing down so I palmed it and grumbled, "Fuck, you have a nice ass."

"Blue, you have a nice everything. Why do you think I made you put a shirt on? I saw Keller staring at you all day today."

I couldn't help but laugh. "Funny, I thought he was looking at me too, but I thought he was giving me the evil eye rather than fuck-me eyes."

"He didn't know about us. How could he have been at the wine tasting and not known about us? Especially after what Aunt Tilly said."

"So what did you tell him?" I asked.

"I told him we were... together. Then he lost his shit. Didn't you hear him?" Tristan pulled out some bread from the oven and pulled down bowls from a cabinet.

"No, maybe it happened after I fell asleep. What did he say?" I asked.

He ladled out some soup and brought two bowls to a small kitchen table. Then he returned for the bread and butter, asking me what I wanted to drink.

"Water's fine," I said, grabbing bottles from the fridge myself.

After we sat down, he continued. "First of all, he came over to tell me that Art, his grandfather, is in the hospital with pneumonia. Keller and his mom are the only family Art has left so I told him to go be with him in Florida. I'm sure Uncle Henry is there since they live together, but Art will appreciate Keller's company."

"Is Art going to be okay?" I asked.

Tristan shrugged. "Not sure. I'll call Uncle Henry in the morning. I think Keller is worried that something else is going on. He wanted me to go with him."

"Do you want to go?" I asked.

"I can't miss John's wedding, and I don't think a bout of pneumonia is worth me dropping everything," he said as he ate. The soup was homemade butternut squash he'd had in the freezer. It was delicious and I told him so.

"How did he react to you saying you were going to stay here?" I asked.

"He understood. It was when I told him about you that he shoved me against the wall and put his hand on my throat," Tristan said as if he was describing someone passing the salt.

22

TRISTAN

"What?" Blue demanded. "Are you kidding me?" He began to stand up, but I put a hand on his arm.

"Sit down. What are you going to do? He's gone, Blue."

"That fucker. I can't believe he put his hands on you and I fucking slept through it. What happened next?" His anger warmed something inside me, and I realized it felt nice to have someone want to stand up for me.

"I pushed him off and told him to calm down. Then I asked what the hell he thought he was doing. He said he didn't understand how I could be hooking up with you when I'm straight."

Blue huffed out a laugh. "Did you tell him I wondered the same thing?"

I gave him the eye. "No, smart-ass. I told him I was realizing I wasn't straight after all, and you were part of that realization."

"I'm sure he loved hearing that. It sounds like he wished he was part of your realization instead," Blue grumbled.

"Well, you might be right about that. But I told him to go home and calm down. Then I implied that he was acting the way he was because he was upset about Art. Hopefully, that will give him the out he needs to let it go without things getting weird between us."

I could tell Blue was still pissed. Never had I ever seen someone butter a piece of bread angrily. Unfortunately, a laugh snuck out of me at that thought and his blue eyes bored into me.

"What?" he asked.

"Nothing." I laughed.

"You're not laughing at nothing," Blue griped.

"Fine. I'm laughing at you. You're so pissed about this and it's really sweet. Jealousy is kinda hot on you."

Blue glared at me some more. "Fuck you."

"Gladly." I waggled my eyebrows and he rolled his eyes. "But you have to admit that turnabout is fair play. I had to watch Jeremy trying to get your attention all day."

"Pfft," Blue scoffed. "Jeremy's with someone else. Keller isn't."

He stood up and took his dishes to the sink, so I did the same. When he got to the sink, I put my dishes down on the counter and slid my arms around him from behind and put my mouth by Blue's ear. I was starting to learn how much that drove him crazy.

"When I'm with you, I can't keep my hands off of you. When I see you, I can't stop staring. You've turned my entire life upside down in twenty-four hours. I may be confused as shit about my sexuality and my life up to this point, but I am not at all confused about who I want to sleep with right now. And it's not Keller."

Blue turned in my arms and had a smile on his face. "Aunt Tilly?"

I laughed. "Shut the fuck up and put your hands on me before I start whining like a little kid."

He leaned in and kissed me, running his hands under my shirt and leaving goose bumps in their wake. We kissed hungrily by the sink—hands searching, hips grinding, and lips locking. I wanted him so badly that I felt like I was going to come out of my skin. Was it because I was so hungry for a male body against mine? Or were these feelings specific to Blue?

I felt as though it was specific to Blue, but I had nothing to compare it to. And I had absolutely no desire to do so. How could any other guy possibly be better than this man in front of me? He was smart and beautiful, creative and funny. Sweet and attentive. Even my dog fucking loved him. And when his body was against mine... all was right in my world.

My hand ran down his shorts to grasp his dick and I realized I wanted to taste him again. I pulled his T-shirt off and then pushed down his shorts and dropped to my knees on the kitchen rug.

This gorgeous man stood completely naked in my kitchen and wanted me. I looked up at him in appreciation. Blue's hand came up and brushed the hair back from my face. The gesture was the same kind of tender sweetness he always seemed to show me when I felt most vulnerable. My stomach twisted with nerves, and I knew then I was really falling for this guy. I had known him for ten seconds and I already felt as if he was as critical to my survival as food and water.

I leaned my head against his belly, my hands resting on his hips. His hands ran through my hair and we stayed like that for a few moments. He seemed to know I needed to go at my own pace.

My tongue reached out and dipped into his navel, causing his ab muscles to contract and ripple. I moved my mouth down the light fuzz of his happy trail, nipping along the way to keep his abs responding. My lips drew kisses along his hips and down to his upper thighs before moving toward the junction of his legs.

His erection was straining upward, precum leaking out. I ignored it and pressed my nose into the nest of curls at the base. He smelled amazing. A combination of my soap and his own musky scent. His breaths were coming quicker in anticipation and I could sense the smallest tremble in his leg muscles.

I held him around the base of his cock and guided the tip onto my outstretched tongue. The moisture at the tip fell onto my tongue and I savored it, licking the slit to search for more. Blue hissed at the sensation as I wrapped my mouth around his crown. Swirling my tongue around the crown, I got him as wet as I could. My mouth and tongue slid up and down his shaft, spreading my saliva all over him until my mouth and hand could work him together. He was moaning and shuddering with each move of my mouth on and around his straining cock.

Trying to remember every trick that had ever worked on me, I took him as deep as I could and then sucked in my cheeks before pulling up. I cupped his sac with a free hand and gently pulled it. I felt his balls tighten and his hips buck as his cock hit the back of my throat and made me gag. I recovered quickly and kept sucking and licking, pulling and twirling. His hands buried in my hair as he began to beg in a raw, desperate voice.

I stuck my thumb in my mouth alongside his dick and then ran it firmly down the trail from his sac to his pucker, pressing gently in when I got to his hole. That did the trick, his hands tried pulling my head away but he came too fast. I was ready and willing, and relished the chance to swallow it all down.

When he was finished and I smacked my lips in smug satisfaction, he let himself slide down to the floor. We sat side by side with our backs against the kitchen cabinets.

Blue swiveled his head to look at me, eyes still semi-glazed over with lust. "Fine. Maybe you really are gay."

I snickered. "Right? I told you."

After making our way back to the bedroom, I stripped and followed Blue under the covers. I knew he wanted me to get back to the story I promised him, but I was beginning to lose my nerve. Maybe we could pretend I hadn't said anything and go to sleep. Or maybe I could distract him with dirty talk and more sexual favors.

Blue eyes pierced my thoughts. "I can tell what you're thinking, and you're wrong."

"I don't think so. We both know that if I put my lips against your ear and started talking dirty to you, you'd forget all about anything else," I said.

His pupils grew but his forehead creased. "Maybe. But you're not going to do it because you respect me too much to blow off this conversation. For the record, I'm not refusing the dirty talk, just postponing it. That's an important distinction to note."

I huffed out a laugh. "Duly noted, counselor. So, we're talking about me then."

"Yes. And you can trust me, Tristan. I swear I would never do anything to hurt you, and that includes repeating your words."

I looked into Blue's eyes, full of sincerity. "I know that. I do. And thank you."

Rolling him over so I could spoon in behind him, I explained. "I'm not sure I can look at you while I'm talking. You're too sweet and I'll start to get all... whatever. Just, stay like that, okay?"

He squeezed the hand intertwined with mine across his chest. "Whatever you need."

I kissed the back of his neck and then settled my head on the pillow and started talking. I told him about losing my virginity to Amber and then hooking up with her twin brother, Adam, the summer after high school. About how I never felt as sexually excited sleeping with Amber as I had just getting head from Adam. So I went in search of a man I liked well enough to fuck in college.

"It took me almost a year before I found a man I wanted to really fool around with. I consider myself sexual, but I'm not really a casual sex person. Like searching for a quick-and-easy orgasm. If I want that, I can do it fine myself, you know? What I wanted was someone I could connect with in multiple ways. Sexual compatibility but also personal compatibility.

"So at the end of my first year in college, I met a man named Glenn. He was older by about seven years and was a medical student doing his residency in the ER at the university hospital. I'd met him when I took one of my roommates to the ER for stitches. Glenn and I met for coffee later and hit it off. He was really nice. Took it slowly with me, asked me out on dates, and would drop me off afterward with just a kiss or at most a heavy-petting session.

"I really liked him, and the fact he took it so slowly with me made me feel safe and respected. As we got to know each other on our dates, he naturally told me about cases he'd had in the hospital. He told me story after story of gay men who'd been beaten and raped. Rent boys who'd been abused and ended up diseased and addicted. Queer teens beaten by bullies at school, and even domestic situations where married gay men hurt their partners after years of being together."

I felt Blue's body tense against mine as my words came out, but I tried to stay focused.

"These stories came at me slowly at first. The more of them he told, the more freaked out I got until I finally asked him what the fuck he was trying to do. Was he trying to scare me off of being gay or bisexual? He said he just wanted me to understand what I was getting into. Then he told me stories about the spread of HIV, how awful dying of AIDS is, and how there are gay men out there who are so bitter about being positive that they want to spread it to everyone.

"None of this felt right to me. I wasn't stupid, you know? I could tell he was trying to scare me, but part of me thought it came from a good place. That maybe he was trying to protect me. One night he invited me over to his place for dinner and a movie. After we ate dinner, we settled together on the couch. I was relishing the feel of being able to touch him and lie on the couch with him for the next couple of hours and then hopefully fool around with him afterward. I was ready, you know? I wanted to at least swap blow jobs. The sex stuff was moving at a snail's pace, and I had the libido of a nineteen-year-old.

"After the movie, Glenn finally took me to his bed. He gave me a full-body massage and finished it with a blow job. It was fucking awesome. He explained that he wanted to show me how much he cared about me, and he wanted me to understand that he was different than all of those abusive gay men out there. He made it sound like a good gay man was as elusive as a unicorn. And since the words came at me on the tail end of a fabulous orgasm, I soaked them in as truth without spending any brain power evaluating them. The message was clear: I was fucking lucky to have found him. He made me promise not to be with anyone else.

"When I tried going down on him, he said I probably wasn't ready for that yet. Even though I knew I was, I let him set the pace. In my eyes, he was the experienced one and I was the newbie. He promised he would tell me when we were ready for that next step. I thought he was looking out for me and it was nice, you know?

"This all sounds so ridiculous now. It's embarrassing to say it out loud. Every time I think of it, I am mortified by how stupid I was. But then I have to remind myself I was a kid. A scared kid who didn't know what he wanted."

Blue pulled my arms tighter against him and kissed the inside of one of my wrists. I buried my nose in his hair for a moment and just inhaled him.

"So after I went back to my dorm that night, I started to get mad. I was annoyed I'd let him talk me into waiting yet again. I was horny and I wanted to have sex. I at least knew I was ready to suck his dick for god's sake. It's not like we were making a blood pact or getting married.

"I decided to take the bull by the horns and surprise him at his apartment the next day. When he answered the door, he was surprised, but then he got a weird gleam in his eyes. He was wearing a towel and had obviously just gotten out of the shower. Perfect, I thought. He led me into his bedroom and closed the door behind him. He said he wanted to tie me up. That was such a big leap from taking it slow that I laughed, assuming he was joking. When he got mad, I said if he was being serious, then no, I probably wasn't ready for that.

"The thing that stresses me out even now is the knowledge that if it hadn't been for that weird gleam in his eyes, I probably would have let him tie me up. Then this other guy comes out of the bathroom wearing only a towel. Clearly they'd been in the shower together. Glenn introduces me to the guy, but I can't hear anything over the blood rushing in my ears. The guy is huge. Like bouncer-at-a-club big, and he pulls off his towel and looks at me like I'm his next meal.

"I look at Glenn with growing panic and he laughs. He tells me he knew I wasn't really gay because gay men are more open and free with their sexuality. But apparently he wants me to try anyway because then he tells me to strip. I try to make my way out of the room but the big guy grabs me and tosses me onto the bed like I weighed ten pounds."

At this point, I notice Blue is trembling in my arms.

"It's okay, baby. I got away. Ended up going batshit fucking crazy and kicked both of them in the balls before running out of there. But after that I was terrified to try again. The stories in my head, my own experience, the safety of being with a woman who was smaller and weaker than I was. It all just came together in the perfect storm of fear and doubt that sent me into hiding."

23

BLUE

I couldn't stand it anymore. I rolled over and buried my face in his neck and let go. Tears, snot, moans. All of it slid out of me and onto him. The injustice of it all broke my fucking heart.

The robbery of fifteen years of sexual satisfaction and confidence in following his true desires. It made me want to vomit. It was so fucking unfair.

He murmured sweet words into my ear and rubbed my back, trying to assure me he was okay and it was all okay. But it wasn't.

He tried to pull back and look at me, but I chased his neck with my face. I wasn't ready to meet his intense gray eyes until I could figure out how to protect him from ever being hurt like that again.

"Is it too much?" he asked. "I shouldn't have told you. I knew I shouldn't have told you."

I finally lifted my head, sniffing and wiping my face with my arm. "It is too much, Tris. Too much for you. Too much for you to go through alone. My heart is broken for that boy who needed kindness and safe sexual exploration. And instead you were taken advantage of. What would have happened if you couldn't get away? Ugh, Tristan. I can't bear to think of you in that situation. It's just so fucking unfair."

His thumbs came up to wipe under my eyes. "Thank you," he said with a small smile.

"Thank you? What are you thanking me for?" I asked incredulously.

"Blue, don't you understand that you are the person who was kind and gentle enough to let me try again? You are so fucking sweet that it boggles my mind. When I'm with you, I feel like I can just be me and it's okay. I've never really felt that way with anyone else. It's exhilarating. I feel like I've laughed more in the last twenty-four hours than in the past year."

I looked at him like he was crazy. He looked so damn... happy. Relaxed and smiling. Maybe he really was crazy. Maybe I'd landed myself in bed with a psycho. Who else could go through something like that and come out... happy?

I cocked my head at him. "How can you be okay with this?"

He shook his head. "I'm not okay with what happened in college. Of course I'm not. It sucked. It scared me and pushed me into doing something that made me feel even worse. Hiding from myself. Denying myself. Packing the feelings away and trying to choose a different path. I dated women after that. Had casual hookups and a couple of longer relationships.

"When I met Sheila, I realized her life fit together with mine better than anyone I'd come across up to that point. She was busy and ambitious. I was busy and ambitious. We didn't see each other much, so when we did get together, I was horny enough to appreciate any sex. There wasn't much of it because I traveled. We texted and flirted which was fun, and I started to convince myself I couldn't have both. The personal connection and the hot sex. So I stuck with the personal connection."

I asked him a question that had been on my mind for a while. "Why did you split?"

"She... ah... slept with someone else. And I... walked in on them when I got home from a trip a day early," he said hesitantly.

"Damn. In your own bed?" I exclaimed.

"Yep. And it was with someone close to me too. So, obviously it was a deal-breaker. Nothing any amount of couple's counseling could fix."

I stroked his cheek. "Who would be stupid enough to cheat on you?" I wondered aloud.

He scoffed. "Looking back on it now, it's a wonder she didn't cheat on me sooner. And maybe she did. But I already told you, the sex wasn't that great, and I was gone all the time."

He had a point. "Tristan, if she cheated on you, why are your parents so hell-bent on reuniting you?"

"They don't know about the cheating. I didn't tell them that part. Just said that our jobs had finally taken their toll on the marriage."

We sat in silence for a while, my fingers tracing patterns through the hair on his chest. Tristan eventually raised my chin with a finger.

"Why did you and Jeremy split?"

Before I could stop them, my eyes darted away. "I made a business decision that pissed him off. He couldn't get past it so we broke up."

Tristan stayed quiet, but I knew he was waiting for more. I chanced a glance at him and saw the intense gray eyes studying me.

"Your eyes are so exotic," I blurted. "Do people tell you that all the time?"

He smiled, the skin by his eyes crinkling and the goddamned dimple appearing. "You're good at stalling," he said. "Do people tell you that all the time?"

I huffed. "Asshole," I muttered, sitting up and leaning back against the headboard.

I rubbed my hands over my face. "Jeremy is a media buyer. He works for a big ad agency that represents several companies, and his job is to plan their advertising campaigns and execute them. Part of that includes buying ad space in magazines like the ones I design for. He was so excited when his company landed a big vitamin company as a client. It was important to his agency, and I knew it was a big deal for him.

"When he approached my company's ad execs about purchasing ads for one of their products, the ad graphics ended up on my desk for approval. They were for a nutritional supplement that boasts added energy, weight loss, and all the usual claims. You know, the solution to all of your body problems.

"While I'm not a fan of those products, especially marketed to younger audiences, I wasn't allowed to deny the product placement in the magazine. I only had decision-making power over the way the ad looked. In this case, the ad copy was misleading and dangerous. It made unsubstantiated health claims that concerned me from a legal perspective, but it also had a shitty tagline. It said something like, 'Because no one asks out the fat friend.' So rude. Fucking idiots."

Tristan had sat up next to me and sat cross-legged facing me. "So what did you do?"

"I kicked it back to the agency and told them to come up with something that wasn't offensive. They got mad because they thought it was funny and would appeal to our target demographic. I refused to allow it. Ultimately their creative group put the onus on Jeremy as the buyer to convince me to accept the ad. Normally the buyer has all of the power since they're the ones with the money. But I wasn't about to let that ad copy in.

"I tried explaining it to him calmly over the phone at work, but he couldn't stay calm. Said we'd talk about it at home. I never liked bringing work home between us, but he insisted. That night he told me I needed to make an exception for him. That it was important to please the client, and the client loved the tagline. I said he could keep the tagline and just move his ad space to another magazine, one I wasn't in charge of designing.

"I've never seen him that angry. He honestly thought I was making a big deal about it just to piss him off or sabotage his job. I tried explaining why the tagline was offensive, but he thought I was taking it too seriously. He accused me of putting my 'social justice' issues before our relationship and implied that if I loved him, I'd let this go.

"And you know what, Tris? I almost did. I almost let that jackass convince me to go against my better judgement. But instead, I called my brother Jude. Explained the whole thing to him and asked his advice."

"You two are close?" Tristan asked.

"The closest. He's my best friend. I can't wait for you to meet him tomorrow." I smiled.

"I wonder if that ever made Jeremy jealous," Tristan wondered.

"You have no idea." I laughed. "Drove him nuts. Anyway, Jude reminded me of that John Wooden quote. Something about true character being what you do when no one is watching. Our dad used to say it all the time when we were growing up. So I went to the office the next day and wrote up an official letter rejecting the ad in its original form. Then I got our editor, my boss, to cosign it and send it to the agency. When I got home that night, all of my things were boxed up by the front door."

Tristan's jaw flexed. "You're kidding. That asshole broke up with you because of a business decision?"

I shrugged. "Guess so. Oh, and he also told me that I was boring in bed. I believe the word he used was 'vanilla.' I put the most important shit in my car and drove to my parents' house. The next day my dad told me about a woman at his office who was subletting her apartment. I've been there ever since. Which turned out to be a good thing because of my move."

Tristan squeezed my hand. "Sounds like things are working out. A fresh start in a new place."

"We'll see. Jude keeps pestering me to sculpt or teach sculpting. I think it's his way of keeping me around. I tried explaining that sculpting and teaching don't pay the rent. Jeremy had told me it was stupid to spend money on studio space if I wasn't good enough to sell the finished pieces. Funny how easy it is to let doubt sneak in and fester, isn't it? Fuck him. I swear. What an ass."

24

TRISTAN

I felt like jumping up and doing a celebration dance. Hearing Blue realize Jeremy wasn't good for him was music to my ears. I wasn't sure I could keep the silly grin off my face.

Blue gave me the side eye. "Smug much?"

So much for hiding it. "Yup. And proud of it. That guy is an ass. He doesn't deserve you; I've already told you that. You deserve to find someone better."

"Easier said than done," he muttered. I have to admit, the words stung. Did he not think I was better? Blue continued, "I just have to find someone whose favorite sex flavor is vanilla."

Oh, right. The part about him being boring in bed. The idea was laughable. I grabbed his face with both hands and put my nose against his.

"I. Fucking. Love. Vanilla." And then I kissed him so hotly he couldn't dare describe it as vanilla.

Hands joined in and we ended up tangled up and panting in the middle of the bed as we tried to find every way possible to get inside each other. We had determined earlier we didn't have more lube for sex even though I did have condoms. So I found myself turning around so we could blow each other at the same time.

"Aloe," Blue gasped. "Have any aloe?"

"What?" I snapped, annoyed that his tongue was no longer on my dick.

"Do you have aloe, like for a sunburn?" he asked again.

"Uh, yeah, maybe under the bathroom sink. Why?"

Blue just grinned and jumped off the bed. He must have found some because I heard a triumphant squawk before he came rushing back to the bed.

"Lube," he explained. "Condoms?"

I reached over to the bedside table and came up with some. Blue grabbed one and ripped it open with his mouth before sliding it onto my throbbing shaft. I groaned in appreciation of his attentive fingers.

He picked up the bottle of aloe and smoothed a healthy amount over my cock before tipping out more onto his own hand. He positioned himself on all fours and the sight of him like that made my dick stand up. His hand reached around to slide his own lubed fingers into his ass, taunting me. Vanilla in bed, my ass.

I watched as he fucked his fingers for me. He looked over his shoulder and caught me drooling at the sight of him. Leaning up to kiss his hot mouth, I growled, "I'm going to shove myself so deep inside of you, Blue. It's all I can think about."

His body shuddered beneath mine as I lay over the top of his back and kissed my way down his spine. My thumb traced a line from the top of his ass down the crevice to his lubed entrance and then pressed gently inside. I felt his channel contract around my thumb and I teased it in and out, making him moan and shudder again.

Finally I guided my cock to his opening and began to push inside. The tight ring of muscle gripped me as I slid through, reminding me of how good it felt to be inside him. He hissed and pushed backward, his body asking for more of me.

Little by little I rocked my way in until I could feel my pubic hair brush against his skin. He was begging me to fuck him faster and harder, but I was still scared of hurting him.

"Baby, wait, just wait a second," I begged.

"No, dammit, stop being afraid of hurting me. I want you to pound me into this mattress. God, Tris, fuck me *please*," he cried.

So I went for it. I slammed into him the way I really wanted to. My body began to sweat as I pounded him over and over, both of us grunting and moaning. It was hard and bordering on brutal, our bodies rutting against each other like animals. The sound of my balls slapping against his and the slide of my slick chest against his sweat-soaked back making it carnal and wholly masculine.

My mouth devoured the skin of his neck as I continued to roll my hips into him. I wrapped one arm around his neck and pulled him upright onto his knees, my other arm wrapped around his middle. My hips continued to thrust upward as he made unintelligible noises and reached to jack himself

"*Fuck, Tris, fuck*," he cried.

"*So good, baby, so fucking good*," I gasped into his ear.

My thrusts were so strong that he had to keep one hand on the headboard to stay upright, his other increasing its tempo on his straining cock.

One more angled thrust and he erupted, screaming my name and coming all over his chest. His body squeezed my dick again and that was it for me. White sparkles shimmered in my vision and electric pulses shot through all of my muscles. I came inside of him until my balls felt empty and my entire body felt boneless.

Blue dropped back down on all fours and I collapsed against his back, both of us struggling to regulate our breathing. Finally, I pulled out of him, dropping the condom into the trash.

I gathered Blue's body into mine and just held him close.

I couldn't help but think about how ridiculous the idea of being pretend boyfriends had been. When it came to showing affection for Blue, I had never needed to pretend.

The irony hit me hard: the only pretending I was doing now was pretending I wasn't falling stupidly in love with a man I'd known for only a single day. The idea was so far fetched that I chastised myself for being overly dramatic. It wasn't love. It was just lust. Horny, newly gay lust.

Right. Because lust made you think of how to refit one of the barns into a welding studio. And lust made you happy the guy had loved your soup. Lust made you secretly thankful your dog adored the man more than anyone else. Lust. Just lust.

25

___

BLUE

Waking up wrapped in Tristan's arms was like opening the front door to the Prize Patrol and learning you were a millionaire. He was so fucking gorgeous and indescribably kind. I had no idea how I'd gotten lucky enough to end up in his bed that week, but I was going to embrace it.

In an effort not to seem desperate and clingy, I told him I needed to spend some time with my family. I figured he had work to do anyway, or at least had his own family to spend time with.

After a quick scrambled egg breakfast, we made our way over to the lodge. Tristan went in search of his granny but Piper stayed by my side, causing Tristan to roll his eyes and accuse her of betrayal.

When he turned his accusatory eyes on me, I batted my eyelashes. "What? Maybe she thinks blonds really do have more fun."

He laughed and leaned in to kiss me on the cheek. "Feel free to put her in my backyard or text me if you need me to take her off your hands, okay?"

"She'll be fine," I assured him. "If I can find Jude I'm going to see if he'll take a walk with me."

After Tristan went in search of Granny, I joined my parents at a table on the patio for a cup of coffee.

I asked my parents if Jude was there yet and they pointed me in the direction of his room. Piper and I made our way down the hall to find the correct door and knocked.

He answered the door and I gaped. "Dude, you look like ass."

Dark eyes punctuated with even darker circles glared back at me. "Tell me something I don't know, Bee."

I hugged him and heard him let out a shaky breath as he sagged into me. "That bad?" I whispered.

"Worse," he said, pulling back and inviting me in.

"Well, I was going to talk you into a walk, but I can see that you need sleep more than anything," I told him.

"No. Actually a walk sounds good. This place is nice and private, and I'd love some fresh air."

While he changed into track pants and a T-shirt and found his running shoes, I asked him about last night's show.

"It was sick, man. Bon Jovi was there. Sat in the front row. During one of the encores, I gestured for him to come up on stage and *he did*. Sang 'Livin' on a Prayer' together and I about fangirled my ass off." He laughed.

I blinked at him as my jaw dropped. "Holy shit, Jude. You're fucking with me."

"Nope. Afterward he hung out with us and told us how much he loved our music. Said 'Heavy Chevy' and 'Bluebells' are his favorites. I wanted to tell him that his entire body of work was my favorite." He laughed again.

I chuckled. "God, that guy is beautiful. Did you get any pictures?"

"Of course. My PR people went nuts over it but I also had someone take a few with my phone. Hang on," he said as he grabbed his phone from the dresser.

When he showed me the pics, I drooled. The chin dimple. The hair. The lips.

I looked up at Jude with a smirk. "Did you tell him about the posters of him on your bedroom walls?"

He blushed. Jude fucking blushed. "Yes, goddamn it. I admitted to being a big fan and told him they were still up on my walls because

Mom thought he was hot. He laughed and then offered to sign something for her."

"Right, it's because *Mom* thinks he's hot," I teased, looking at another shot on his phone. "Who's this muscle guy in the background who looks like he wants to kill Bon Jovi?"

"That's my new bodyguard. You'll meet him in a minute. I think he just looks pissed because the person taking the pictures with my phone was kind of a weirdo."

We walked out of the room and Jude knocked on the door next to his. The bodyguard from the photo answered the door.

"This is my brother, Blue. Blue, this is Wolfe. We're going to take a walk," Jude told him.

The guy was enormous compared to my brother. He looked like an action hero or some shit. I almost took a step back in reaction to his piercing stare.

"Blue, nice to meet you," the man said in a quieter voice than I imagined.

I reached out a hand to shake. "Nice to meet you. Thanks for keeping an eye on this guy," I said, jerking my thumb at Jude.

Wolfe's eyes softened. "My pleasure. Just let me change my shoes and we can go."

Jude stiffened next to me. "No, it's okay. We can go on our own. There's no one around here and it's pretty secluded."

The man gave Jude a look and my brother sighed. "Fine, but can you stay far enough back so we can catch up in private at least?"

He nodded. "Sure thing, boss."

We stepped back into the hallway to wait for him. I raised a questioning brow to Jude. "What's with the increased protection?"

"I've gotten some threats that seem a little weirder than normal. No big deal. My agent is overreacting. Please don't tell Mom and Dad."

"Don't worry, I don't have a death wish," I joked.

As the three of us made our way out of the lodge, I asked the woman at the front desk to point us in the direction of a good walking trail.

Once we found the trail, the bodyguard hung back as promised. We walked in silence for a few minutes before Jude spoke up. "Who's your dog friend?"

"Oh, right. This is Piper. She's Tristan's dog."

Jude reached down to introduce himself to Piper and scratched her back. "Why is she hanging out with you?"

I laughed. "Because she likes me better. And I told Tristan I was going to be taking a walk."

"Tell me about him," Jude said, standing up and giving me a look. "Start with the part about him being straight."

"Right, well, he might not be as straight as I first thought. We had a long talk about it last night." I told him about what had happened so far between us, leaving out the part about Tristan's personal sexual history.

We walked down a shaded lane with hardwood trees on either side. Piper enjoyed chasing through the bushes under the trees and coming out ahead of us on the lane before racing back to my side and then wandering off again.

"Jude," I said hesitantly. "I think I might be in trouble with this guy."

Jude let out a soft laugh. "Sounds like it."

"I mean, I can't stop thinking about him. He's so easy to be around. When we're together we can talk for hours and not run out of things to say. He makes me laugh. Even when we're not talking, it's easy. He's so sweet to me and he's not afraid to show his emotions. Fuck. I don't know what I'm doing." I saw a thick, broken piece of basswood on the ground and bent to pick it up. It was about the size of a softball. I rotated it around in my hands, searching for pests or imperfections.

Jude stopped to look at me, warm brown eyes looking out from the curtain of his shoulder-length brown hair. "How do you think he feels about you?"

I shrugged. "That's the million-dollar question, isn't it? He seems to like me quite a bit, but I wonder if he can distinguish between liking me and liking being with any man."

Jude hummed in disapproval. "Blue, that's a bit self-deprecating, even for you. I don't think you'd be into someone who would be so fickle."

I barked out a laugh. "Oh shit, Jude. You haven't seen who Jeremy brought with him this week."

"Jeremy is an ass," he said matter-of-factly.

"Everyone keeps saying that. Why didn't anyone say it when we were together? Jesus."

"We did! We totally did. Even Mom asked if she could set you up with someone she met at the fucking grocery store. She was desperate to show you there were better guys out there for you," Jude said.

"I thought she was kidding. She said she could set me up with a bag boy from Safeway. How was I supposed to know she was being serious? And, really, a bag boy from Safeway?" I mocked. "How fucking romantic. Why would I leave a successful media buyer who loves me for a grocery bag boy?"

Jude shot daggers at me. "'Because no one asks out the fat friend.'"

Fuck. "You're right. Ignore me. I'm sure Bag Boy is perfectly nice regardless of his career ambitions or lack thereof. But to offer to set me up on a date when I'm living with a long-term boyfriend is kind of rude. Maybe I should ask Mom for the guy's number now that I'm single."

That made Jude laugh. "Let's not go that far. I'd definitely rather see you settled down with a vineyard owner than a bag boy."

The idea of settling down with Tristan was too lovely to contemplate so I changed the subject.

"Speaking of settling down, let's talk about Simone and John for a minute," I suggested.

"I saw her this morning and gave her a hug. She seems excited," Jude said as we began walking again. I could hear the bodyguard's steps crunching about twenty-five paces behind us. Not for the first time I wondered about what it would be like to be live Jude's life. It seemed very lonely. Unable to shop in public. Worrying about people using you for money or fame. Being threatened for no better reason than having a nice voice and making something of yourself.

"It's not really Simone I'm concerned about. It's John. He's an ass, Jude. I never liked the guy, and now I've heard a few more things and seen him spouting off. He's homophobic and disrespectful. I hate to think of Simone tied to someone like that for the rest of her life."

Jude sighed. "I know, Bee. But you can't ask her to give up the man she loves because he's narrow minded. Don't you think she knows that about him by now? You have to respect her decision. She won't be tied to him forever if she doesn't want to be. If the time comes she decides he's not right for her, she can always leave him."

"I have a bad feeling about this, Jude. I don't want her to get hurt," I explained.

"You have to let her stand on her own two feet. She's a big girl. I know she'll always be our baby girl, but she's twenty-six years old. We can't keep her safe forever, Blue."

He was right, so I let it go. Part of me wanted to talk to Tristan about it but knew that would be crossing a line. John was his brother. It was one thing to call your own brother a jerk, but to hear someone else do it was another. I couldn't do that to Tristan. And I didn't want to jeopardize whatever it was we had going on by putting him in that position.

When we circled back to the lodge, I noticed the bodyguard come up to whisper in Jude's ear. Jude nodded and then told me he was going to go lie down after all. I wished him some good sleep and told him I'd at least see him at the poker night later that evening.

As I walked into the lodge to get my phone charger out of my room, I passed Tristan's mom walking through the lobby. I smiled and greeted her but she just kept looking ahead of her as if I didn't exist. Uh-oh. That was going to be a problem. About ten strides later, I saw Tristan's dad walking to catch up with Mrs. Alexander. I smiled less confidently this time and said hello. He smiled and returned the greeting before rushing past me to join his wife on the sidewalk outside. So, Mr. Alexander okay with it, Mrs. Alexander definitely not okay with it.

As I continued to my room with Piper in tow, I texted Tristan.

Blue: I just saw your parents in the lodge lobby. Your mom pretended I was invisible. I wonder if maybe we should talk about it.

Tristan: Ignore her. She's trying to manipulate you with her attitude. She thinks she knows what's best for me, but she's wrong.

Blue: If you say so. Makes me feel bad though. Causing problems for your family.

Tristan: Do you think my mom wants me to be happy?

Blue: Don't most parents want that for their children?

Tristan: Yes. So let's assume she does.

Blue: Okay?

Tristan: Baby, you make me happy.

Fuck, when he calls me that... it makes my heart race like an idiot. I shook my head and put my phone in my pocket before digging out my room key to open my door. I found my charger and began to put down the chunk of wood I'd gathered on the path during my walk. I had a thought and texted Tristan again.

Blue: Do you have any carpentry tools on the property? Specifically, a wood carving knife?

Tristan: There are a ton of tools in a room in the barn. Do you know how to get there? I can walk over to meet you. I'm sure you'll find something useful in there.

Blue: The main barn with the horses?

Tristan: Yes, can you meet me in ten minutes?

Blue: Ok.

I charged my phone for a few minutes and then walked back out of my room, calling Piper from her curled-up spot in a sun patch by the window.

We walked over to the barn in time to see Tristan talking to an older man who was mounting one of the horses. When Tristan saw me, his eyes lit up and the dimple came out. *Motherfucker.*

By the time I got to the entrance of the barn, the man had tipped his hat and trotted off.

I had fallen back into the awkward attitude that Tristan probably wasn't as interested in me as I was in him, so I was unsure how to greet him. What I really wanted to do was run and leap on him, arms and legs hanging onto him for dear life. But what I did was walk up to him and stop a few feet before I got to him, my hands sliding into my jean pockets to keep them from reaching out to maul him.

He tilted his head to study me with furrowed eyebrows. His eyes darted down to survey his own body and then he looked back at me in confusion.

"Do I have cooties?" he asked.

I felt my face flush with embarrassment before I let out a laugh. "Apparently I'm playing hard to get. Is it working?"

"Well, your body language says, 'Don't touch me,' but those baby blues are talking real dirty to me," he said, smiling wolfishly as he stepped closer. He drew out the words "real dirty" as if he was speaking in Matthew McConaughey's drawl.

26

TRISTAN

If there was one thing that made Blue even cuter, it was a good blush on his light skin. It made the tips of his ears pink and his neck blotchy. Fucking adorable.

I strode slowly toward him, watching him in an effort to determine whether he was keeping his distance because he didn't want me to touch him or because he was nervous to touch me.

Fuck it. I sped up the last few steps and crashed into him, grabbing him around the back to keep him from pitching onto his ass. My mouth landed over his. He may have been unsure of how he felt, but I sure as hell wasn't.

He melted against my body, pulling his hands out of his pockets to grab fistfuls of my shirt as I deepened the kiss, and I smiled against his lips in triumph. I turned him, still kissing, and began walking him backward into the barn, stopping once we were out of sight of the yard.

I started to pull back to tell him how damned happy I was to see him, but he shoved me backward against the wall of a stall and kicked the intensity up a thousand notches. His hands pushed under my shirt, short fingernails catching the skin of my back, his knee shoved between my legs, forcing his thigh against my swollen cock. His tongue took complete possession over my mouth and his chest pushed mine so my body was pressed completely against the wall.

"*Fuck*," I mumbled against his onslaught. "What's gotten into...?" My words were replaced by a groan when his hand gripped my hard-on through my jeans.

"Stop, stop, Jesus, baby, *stop*," I begged, pushing him off. He started laughing smugly, hands on his knees, while I stood there panting and readjusting myself.

"What are you laughing at?" I asked indignantly.

"That is exactly what happened to me when you kissed me in the bar that first time. You got me so hot and bothered and then just sat up on your stool like it was no big deal. I was practically sprawled out across the bar begging for more."

I looked at Blue and started laughing. "You did that on purpose just now," I accused.

"Right, because I don't actually want to jump your bones every time I see you." Blue laughed.

"Didn't think so." I smiled back at him. "What are we here for? You said you wanted to manipulate my wood or something?" I winked.

He smacked my ass. "Something like that. Where are the tools?"

As I led him deeper into the barn, I adjusted my jeans again and heard him snicker behind me. I turned around to give him a dirty look when I noticed his own hand doing the same.

"Busted." He blushed. Damn, those ear tips again.

We arrived at the locked door to the tool room. I punched in a code and slid the door open on its rail. Inside were hundreds of random tools accumulated from a century of makers and fixers on the vineyard. They were kept somewhat organized but neither the agriculture guys nor I knew what some of them were for.

Blues eyes went wide and he looked awestruck. "Holy shit," he breathed.

"It's pretty cool. There are some amazing antique tools in here."

"No kidding, Tris. I could spend a month in this room and never get bored." He walked around the room like he didn't know where to start. He picked up a welder's torch and turned to look at me.

I bit the tip of my tongue to keep from offering him everything I owned, including the entire vineyard. Instead, I raised my brows in question.

"You have a complete welding setup here. Did you know that?" he asked.

"We have quite a bit of metal equipment in the winery that needs maintenance and customization. But I don't do that work. I've never welded anything. I'm pretty handy with electrical stuff though," I added lamely. Didn't want him to think I was useless around the place.

He put down the torch and wandered over to the carpentry equipment where he focused in on a group of small hand tools. Running his fingers along their seasoned wooden handles, he selected three of them to pull down from the wall and examine more closely.

"Is that what you were looking for?" I asked, stepping against his back and resting my chin on his shoulder. He laid the three tools on the workbench in front of him and held each one in turn.

"These must have been pretty special to someone at one point," he said.

"Probably Uncle Henry's father. He made some of the furniture around the vineyard properties," I explained.

"This one is a chip carving knife. If I could only borrow one, this is the one I'd need. Then this one is a double bevel straight chisel. And this one is a palm-handled gouge," Blue described as he handled them with care.

He had told me his idea for carving a small gift for John and Simone out of a hunk of wood he found on the property. It sounded like a great idea.

"You know you're welcome to use whatever you want, Blue. What about a mallet or a vise? How big is your wood?" The words weren't out of my mouth before I begged for them back.

He turned in my arms with his upper lip held in place by his lower teeth, trying to hide a big smile.

"Babe. Is my wood that unmemorable?" Blue teased.

"You're an ass." I laughed. "Believe it or not, my next question was going to be asking you if you needed any of my wood. Shut up."

By the time we locked up the tool room, Blue had decided to start with just the chip carving knife and return later for detailing tools when he knew what he wanted to make. We walked out into the sun still making each other laugh, swapping ideas for dirty wooden figures he could carve for the lovebirds when a voice called out my name, halting my steps and turning my blood cold.

Blue stopped beside me and shot me a questioning glance. I looked at him, feeling the blood drain from my face. He raised an eyebrow as I slowly reached out to take the carving knife out of his hand and switch it to my opposite hand.

I leaned over to speak into Blue's ear. "I'm so sorry. Please don't leave me no matter what I say or how mad you get."

He opened his mouth, probably to ask me what the hell I meant when I heard the voice again.

"Tristan!" she called, and I could finally make out her silhouette walking toward us from the estate house.

"Coming," I acknowledged, sensing Blue's head snapping up next to me to seek the source of the voice.

As she approached, I tried to imagine seeing her from Blue's perspective. She was tall and beautiful in a cold kind of way. Platinum-blonde hair cut short in a trendy but no-nonsense cut. She had obviously come from work because she was dressed in a slim skirt and semi-sheer blouse with high heels. It would have been topped with her lab coat while making rounds.

The only feeling I had when seeing her was annoyance.

"Hi," she said, eyes flicking from me to Blue and back. I leaned in to kiss her cheek out of habit.

"Hi," I answered before remembering my manners. "Sheila, this is Blue Marian. Blue, this is Sheila Alexander. My ex-wife."

27

BLUE

I felt the urge to bolt so strongly that my entire body vibrated with it. Hearing her last name was like a blow to the chest. This woman had been naked in bed with Tristan. For *years*.

She knew about ten million more things about him than I did, and no matter what happened between Tristan and myself, Sheila would always have known him longer.

To add insult to injury, she had body parts I would never be able to provide for him. Damn, this sucked so badly. I wanted to walk away. Just turn and wander back to the lodge. Either that or cut a bitch. No wonder he took the carving knife out of my hands. The fucker.

I reached out my hand to shake hers. "Hi, Sheila. It's nice to meet you." Lie, total lie.

Her lips tightened into a grimace as she nodded her acknowledgement of my words, but she didn't respond in kind. It sort of reminded me of another Mrs. Alexander we all knew.

I looked over to Tristan and saw his jaw clenching. My eyes moved back to Sheila, who was trying to make significant eye contact with Tristan. He looked down at the very interesting gravel we were standing on.

The silence was deafening. "So, Sheila, what brings you to the vineyard today?" I asked like a cheerful faker.

She looked at me, almost as if she was surprised I could speak. Didn't I know she and Tristan needed to have words in private? Why, yes, yes, I did.

"Did my mom call you?" Tristan asked her.

"No, John called me," she answered. Her eyes glinted with something strange, like pleading.

"Ah, John. Keeping in touch then?" Tristan spat. What the fuck was that about?

"Leave it alone, Tristan. Can we go somewhere to talk, please?" she asked.

"No need. We don't have anything to talk about Sheila. But John and my parents are probably up at the lodge if you'd like to go find them," Tristan said as he started to walk toward the estate house. I followed along like a duckling.

As Tristan passed Sheila, she reached out and grabbed his arm to stop him. He looked down at her hand and back up at her, causing her to drop her hand faster than I would have imagined possible.

His entire body was radiating annoyance and it was starting to border on anger.

"Don't be a jerk, Tristan. I just want to talk to you for a few minutes. Let's go into your office," she said in a commanding tone that explained why he found her so goddamned annoying.

"Fine. Let's," he said in a clipped voice. I may not have known him well, but I knew what that tone meant coming out of anyone. Trouble.

He reached the wood-and-glass doors of the building and held the door for us. Once we passed into the reception area, he turned in the opposite direction of his office and led us into a small conference room with a round table and four chairs.

Tristan pointed to a seat for me and then sat in the one next to it. When Sheila noticed me enter the small room with them, her eyes widened.

"Blue, would you mind leaving us alone to speak in private?" she asked. Apparently my cheerful faker voice was contagious.

I started to stand but Tristan grabbed my hand and yanked me back down into my chair.

"He's staying," Tris said, surprising me with his need to keep me with him.

She barked out a laugh. "You've got to be kidding me, Tristan. Are you afraid of me? You need your sidekick here to protect you from your ex-wife?"

Oh no she didn't. I sat forward to give her a piece of my mind when I felt Tristan's hand land on my leg. So I gave her my angry eyes instead.

"For the record, I'm not afraid of you, Sheila. I'm afraid of me. Of what I'll say and do when you tell me why you're here," Tristan explained coolly. It was almost like the more worked up I felt, the calmer he acted.

"What if I'm here to talk about him?" She gestured toward me.

"What about him? And he has a name," Tristan said.

"Are you really pretending to be gay?" she asked.

"No, I'm not. And it's none of your business anyway. Explain to me why you're here and how any of this is any of your business anymore."

"So you two aren't fucking around?" she asked in relief.

I couldn't help it. I had to answer that one. "Oh, we're for sure fucking around."

Tristan barked out a laugh. Sheila's eyes darted to him and he spoke up. "He's right."

"But you said you aren't pretending to be gay." I could practically see her mind at work as she tried to work it out in her head.

"I'm not pretending. I am gay. But like I said, it's really none of your business."

"Your mom's worried about you," she said. "And so is John."

Tristan's entire demeanor changed and a quiet rage seemed to overtake him. His words came out through clenched teeth. "Don't fucking tell me shit about John. Don't say his name, and don't you dare imply that he cares about my love life. I can't believe your gall in coming here to tell me that. Do you even hear yourself?"

Sheila's eyes darted to me again and I had nothing for her. I had no idea what he was talking about.

"Tristan, I told you a million times how sorry I was. It was a mistake. It's been three years. Can't you get over it already? I thought you'd forgiven us. If you can't forgive me, at least forgive John."

I felt like I was watching a tense game of tennis. Back and forth, who was going to lose their shit first? My money was on Tristan at this point. Wait. *Wait.*

"Sheila, I'm over you. Really over you. I don't even give a shit about your part of it anymore. Our marriage sucked. The sex sucked. You sleeping with someone else was almost inevitable. But my brother? That's not something I can just get over."

Blood started rushing in my ears as the truth of what they were saying sank in. John was the person Sheila was sleeping with in Tristan's bed? Tristan walked in on his wife and his *brother*?

Oh god. Poor Tristan. Jesus, how could they do that to him? Without thinking, I reached over to grab his hand. He glanced at me with appreciation and held it tightly.

Sheila's eyes followed the movement and couldn't look away. "So it's true? You two? Really?"

Tristan nodded. "Yes, really."

Sheila let out a big sigh and slumped in her seat, silent for several moments. "I guess it makes sense. Explains some things anyway."

"Yes, it does," he agreed.

She glanced between us some more before sighing and continuing. "Tristan, you look happy. I mean, not right now. Right now you look pissed. But when I saw you two walk out of the barn. You looked... lighter. And really happy. Your family said they were worried about you, but I think maybe they're the ones who are wrong."

Tristan threw up his free hand. "Thank you. Finally someone can see how fucking good this is," he exclaimed.

I raised my free hand too, as if I had a question. "Uh, I saw how fucking good it was from the beginning. Does that count?"

They both laughed and the tension in the room broke.

Tristan asked Sheila if she needed a room for the night and she declined, saying she was going to head back to the city. I tried not to let my relief show but I felt Tristan squeeze my hand again in acknowledgement.

We stood up to walk out and she hugged Tristan goodbye in the courtyard. Then she surprised us by hugging me as well.

"You're really lucky, Blue," she said into my ear.

No shit, I thought. But before her car was even out of the parking lot I realized something that changed everything.

If John had slept with Sheila while she was married to Tristan, my own baby sister wasn't just marrying a homophobic asshole. She was marrying someone who didn't respect marriage vows.

And Tristan had known this whole time.

28

TRISTAN

I wondered how I would know when it was safe to hand Blue back the carving knife. After Sheila got in her car and drove away, I turned to him.

The look on his face told me I would never, ever be able to give him the knife back. His blue eyes took on the deep color of the Mariana Trench and his entire face looked pinched with betrayal.

I subconsciously took a step back, stunned by the swift turnaround of his mood. What the hell happened?

Blue turned on his heel and took off running in the direction of the lodge, Piper perking up and bolting after him. I stood there, stunned for a minute while I tried to figure out what to say.

"Wait," I cried out. "Blue, hang on."

Before my words had a chance to carry, he was out of sight. *Well, fuck.*

I followed him to the lodge, forcing myself to smile and nod politely to the family members and friends I passed in the lobby before making my way to Blue's room.

My knock on the door went unanswered so I knocked again.

"Blue," I called through the door. "Don't make me use my master key. Open the door, please, and talk to me."

After a moment, the door opened and I stepped in, closing it behind me. Piper was already curled in a spot by the windows, but she picked her head up when I walked in.

Blue stood in the middle of the room with his arms crossed defiantly in front of his chest.

"What the hell happened back there?" I asked. "Is this you being jealous of Sheila or something? How could you think I still have feelings for her?"

His nostrils flared and his eyes narrowed. Being on the receiving end of his anger made my stomach twist in knots.

His voice came out in a low, controlled tone. "It's not about Sheila. Your brother is a homewrecker, and you knew about it all along. Does my sister know? Does Simone know about John and Sheila?"

Oh shit. It all made sense to me now. "I... I don't know, Blue," I answered.

"Well, don't you think she deserves to?" he asked in the same low, angry tone.

I stood there, trying to think about what he was asking. Before I had a chance to think it through, he spoke again.

"What if you'd just found out that Simone slept with Jeremy when Jeremy and I were together? How would that make you feel about Simone marrying your brother?" Blue asked.

"I get what you're saying, Blue, and I don't disagree with you. But that's like you trying to convince me John isn't good for Simone, and I already knew that. But what was I supposed to say? 'Uh, Simone, you shouldn't date my brother, he's an ass.' That shit with Sheila happened three years ago, before he even met Simone. And there's more to this story than I can tell you."

Blue rolled his eyes at me. "What could there possibly be that would justify his actions?"

I threw up my hands at him. "What do you want me to say, Blue?"

"Nothing. I don't want you to say anything. I'm fucking pissed at you for not telling me. I'm worried about what it means for my sister. I just... I need to be alone right now," Blue said, sounding defeated.

I took a few cautious steps toward him but I saw him bristle. Seeing him react that way to me made me want to scream.

"Okay. Okay, Blue. If that's what you want, I'll give you some space. But..." I tried to think of how to say what I needed to say without fucking everything up worse. "But... can I please just hold on to you for a second?" My voice broke on that last part and I couldn't look at him. I hated sounding so needy, but I couldn't bear walking away without touching him.

He uncrossed his arms and stepped into me, his face immediately going into my neck. I did the same and we just stood there, holding on to each other. There was nothing sexual about it at all. It was just me grasping the most important thing in the world and trying desperately not to think about losing it.

That was the moment when I realized I was in love with him. The idea of something coming between us terrified me because *I loved him*. A desperate, all-consuming love that left me breathless and scared. And more vulnerable than I'd ever felt in my life. In less than a week he was leaving to move half a world away.

When I had woken up that morning, I hadn't expected to hand over my own heart to somebody else, but no one ever does. The end result was the same. My body may have walked out of that hotel room a few minutes later, but my heart stayed behind, entrusted into Blue's care whether or not he realized it.

29

BLUE

I needed to stop thinking about the man with the gray eyes who seemed to draw my attention away from everything else in the world. Remind myself I was there for Simone's wedding. A wedding to a man who I'd never liked and who was turning out to be even more of a selfish ass than I'd expected.

Getting involved in other people's relationships was swimming in dangerous waters. I needed to be smart about this and figure out if it was even my place to speak to Simone about what I'd learned. I lay on the bed and pulled a pillow over my face, trying desperately to ignore Tristan's scent on the pillowcase.

My brain flipped through different scenarios of how to deal with Simone and John. I realized quickly that telling Simone was a bad idea. She already knew John wasn't my favorite person, and she might think I was deliberately sabotaging her wedding week by causing trouble.

Maybe I should talk this through with Jude. He was always my go-to guy for strategizing shit. But then I remembered how shattered he'd looked and how badly he needed rest and relaxation to recover from the exhaustion of his tour. I didn't want to put this stress on him.

One thing I knew was it would be way better to bring this up now, on Wednesday, than to wait until we were all closer to the actual wedding day. I finally decided on a plan of action. I would confront John himself.

The idea of getting into it with John made me want to hurl. After his nasty words at Tristan's cabin the day before, I was feeling more intimidated than usual by him. I didn't want things to get ugly, and one of the ways I could imagine that happening included his fist and my face. Maybe the best thing to do would be to wait an hour and cool off.

Simone texted me to ask if I wanted to hang out for a little while. I knew I wouldn't be able to hide my unease from her so I begged off, asking if we could maybe hang out later in the day before her spa night.

I called Piper up to the bed with the idea of taking a short nap, but when I came out of the bathroom, I noticed Tristan had left the carving knife on the dresser next to my block of wood. I took the two items and Piper outside, wandering until I found a bench under a shade tree off the beaten path. I closed off my brain and started whittling, not knowing what I wanted to carve yet, but knowing I had quite a bit of wood to hack off before getting to a useable base for anything.

When I looked at the clock on my phone again, I realized two hours had passed. I felt groggy and slow when I tried to look up and focus on the real world. After dropping the wood and knife back off in my room, I fixed a cup of coffee in the lobby and took Piper back outside through the patio doors.

While she sniffed her way around the yard, I sipped my coffee and let it do its job. I texted Tristan to ask him what room John was staying in.

Blue: Do you know what room your brother is staying in?

Tristan: Blue, don't do anything stupid.

Blue: I'm just going to talk to him. What room?

Tristan: Let me come with you.

Blue: Never mind. I'll ask Simone.

Blue: BabyGirl, what room is John in?

Simone: 126, why?

Blue: I just wanted to ask him something. We still on for 3pm?

Simone: Yep. I'll meet you in lobby.

I called Piper in and headed to John's room. It was a suite with a door that opened to a sitting room. John didn't seem thrilled to see me, but I assumed it was from general annoyance about me being with his brother rather than knowing what was going through my head.

"Can we talk for a minute?" I asked.

"Sure, have a seat." John pointed to the sofa and I sat down, Piper sitting next to my foot and leaning against my leg. She seemed uneasy, and I assumed she was reacting to my nerves. John sat in an armchair next to the sofa.

"I met Sheila a little while ago," I began. John immediately tensed. I was sure he wondered how much I knew.

"Doesn't surprise me," he said arrogantly. "She was pissed about you and Alex."

That's when I remembered John didn't call Tristan by his name. It was a strange thing, one I wanted to ask Tristan about later.

"First of all, she wouldn't have known about it unless you called to tell her. Secondly, what business is it of hers exactly?" I asked.

"It's her business because she's family, dammit. She was with him for years."

I returned his glare with one of my own. "I get that. But they're over. They've been divorced for years. Why call Sheila?"

"Because she knows him better than anyone. She would know how to talk some sense into him," he replied angrily.

"Sense? As in, he should have the good sense not to be gay?" I accused.

"Among other things," John retorted.

The implication being that even if Tristan was gay, he shouldn't choose me?

"Is she good at talking sense into people, John? Is that what she was doing with you when Tristan walked in on you naked in his bed?" *There. Let's get this party started.*

His eyes narrowed and shot fire at me. "This is none of your goddamned business, Blue. You have no right sticking your nose in this when you've only known Alex for ten minutes."

I didn't hear the click of the door latch or see Tristan enter the room.

"Yeah, well, I've known Simone for twenty-six years," I barked. "And she doesn't deserve someone who shits all over someone's marriage vows."

"You leave Simone out of this!" John stood up to lunge at me, and I jumped up in response. Tristan got there just in time to grab John's arm before it took a swing at me.

"Stop, dammit," Tristan ground out between gritted teeth. "Stop."

"Get your fucking hands off me," John shouted.

"No. Not until you sit down," Tristan said in a tone more calm than he looked.

"He needs to know about Simone, Alex, so he'll get off my fucking back. Tell him what you did." John shook off Tristan's hold and threw himself back down on the chair.

Tristan shot John a look. "No, John. He doesn't. And you need to shut your fucking mouth before you say something you can't take back."

I looked from Tristan to John. "What about Simone?"

Neither man said a word. I looked at Tristan, desperate to understand what I was missing. "Tell me, Tris. What about Simone? What did you do?"

"Let's go, Blue. We can talk about this somewhere else." Tristan reached out his hand for me but I ignored it, passing him and exiting the suite. Piper trotted after me down the hall to the lobby and out the front doors. I didn't look back to see if Tristan followed me.

I saw his utility vehicle and sat in the passenger seat, Piper sat behind me in the cargo bed. Tristan came striding out of the double doors, long legs eating up the distance to where I was. His face was set in a serious mask of determination and my gut roiled at the possibilities of what he was going to tell me about my sister.

He drove us to his place in silence while my mind churned with possible scenarios. A horrible thought occurred to me, and it almost made me want to vomit. Was he going to tell me he had slept with Simone to get back at John?

Fuck, oh fuck. I couldn't handle that. No, no way. Please no.

My breathing started coming in quick gasps, scaring me with its intensity. My lungs couldn't keep up and worried I was hyperventilating. When Tristan parked in the gravel drive, the sound of my labored breathing stood out. He turned to look at me and noticed my distress.

"Blue, are you okay?" he asked with concern in his eyes.

"Did," gasp, "you," gasp, "sleep," sob, "with *Simone*?"

"What? No! God, no. Of course not, Blue. Slow down. Slow your breathing down." He ran around the other side of the vehicle and pulled me up from my seat, leading me into the cabin and settling me on the sofa.

He knelt on the floor in front of me, holding both of my hands and looking into my eyes. "You're okay, baby, just calm down and breathe. Slowly."

As my breathing came under control, his hands came up to smooth my hair back from my face. God, he was so fucking sweet. The look of concern and tenderness in his eyes made me want to crawl into his lap and stay there.

He sat next to me, pulling me down to lie next to him on the sofa with my head resting on his heart. One of his arms wrapped around me and the other hand held my head against his chest.

I felt the rumble from his chest a split second before I heard the words. "Just catch your breath for a minute. And then I'll tell you whatever you want to know. I promise."

We lay there quietly for a while until sound of my phone rang from the coffee table. I lifted my head up in time to see Tristan answer it.

"'Lo?" he mumbled.

I thought I heard my sister's voice on the other end and remembered I'd been planning on meeting her at 3 p.m. I wondered what time it was.

"Yeah, he's right here. Hang on," he said, handing me the phone. "Sorry, thought it was mine."

"Simone?" I answered.

"Dude, where are you? Did you get caught up in a postcoital haze?" she teased.

"No, just dozed off on the sofa. What time is it?"

"It's after three. Want me to give you an hour? Spa night doesn't start until seven, so it's fine."

"Sounds good. I'll see you at four." We disconnected and I sat up, rubbing my face and putting the phone back down on the coffee table next to Tristan's. I turned to look at him and felt familiar butterflies in my stomach. He was so fucking hot, hair sticking up and face red where his cheek had been resting against my head. He grinned sleepily under my gaze and it made my dick twitch.

It was really hard to be mad at someone that good looking. I rolled my eyes and he laughed.

"What?" he asked with a smile.

"You know what," I muttered.

"No," he said. "I don't."

"You're looking at me again. You know what that does to my dick."

He leaned forward and grabbed my hand, pulling me back down on top of him. "It makes your dick want to dive into my hot, wet mouth?"

"Don't give it any ideas," I said, grinding my hard-on against his. "We're supposed to be talking. Not fucking."

"Speaking of fucking, Amazon is bringing us some lube today." He smirked.

I laughed. "You're joking."

"Nope. I had myself a little online shopping spree yesterday before the vineyard tour. And, this ought to make you feel special, I even upgraded to overnight shipping." He waggled his eyebrows.

"Horny bastard," I snickered. "When you say spree... what else did you get?"

His face dropped. "Just lube. What else is there?"

I laughed again. "Dude, you might not be ready for me to answer that. But lube is a good start. Baby steps."

He grabbed my ass and squeezed. "As long as I have this and some lube, I'll be happy for a while."

I leaned forward and kissed him, crawling up his body to kneel on either side of his hips so I could cup his face in my hands. His own hands rested on my thighs, rubbing up and down the worn denim of my jeans as we kissed.

After a few moments of savoring each other's mouths, Tristan pulled back, and I noticed a serious set to his face. "A year ago Simone slept with one of John's friends. One of his *married* friends."

I sat up, the blood draining from my face. "Liar."

30

TRISTAN

"I wish I was. I'm sorry." I sat up as Blue slid off my lap to take a spot next to me on the sofa. I reached for his hand and threaded my fingers through his.

"But... who? Who did she sleep with? She's dated John for at least two years. She cheated on John with a married man?" he stammered, obviously trying to figure it all out.

I hated being the one to tell him this, but I knew he would push and push until it came out anyway. He needed to understand Simone and John's shit was between the two of them.

"Yes. He knows. They've worked it out and gotten past it together. Blue, it's their business. It's not for us to get in the middle of. Like I said, it was one of John's friends. Actually, he's the one who set the two of them up in the first place," I explained.

"Billy? She fucking slept with Billy Treadway?"

"Yes. I didn't realize you knew him. He and John went to high school together," I said. "I think Simone was friends with his wife, Kim. I saw Billy kissing Simone in his car one night and went ballistic. I confronted them and punched Billy in the face."

Blue sounded utterly deflated. "How could she do that to Kim? They grew up together. Kim lived on our street. Are you sure?" His eyes met mine; I could tell he was desperate for me to tell him it was all a misunderstanding.

I nodded and pulled him in close again with an arm around his shoulders. He leaned his head onto my shoulder and let out a big sigh. "How could she do that? I'm so disappointed."

"Baby, not everyone is perfect. People make mistakes, even little sisters," I said gently. He raised his head to look at me.

"Do all people cheat? Am I the only person in America who thinks cheating is more than just a mistake some people make? Have you ever cheated?"

I shook my head emphatically. "No, Blue. I have never and would never cheat. I abhor cheating. I think it's unfair and disrespectful. But that's between me and my partner. What happens in someone else's relationship is between them. Some people have open relationships. Some people go into a relationship knowing they're with a cheater. I'm only saying that if both Simone and John have made similar mistakes, maybe they are able to forgive each other."

He looked at me with those blue eyes that seemed to show me everything he was thinking. "For the record," Blue said, "I have never cheated. I would never cheat. Even when I'm just hooking up with someone, I'm not hooking up with anyone else."

My heart warmed at his words because they were clearly meant for me. But there was a little bit of unease at his use of the phrase "just hooking up." Was that what he thought we were doing? Just hooking up?

If I wasn't already sure it was too soon to make a declaration of my feelings to him, that phrase was a reminder. He would most likely flip out, and then I would come across as this crazy fickle guy who goes from straight to gay and hooking up to the L-word in about sixty seconds. Surefire way to scare someone the fuck away. And what was the fucking point anyway? He was leaving. Why did I let this happen?

"So," I said, stretching and knocking the mood up several hundred notches. "We playing poker tonight?"

Blue looked a me for a beat, probably deciding whether or not to accept my abrupt topic change.

"Poke her? I don't even know her," he said with a wink and stood up. "Yes, but right now I have to go meet Simone."

I gave him a look.

"Don't worry, Tris. I'm not going to bring it up. Plus, I'm pretty sure she's planning on grilling me about you the whole time anyway."

"What are you going to tell her?" I grinned.

"How you stink at blow jobs and have a tiny dick," Blue deadpanned.

"Fuck you," I cried. "Oh my god, you're so mean." I laughed and pinched his ass. "If you think my dick is so tiny, how come you ejaculate every time I wave it in your direction?"

"Okay, okay." He laughed. "You have a big, beautiful cock. Remind me to have Aunt Tilly cross-stitch that on a pillow for you for Christmas."

We kept flirting and giving each other hell while I drove him back to the lodge. I decided to check in with my parents while Blue visited with Simone.

When we walked into the lobby, there was a big group of people standing around talking excitedly. As we got closer, I could see the group was mostly made up of the Marian clan.

Blue grabbed my hand. "My brother Thad is here and you can meet Jude too. Come on."

He introduced me to Thad, who had just flown in from Africa. He looked jet lagged but happy. He had the same brown hair and brown eyes that all the Marian siblings had except for Blue. My first impression of Thad was that of a puppy. Young, open, and eager to please. I knew he was thirty years old but he seemed younger than that.

Then I met Jude. I recognized him from the media but he was smaller in person than I'd expected. He, too, looked jet lagged even though I knew he had only come from Los Angeles. His thick brown hair was shoulder length and he had a kind face. When he shook my hand, he gave me a sincere smile that went all the way to his eyes.

"Tristan, it's very nice to meet you. I can tell Blue thinks you're pretty special," Jude said in a clear but quiet voice. "Hopefully we can get a chance to hang out this week. You have a beautiful place here."

"Thank you. I'd love a chance to get to know you better. Blue thinks the world of you too, and so far all I know is that you have quite a way with an acoustic guitar."

His smile widened. "Thanks, man. I brought it with me. Simone made me promise to play for her one night. Hopefully you and Blue will join us."

"Wouldn't miss it. Just don't make me sing along. You'll regret it," I promised.

"Have you heard Blue sing? He has a killer voice."

Blue shot a dirty look at his brother. "Zip it, Jude."

Jude laughed and looked back at me. "He knows I always make him sing duets with me, so don't worry. You'll get to hear him sing. Maybe I can get him to sing the song he wrote for Mom when he was thirteen."

"Fat chance." Blue laughed before putting Jude in a headlock. They were laughing and starting to wrestle when a giant man stepped in and calmly removed Blue's arm from around Jude's throat. I stood there staring and wondering what was going on when Jude held up a hand to the man to tell him it was okay. Then Jude smiled at Blue.

"Dude, fucking finally, after twenty-eight years I have someone to defend me from you." He laughed and then turned back to the big guy. "Thanks, Wolfe. I owe you one."

The man chuckled. "Just doing my job. Even family's not allowed to mess with your voice. Maybe you need to remind Blue how much it's insured for."

Ahh, the guy must be a bodyguard. How crazy was that? And of course I was dying to know how much his voice was insured for. I wondered if Blue knew. I had heard one time that Bruce Springsteen's was insured for six million dollars.

I said my goodbyes and detoured to the front desk before making my way to my parents' room. The Marians seemed like a pretty amazing family. Loving, accepting, and tight knit. I could see those influences in Blue's personality and was grateful to know he was so well loved.

31

BLUE

Instead of spending time with just Simone, my whole family spent time together on the back patio of the lodge. Apparently Tristan had sent someone to arrange for wine and snacks to be brought out, so we had an impromptu happy hour.

Ginger and Pete's girls found a tennis ball and threw it for Piper the entire time, wearing all three of them out. Jamie propped an injured knee on a second chair and had an ice pack on it. My mom fluttered around him, making sure he had wine and a little bowl of his own bar snacks. At one point after she fussed over him for the millionth time, Jamie winked at me behind her back. I stuck my tongue out at him and mouthed *brat*.

Simone was in heaven surrounded by all of us. It wasn't often any more that the eight of us were all together anymore. Simone was twenty-six and Pete was thirty-six, so everyone was busy with jobs and kids and their own adult lives. We were fortunate that almost everyone had stayed in California.

After about a half hour, Tristan's cousin Sarah wandered out and joined us. I introduced her to the people she hadn't already met, including Thad, Jude, and Jamie. She seemed overwhelmed by the three single men standing in front of her, but she impressed me by treating Jude the exact same as everyone else. Luckily she seemed most interested in the only one of them who wasn't gay.

Thad told us about his project in Kenya and said he was happy his next project was close to home. He had a grant to implement a child poverty program in Fresno.

Mom and Dad asked Jude what he was doing now that the tour was over. He said he was spending a few months on a new album and then recording it. If all went well, he'd be starting a new tour in six months.

"But I don't even want to think about another tour right now. I just want to go home and hole up behind my tall fences and be by myself for a little while. No offense." He smiled. I could tell he was ready to be away from the crowds.

Aunt Tilly walked up with Granny and Irene. Pete and I gave up our seats to make sure there were three patio chairs together for them, and then Pete fixed them each a glass of wine. They told us about playing bridge earlier with one of the older gentlemen who worked at the vineyard. I wondered if it was the same man I'd seen on the horse.

Granny looked at me and raised an eyebrow. "Where's your side-kick, Blue?"

"He went to find his parents a while ago, so he might be in their room," I answered from my spot on the stone step by her feet.

"Well, text him and tell him to get his sweet ass out here," Aunt Tilly commanded.

"Yes, ma'am." I laughed, pulling out my phone. "You don't have to ask me twice. It certainly is a sweet ass."

Irene blushed. Aunt Tilly nodded enthusiastically in agreement, muttering, "You can say that again."

Blue: Save me. Happy hour in full swing on patio. Three grannies asking me about your sweet ass.

Tristan: Why do you think I sent wine? Just keep refilling.

Blue: My glass or theirs?

Tristan: Both.

Blue: So you aren't going to come?

Tristan: Oh, baby, I'm definitely going to COME.

Blue: Dirty old man.

Tristan: Lemme track my Amazon package.

Blue: You know I have everything we need in my room right?

Tristan: Meet me there?

As I stood up, Aunt Tilly interrupted me. "Quit sexting him; he's standing right behind you."

I whipped around and bumped my shoulder against Tristan's chest. If he hadn't reached his arms around me, I would have tumbled backward down the stone step and into the yard.

"Whoa, baby." He laughed. "What's your hurry? Going somewhere?" The laugh was accompanied by a wink, and I gave him a dirty look. He chuckled even deeper.

"Well, I was going to my room to... ah... talk to a guy about a thing." Why couldn't I ever come up with something better than that?

Granny piped up. "Right, to talk to Tristan about *his thing*. You're busted. Might as well stay here or else we're all going to talk smack about you two behind your backs."

My face had never been so flushed and hot in all my life. I shot a *help me* look at Tristan, but he just covered his own blushing face and kept laughing. At least I wasn't alone.

"Walk with me to at least get you a glass of wine," I told him. "You're obviously going to need it."

We walked together to the table where the ice buckets and bottles were set up next to the open French doors.

As he selected what he wanted and begin to pour, he turned to wink at me. "You okay?"

"Better now that you're here. Those old ladies are mean," I joked. "Where are your parents?"

"They're coming. Mom wanted to freshen up first, I think." Tristan took a sip of wine and sighed appreciatively before leaning in to kiss me.

"Mmm, white tastes good on you," I whispered. "I gotta be honest. It's still strange to me that you're just suddenly gay and out, kissing in front of people."

He shrugged. "I know. It's a little weird. But I keep reminding myself I'm an adult and I know what I want. And what I want is to fucking touch you every minute of the day and also to show you I'm proud to be with you. It wouldn't be fair to you to treat you any differently in public than I would a woman I was this into. And for the record, I've never been into a woman as much as I'm into you."

His words were too good to be true. I mean, really. This guy just couldn't be for real.

"Are you really this brave?" I asked skeptically. "You make it sound so easy."

"I've had too many gay friends struggle to compartmentalize their lives. It's painful to watch. Don't get me wrong, Blue. I think things might have been different if I was still a corporate attorney. It might have taken me longer to get up the courage. But owning my own business makes it very easy to do what I want. Was it hard for you? I never did ask how and when you came out."

Jude had walked up in time to hear the last part. He refilled his wineglass and then asked if he could tell Tristan the story about how I came out. I rolled my eyes and agreed, smiling at the look of anticipation both Jude and Tristan had.

We found seats around a patio table and settled in. Aunt Tilly caught wind of the story and joined us while Wolfe sat a few feet away on a chair by the patio doors.

Jude's voice was mesmerizing, so I loved it when he told a story.

"So Blue is sixteen and I'm twelve. Our parents had always been super cool and open and liberal, right? We had gay neighbors and friends, so Bee already knew our parents weren't going to lose their shit. It was really just one of those things that needed to be said before moving on. No big deal.

"Blue had suspected he was gay around age fourteen, but it was irrelevant until he was ready to date someone or hook up. He decided to just stay cool until the time came and then he'd tell everyone. Well, that hadn't happened yet by the time he turned sixteen. The homecoming dance was coming up and he planned to take his friend Ginger."

Tristan looked at me. "Ginger? Pete's Ginger?"

I laughed. "One and the same. For the record, she was my Ginger before she was Pete's Ginger."

Jude laughed. "Right. They were really close friends in school. When Ginger and Pete started dating, it was a whole big thing. But that's another story. Totally worth telling, but later, right? Anyway, Blue asked Ginger to the dance and she said yes, knowing already that he was gay. At that point, Ginger and I were the only ones Blue had told about being gay.

"One night at dinner Blue tells Mom and Dad that he's taking Ginger to the homecoming dance. It wasn't an announcement or anything, more like just informing them he was going.

"The entire family just sat there, shocked and silent. Blue finally looks up into everyone's faces, noticing they've all gone pale and awkward. So then Simone, who just turned ten, pipes up."

At this point, Jude started giggling uncontrollably, which set Aunt Tilly off.

I couldn't help but laugh too, and we were laughing so hard that Jude couldn't finish the story.

Jude snorted. "So then... oh my god, so then..." More giggling. I noticed the bodyguard watching him and laughing too.

I tried finishing it. "Simone says..." More laughing.

Tristan shouted, "Hey, Simone! We need your help over here."

When Simone came over and he explained he was left hanging, she started chuckling. "I still remember it like it was yesterday."

Jude said, "No, I got it, I got it. So then Simone stands up with this confused look on her cute little face, slams her palms on the dining table and yells, 'You're *straight*?' and the whole family bursts out laughing. They had all already assumed he was gay. So when he said, 'Well... uh, no,'" it was a bit anticlimactic. He accidentally inned himself instead of outing himself. We still call it his 'coming in' story."

Simone looked at Tristan. "Did he tell you about the time he thought Dad was gay?"

Aunt Tilly almost spilled her wine. "Where is Kevin? He should be here. Such a sweet man." She winked at me.

Tristan laughed and told them I'd already told that story. So of course they came up with more and continued telling Tristan embarrassing Blue stories for the next half hour. The only good thing I got out of it was Tristan's warm, strong hand on the back of my neck tracing lazy circles with his thumb on the edge of my hairline at my nape.

32

TRISTAN

As the clock neared 6 p.m. more and more people joined us out on the patio. Several of John's and Simone's friends had arrived that day as well as extended family members from both sides. The lodge was filling up and introductions took the place of Blue's childhood stories I enjoyed hearing.

John and Blue seemed to have settled into an unspoken truce and even my parents were being cordial to Blue and his family. I had a flash forward to future family gatherings of the Alexanders and the Marians. The thought was both exciting and nerve wracking.

Exciting if Blue and I were still together and could share family functions. But fucking heartbreaking if we weren't. Even more heartbreaking if he didn't come at all because he lived too far away. I couldn't imagine ever coming together with our families and having to watch him with someone else. The mere thought of that made my stomach roll. I tried to shove the idea aside and enjoy the moment.

Blue was across the patio speaking to a good-looking man I hadn't met. The guy was standing so close to him it was starting to bother me. I didn't realize I'd stopped listening to Irene and Granny until Irene said, "Why don't you go over there and join him, honey? There's nothing wrong with marking your turf."

That was all the permission I needed. As I began to make my way over to him, I saw Jeremy join them and take hold of Blue's arm. The stranger laughed and kissed Blue's cheek before walking off. Then Jeremy led Blue toward the trees. *Oh hell no.* I picked up my pace at the same time I noticed Brad watch the scene playing out. He stood frozen in surprise as he watched Jeremy manhandle Blue toward the seclusion of the woods.

Before I got to the edge of the patio, Blue came storming back from the edge of the trees, turning to bark something at Jeremy. I stood there, waiting to see what happened next and wondering what Brad was going to do. I couldn't figure out if he was sad, angry, or a little bit of both.

Blue walked straight toward me, grabbed my hand, and led me into the lodge, turning down the hallway toward his room. I belatedly whistled for Piper and she raced to catch up with us.

When we got into Blue's room, he turned and put his face in my neck. I was learning he found comfort in doing that, and I loved the feeling of providing him any small measure of comfort I could. I wrapped my arms around him and held him while he grumbled about Jeremy.

His fingers rucked up my shirt to find their way onto my back, and I winced at how cold they'd gotten while we were outside.

He snickered and slid the cold fingers down under my waistband to press the icicles against my ass cheeks.

"Mean bastard," I chastised. "The joke's on you when you can't find my balls later."

"Your ass is like a toasty furnace. Side benefit of having a hot new piece of ass," he teased.

Now I was the one grumbling.

Blue leaned up to kiss me with a grin on his face. It was playful and flirty. We smiled and toyed with each other's lips, nipping and teasing. I'd never felt so free and open, and I knew I was grinning like a fool. Again.

We stopped long enough for me to ask him what was up with Jeremy.

"He keeps begging to talk to me, Tris. I don't know what his deal is. I keep brushing him off and telling him I don't want to talk. He won't get the message. I feel sorry for poor Brad, you know?"

"Did you see Brad just now? He watched the whole thing happen," I said.

"No, I didn't see him. I was looking for you." Blue reached up to smooth one of my eyebrows. The gesture was almost maternal and it made my chest feel tight.

"What?" Blue asked me. "Why are you looking at me like that?"

Because I'm so goddamned crazy in love with you.

"Because you're beautiful," I said instead. "Inside and out. Truly."

Ear tips went red. *Fuck what that does to me.*

"Thanks, babe," Blue said. "Now I'm blushing. I'm beginning to think you get a kick out of making me blush. Cruel bastard."

If you only knew.

I let out a deep breath. "We'd better go to the poker thing. It's starts at seven."

"Oh no. I forgot to tell you. They pushed it to eight because some of John's college friends are on a flight that was delayed."

I looked at my phone to check the time. "So we have an hour and a half before we need to be anywhere?" I asked him, aiming my gray eyeballs right at him and hoping they carried the sex magic he accused them of.

"*Jesus fuck*," he murmured.

"Exactly." I grinned.

And, because I was terrified of a repeat from the day before when having sex with Blue made me cry my eyes out, I was determined to replace my love with lust for the next hour. With my emotions so raw from the day, I couldn't afford to make love to the man in front of me. So I tried my hardest to fuck his brains out instead.

I landed my mouth on his in a crush of lips and tongue and teeth, walking him backward toward the bathroom while practically ripping his clothes off. By the time I got him to the bathroom threshold, we were both naked and my mouth was devouring every inch of his skin I could find. My hands were everywhere, pulling and searching and grasping.

His breathing turned into panting and he barely knew which way was up. Blue gasped when I picked him up and sat him on the granite countertop of the bathroom sink. I nipped his earlobe and then traced a path with my wet tongue down his neck to his tight nipples to his navel.

His hands were in my hair and he made small sounds that went straight to my dick. I was so hard for him and I ground my cock against his thigh before leaning down to take his straining erection into my mouth.

"*Fuck,* Tris," he gasped.

My tongue swirled around his tip and then slid down the underside of his shaft. I teased him with light kisses and then took him completely into my mouth, concentrating on opening my throat and staying calm. The grip on my hair tightened as I sucked him in and out before doing the same to his balls, one at a time. He took his hands out of my hair and leaned back, bracing his palms on the counter behind him and trying to thrust up into my mouth.

"Not yet, baby," I told him before licking a trail from his balls to his hole. "I'm going to fuck you over this sink and you're going to come screaming my name."

"Oh *god*," he groaned, panting faster. "Please, Tristan, please fuck me."

I stepped back, letting him slide off the counter and grab what we needed out of the dopp kit on the bathroom sink. Once he handed me the condom and lube, I turned him around to face the mirror.

Hopefully he was seeing what I saw. His cornflower blue eyes glazed over with desire, his cheeks red from my beard, his hair tousled from my greedy fingers, and his lips swollen from my bites. He was the hottest vision I could dream up.

"God, you're gorgeous," Blue said. And I realized he wasn't looking at himself. He was seeing only me.

We locked eyes in the mirror and I slowed down long enough to kiss between his shoulder blades and drop my forehead to that spot for one quick moment while my brain cried out, *I love you. I love you.*

I stepped back, rolled on the condom, and lubed up my fingers, slipping them inside him one at a time until his hisses turned to begging and his hands were spread out on the counter in front of him.

Seeing him splayed on the bathroom counter with his ass ready and willing was enough to make me dizzy. I slid into him and let out a pent-up breath while I dropped kisses on his spine. Then I pulled back, feeling his muscles stroke my cock as I thrust back in.

His cries were nonsensical and needy. His thighs quivered and his back muscles rippled under my touch. After placing his hands far up on the counter and gently holding both wrists together there with one of my hands, I ran my other hand down to his hip and grabbed on, using it to pull me deeper into him with each thrust. He felt fucking amazing.

"Please. God... Tris," Blue begged and pleaded in a series of whimpers.

In, out, slow, fast, hard, soft. I couldn't get enough. Every time Blue pulled a hand out of my grip to stroke himself off, I grabbed it away and placed it back on the counter. It was driving him insane until his cries were almost sobs, and it was just the word *please* over and over.

I quickly squeezed out more lube with shaking hands. When I absolutely couldn't hold my climax back any longer, I grabbed his leaking cock with my slick hand and stroked him to the rhythm of my thrusts deep into his ass. He came in a split second and I felt the now familiar ecstasy of his tight channel contracting around me, sending me over the edge in a blast of fireworks and heat.

Blue started to slide to the floor and I caught him under the arms.

"I've got you, baby. Hang on," I said as I quickly tossed the condom and cleaned us up with a wet cloth.

We made our way to the bed and collapsed under the covers. I had just enough foresight to set my phone alarm for 7:45 p.m. before letting myself drift off, Blue cocooned in my embrace.

I fell into an amazing dream where the first thing I heard was the faint echo of Blue whispering the words I hoped one day to hear in real life: "I love you."

33

BLUE

I had come undone. The look in Tristan's eyes as he nailed me in the bathroom had been stark and raw. Naked lust had been there, but those gray eyes had told me there was much more to it than lust. What I had seen was a mirror image of my own intense feelings for him.

There was no doubt in my mind I was head over heels in love with Tristan. I'd tried denying it, doubting it, ignoring it. But there was no use. I was all in. The idea of any of this being "pretend" anymore had been incinerated in the blast furnace of our connection, the last trace of ash blown away with the breath it took for me to whisper those three words to his sleeping form.

I love you.

What in the hell would I do if he rejected me? Rejected the idea of us? It wasn't that I worried he didn't return my feelings. I knew he did. I could feel it in every fiber of my wracked-out body. Whether or not he knew it, Tristan loved me as intensely as I loved him. But there was a difference between loving someone and choosing to build a life with them. And what kind of life would that be? He was committed to this land and I was leaving.

And how the fuck did you fall in love with someone so damned fast? I mean, maybe I was crazy. Maybe this was just prostate-searing lust and I was misinterpreting my exuberant sexual satisfaction as love. But if that was the case, if you couldn't fall in love this fast, then how could I feel more for him in a couple of days than I'd ever felt for Jeremy and anyone else I'd ever been with all put together?

No. Lust wasn't what I felt when I saw Tristan giving piggyback rides to my nieces on the back lawn of the lodge. Lust wasn't what made my hands start subconsciously shaping the basswood into something for Tristan instead of my sister. Lust wasn't what puffed my chest out with pride when I heard several people compliment Tristan on the wine selections earlier that evening. And lust wasn't the feeling I had wrapped in his warm embrace and held protectively against his body.

I drifted off, unsettled by my thoughts and warring with myself about whether or not to expose my true feelings to Tristan. When his alarm went off, Tristan kept one arm around my chest while he reached for the phone with the other. He turned off the alarm and settled back around me, nuzzling his nose into my neck.

"Mphf, that sex was unbelievable, Blue," he mumbled against my skin.

"Mmm-hmm," I purred in agreement. "Kinda makes you hate the game of poker, doesn't it?"

"My thoughts exactly, but you know I can't skip."

I rolled over to face him. "I know. Just give me a minute to come to terms with the reality of having to get out of bed."

"Hey, who was that guy you were talking to before Jeremy tried kidnapping you into the forest?" Tristan asked, brushing my hair off my forehead.

I chuckled. "Oh, that's Zane. He's one of Simone's coworkers at the vet clinic. Apparently she'd been planning on setting us up this week and had been singing my praises to him. I think he was her best attempt at mitigating the fact that Jeremy was going to be here. She must have thought that having a good-looking guy flirting with me would be a good idea. Too bad you beat her to the punch."

Tristan frowned. "That explains why he was falling all over you."

I pulled back to get a better look at Tristan's face. Eyebrows gathered and wrinkles deepened on his forehead. A laugh escaped me again.

"Oh my god, you were jealous of Zane before you had to switch to being jealous of Jeremy again? You poor thing. You've had a rough night."

"Shut up," he grumbled. "That guy might as well have been groping you. He fucking kissed you, Blue."

"Dude, he kissed me on the cheek. But keep going. I like this. Makes me feel wanted. What else pissed you off?" I grinned at him.

He directed his piercing glare at me before the stormy gray eyes suddenly cleared and a wolfish grin appeared. Uh-oh.

"You like me being a little possessive?" he asked innocently in that sexy-as-fuck voice.

"A little, yes." I answered, feeling like I was being lured into a trap.

He leaned in to kiss me, teasing and tasting until my body thrummed with pleasure. By the time his mouth latched on to my neck with a bruising suck, I was too far gone to stop him.

Tristan pulled back in triumph and leaped off the bed. "Shower time," he called cheerfully.

I sat up and pressed a hand to my neck. "You jackass. Do you have any idea the shit my brothers are going to give me for sporting a *hickey*?" I yelled to his retreating form.

After we showered, I tried in vain to find a shirt in my suitcase that might help cover up the hickey. No dice. So I decided to own it. Turn the tables back onto Tristan since everyone would know whose damned fault it was anyway.

I slipped a T-shirt on over my jeans and turned to Tristan. It was a parody of a Katy Perry concert tee. He saw my shirt and snorted.

"Oh hell no," he said, eyes roaming over the printed words *I Kissed A Boy And I Liked It*.

"What? You appreciate the irony?" I said innocently. "Or did you want to wear it?"

"I think I should wear it. Give my mom's brothers something to finally push them into full cardiac arrest," Tristan suggested.

I laughed and stripped off the shirt, putting a soft oatmeal-colored henley on instead. The concert tee was folded and put back into my suitcase.

Tristan finished putting his clothes back on and slipped into his shoes before propping his ass on the end of the bed to wait for me.

I stepped between his legs and cupped his face. "Just so we're clear. When I am around other men, I only see you. Even if you're not there, I see you. You've cast some kind of juju on me, and I'm lost in its spell."

His face softened and his hands came up to rest over mine on his face. "Thank you. I didn't realize how much I needed to hear that. Sorry about the hickey."

"I'm not. Because I've decided that every time someone gives me hell about it tonight, you're going to have to use the word 'balls' in conversation with a straight face. Do we have a deal?" I smirked.

"Deal." He laughed before leaning forward to kiss me softly. After the kiss, he winked at me. "Let the games begin."

34

TRISTAN

There were about twenty-four of us for poker. Tables were set up in the main dining room in the estate house. There was a full bar set up with plenty of food like wings, sliders, and loaded potato skins. Bowls of chips and nuts dotted around the tables and classic rock played in the background. I would have to remember to thank Keller for his work in planning the wedding events this week.

Of course the first thing anyone said was about the hickey.

Blue's older brother Jamie piped up from his seat at a table. "Baby brother, is that a love bite you're sporting?"

Blue lifted an eyebrow in my direction and coughed. I sighed and returned his look. "Ball's in your court, Blue."

He nodded in approval. "Right you are. Jamie, this is a bruise. I tripped over my feet and landed—" Before he had a chance to finish, Pete jumped in.

"On Tristan's face?" The brothers high-fived as Thad walked up.

"Did someone say hickey? Blue, you kinky whore." Thad smirked.

Jesus, this was going to be a long night.

I thought for a beat and then said, "Who's ready for poker? Let's get the ball rolling."

John walked up and took a sip of his beer before speaking. "Dude, seriously, you gave a guy a hickey?"

Blue snorted, nearly choking on his own beer.

"Don't bust my balls, John. You've done way worse to Simone. Remember that time you accidentally gave her a black eye?"

"That was different. I was having a nightmare and accidentally elbowed her."

I shrugged. "Well, I accidentally sucked on Blue's neck too hard. What do you want me to say?"

Blue winked at me and flashed me a thumbs-up sign while John struggled to keep from gagging.

After we had been playing poker for about an hour, my phone rang. I checked the caller ID and saw Keller's name so I folded my hand to take the call.

"Hey, man. How's Art?" I asked.

"Not great actually. It's not just pneumonia. It's lung cancer. They didn't want to tell me that over the phone. Damn it, I knew there was more to it than pneumonia," he said, obviously shaken by the news.

"Shit, Keller. Any idea how bad it is or what the prognosis is?" I asked as I moved out of the dining room to seek the privacy of my office.

"They're still running tests. My mom is flying out first thing in the morning. That's actually why I'm calling. I need a favor, Tristan."

"Sure, Keller. Just say the word," I assured him.

"Art says there is a wooden box he left somewhere in the barn. He's a little out of it on the medicine but is frantic to get his hands on that box. It might be in the tool room because he kept mentioning it was in a drawer. I get the impression it has memories or something in it. Maybe old photographs?"

"I'll check it out right now and see what I find. What should I do with it if I find it? I can't fly down there until after the wedding."

"Well, that's the favor. I was wondering if you could maybe drive it to San Francisco and give it to my mom. You'd have to get to her before like seven tomorrow morning. I know it's a pain in the ass, Tristan. Sorry to even ask."

I shook my head even though he couldn't see me. "It's not a problem. Art and Henry are like my grandfathers too, Keller. You know that. If this box means that much to Art, I'll do what it takes to get it to him." I looked at the time on my phone. Ten p.m. The drive would take about an hour and a half.

Before I could think about the drive there and back, I needed to see if I could even find the box.

"Let me go look for the box and I'll call or text you back. Actually, it's got to be late there. Why don't I text you in case you're asleep?"

"Sounds good, Tristan. I owe you one," Keller said, sounding tired.

We disconnected the phone and I searched my office for the big flashlight I had somewhere. After I found it, I walked out of my office to see Blue waiting for me in the reception area.

"Hey," I said. "What are you doing out here?"

"Wanted to check on you. You looked upset when you took the call. You okay?" he said. *Sweet man.*

"Not really. That was Keller. Art has lung cancer."

Blue stood up to hug me, wrapping his arms around me and holding me against him. I could smell the hotel shampoo in his hair and the unique Blue scent of his skin.

He spoke next to my ear. "I'm sorry, Tris. What can I do to help?"

I pulled back and raised up the flashlight. "Want to help me search for buried treasure?"

"Is this your way of asking if you can plunder my booty?" he joked.

"No, but I would definitely like to plunder your booty later," I assured him with a smack on the ass. "First, we need to revisit the tool room in the barn."

"Now I know you're trying to make me horny because we both know what that tool room does to me," Blue said as we exited the estate house to make our way to the barn.

I told him about the wooden box that may or may not exist. When we entered the tool room and turned on as many lights as we could find, we got to work.

Blue asked me to tell him about Art and Henry while we were searching. I told him some of my memories of them and how the two men were role models to me. That was part of my sentimental connection to the vineyard. To me, it was a place of goodness and kindness. Growth and hard work.

After about twenty minutes of looking through drawers and deep into shelves, Blue looked over at me. "Are you sure they weren't together? You keep saying they were best friends, but this sounds like a marriage."

I started to laugh but stopped myself. "Fuck, Blue. What if it was? What if it is? How could they be together for a lifetime and not tell anyone? Is that even possible? If so, why? Why not at least come out now? Things are different."

"They were raised in a different era, Tris. You don't know what's in their heads." Blue went back to searching in a filing cabinet that held instruction manuals for years' worth of power tools.

"Found it!" he squawked. He raised up a carved wooden box about the size of a thick stack of dinner plates.

We met in the center of the room, and he set the box down on a large worktable. I opened the lid and saw the box held old photographs and small trinkets. I picked up a small stack of photos, faded and curled around the edges.

In the first one, I recognized Art and Uncle Henry standing in front of a trellis during a harvest. They looked like they were in their early thirties, tan and fit. Happy.

Blue came to look over my shoulder, one hand resting on my waist. I leaned back into him, pointing out who was who.

"I can tell which one is Henry. There is something about him that looks like your dad. But I don't see Keller in Art at all," Blue said.

"No. Keller looks more like his dad. Art is Keller's maternal grandfather. He was married to a woman named Katherine, and they had a little girl. That girl is Keller's mom," I explained. "I have to take this to her tonight in the city."

"Then let's get going. You can look at the rest of that while I drive," Blue said, kissing the side of my face before stepping back.

I turned to look at him. "You don't have to come. It's going to be a long night of boring driving to the city and back. Go enjoy the time with your brothers. I'll be fine."

"I have a better idea. I'll go with you so that I don't spend the next several hours imagining your mangled body on the side of the road. Or, look at it this way, I'll go with you so I don't spend the next several hours adding up how many times you'll have to use the word 'balls' in a sentence tomorrow."

"Are you sure, Blue? It's going to be boring and long. I hate to ask you to—" I stopped talking when Blue interrupted.

"Tristan, do you really think that several hours in the car with me is going to be boring?" Blue huffed.

"Good point."

"Plus, I have an idea. We have to swing by your cabin anyway to deposit Piper so let's grab some overnight stuff. We can spend the night at my place in the city and come back in the morning. We don't have anything planned tomorrow. At least I don't. Do you?"

"No. And I'd love to see your place. Let me text Stacey to have her cover for me here until I get back. You probably should go back in and tell your family where you're going. Find Piper too," I said, pulling out my phone to text both Stacey and Keller.

When we were finally on the road in my Tahoe with Blue at the wheel, I had a chance to study the contents of the box again. It was immediately clear that Blue had been correct. One of the photographs showed Art and Henry looking at each other in an intimate way, and I just knew.

"How could I have missed it, Blue? How could I have spent so much time with them and not known? I feel like an idiot."

Blue reached a hand over to squeeze my leg. "They probably worked hard to keep you from finding out. That's what it means to be in the closet. There's no halfway. You're either in or out with someone. Maybe your parents put the fear of god in them to keep it quiet when you were visiting."

"God, that's so sad. I can't imagine being in love with someone and not being able to touch them whenever I wanted. Or tell anyone who will listen that they're mine. Or wear their family reunion T-shirt in front of everyone I know," I said, winking over at him.

35

———

BLUE

Was he implying he was in love with me? The idea this was actually happening between us both thrilled and terrified me. I promised myself not to overthink it or rush it. Just enjoy the time and let it happen on its own schedule. If this was going to end up being what I wanted it to be, it was okay to savor the early days without pushing for more. Keep it light and fun.

"I have an idea," I told Tristan. "After we drop off the box at Keller's mom's house, let's go dancing."

"It'll be like one in the morning," he said.

"Right. Your point?" I laughed.

"Won't that be kind of late?" Tristan asked.

"I should have clarified. Let's go dancing at a club. Not at senior center bingo night."

"Fuck you. Okay, so maybe it's been a while since I've done anything wild like go to a club."

"Babe, have you actually ever been to a club?" I teased.

"Not really." He smirked. "Other than one or two times when I was too drunk to remember what time it was."

"Well, if you think you might be gay, I'm taking you to a gay club. Think of it as a rite of passage."

"I'm game. Do I need to wear guyliner and go-go boots? Sprinkle myself with glitter?" he joked.

"You joke, but you'll see all that shit there. And more. Much more."

"I'm wearing boring-ass jeans and a button-down shirt. I'll look like I'm coming to audit the place." Tristan looked down at himself.

"You want to swing by my place and I can dress you up in some hot pants and a sequined tank top?" I asked with a serious face.

Tristan blinked, his mouth open in a tiny "O."

I burst out laughing. "Oh my god, I'm joking. The look on your face. Jesus, Tris. Do I look like someone who wears that shit?"

"Well, no. But how do I know you're not putting on your Marian mask for the wedding week when in reality you're Blue the Boy Toy at the clubs?" he said defensively.

"I grabbed some T-shirts at your place we can change into only because it's hot as hell in those places. But lots of guys end up taking off their shirts anyway. That's up to you. Obviously I'll be happy if you keep your shit covered up."

"Oooh, I get to see Blue jealous. About fucking time," he snickered.

"I got jealous when your damned ex-wife was there earlier, didn't I?" I snapped.

We had pulled into a gas station and both got out to fill up the Tahoe. While the gas was pumping, Tristan continued.

"Why would you be jealous of Sheila? I told you things were never that great between us."

I looked at him as though he had two heads. "Are you kidding? All I could think about was how many times you were naked in bed with her and how she had boobs and a vagina and things I don't have."

"Gross. Did it ever occur to you that she doesn't have a dick or a prostate or a sexy as shit happy trail that I want to run my tongue down every time I see it? Did it ever occur to you that she doesn't have a fucking heart?" Now Tristan was getting riled up.

I replaced the gas pump and closed the tank before facing him.

"No. She's beautiful, Tristan. And she's known you for years. I've known you for days. I felt... I don't know. I felt..." Before I had a chance to think of the right word, Tristan's lips were on mine.

The kiss was possessive and consuming. I clutched his shirt front. When Tristan pulled back, his eyes were sparkling with intensity.

"In all the time she and I were together, I never felt about her the way I feel about you after only a few days. Do you hear what I'm saying?"

"I... uh..." I stammered.

"Good, now let's get going. The idea of watching you shake your ass in a dance club is making me horny." Tristan grabbed the keys out of my hand and got in the driver's seat. I stared out the window as the city lights came into view. Tristan turned on the radio and the soft sounds of a female radio announcer came on. Once she was finished promoting an upcoming music festival, my song came on.

"It's 'Bluebells,'" Tristan blurted, reaching to turn up the volume. The familiar refrain was known by millions of people around the world.

With a stomach full of bluebells
In a roadhouse full of nutshells
There sat a whiskey-sipping scarecrow
Busy tossing out bombshells.

"What does it mean?" Tristan asked. And there it was. The question almost no one ever thought to ask, even my parents. Everyone thought it was just rhyming nonsense. But it wasn't.

At my silence, Tristan turned to look at me. I stared straight ahead and he reached over to brush the backs of his fingers over my face. "It's okay," he said quietly. "If you don't want to tell me."

"It's not my story to tell," I said truthfully.

"Then why do you guys call it your song?" he asked.

"Because it's not a stomach full of bluebells like everyone thinks. It's a stomach full of Blue's Bells."

"What does that mean?" he asked.

"Growing up, Jude and I used to talk about how people would know they were in love. Like, how could you tell the difference between really liking someone and being in love with someone. I finally decided that the right person would make my insides play a thousand tiny bells. After that, Jude always referred to true love as Blue's Bells," I explained.

"In that song, are you the one with Blue's Bells or is it Jude?" he asked carefully.

"Jude," I answered. "The song isn't about me."

Tristan seemed to let out a breath he'd been holding in, and we drove the rest of the way in silence.

When we got to Keller's mom's house it was after midnight. I stayed in the car while Tristan handed her the box and gave her a big hug. There had been several other objects of interest in there. Wedding bands, letters we didn't dare read, small polished river stones, and a few metal toy soldiers. I hoped the box gave Art some comfort while he dealt with his new diagnosis and time in the hospital.

After Tristan got back in the Tahoe, I directed him to the dance club. We found a place to park and changed our shirts. I forced myself to look away from Tristan when he unbuttoned his. Had I gotten even one look at his bare chest, I would have mauled him right there in the parking deck.

The club wasn't too crazy on a Wednesday night so we got in easily and made our way to the bar for a drink. The music was contagious and the bartenders were friendly. We got a couple of shots and some beers before making our way closer to the dance floor.

I was curious to see Tristan's reaction to being at a gay club, but then I remembered him saying that Granny and Irene's bachelorette party had ended at Cockblock. Tristan was definitely the kind of guy who looked at ease in most places. He was looking around and I could see the barest hint of moving his hips to the beat of the music. I wanted my hands on those hips.

We clinked our shot glasses together and threw them back before taking a seat on stools against the wall and watching the dancers. Tristan had one hand on my thigh while he drank his beer with the other. Periodically he would lean over to point something out to me like a man with a beard down to his navel dancing with a bald guy.

"If only they could share the hair," he said into my ear. When he leaned in to talk to me, I shivered, catching his scent and feeling his stubble graze the tender skin of my ear.

When we'd put a nice dent in our beers, Tristan set them both down and grabbed my hand with a flirty waggle of his eyebrows. "Dance with me, gorgeous," he yelled over the music.

A thousand tiny bells started tinkling in my stomach the same way they did the night we first met and every other time I set eyes on Tristan Alexander. I was such a goner and had known it from the beginning. Somewhere in the back of my mind, I knew there were beautiful men nearly naked all around that club, but I could only see the tall, dark, and handsome one in front of me in his blue jeans and plain black T-shirt.

We danced together to the house music, laughing and touching and sweating. After a while, he said he was going to get another beer. I asked him to get me a water while I visited the men's room.

When I returned to find him at the bar, there was a good-looking man flirting with him. I wasn't surprised, and Tristan was giving him his usual friendly smile. But when Tristan saw me approaching, the dimple came out, and I winked at him in return. As I struggled to make a path to him, I saw the handsome stranger put his hand on Tristan's shoulder and gesture to the bartender like he wanted to order them both drinks. *Jackass.*

Tristan shook his head at the guy and pointed to me. The man turned to look, eyes widening as he pointed to me, and then Tristan with a quirk of his eyebrow. *You two together?*

I nodded with a smile and tried so damned hard not to look as smug as I felt as the guy shrugged and moved away. Tristan held out his hand to me and I squeezed against his side, giving him a kiss on the lips and taking the water bottle he offered me.

After we finished our drinks, we returned to the dance floor. We danced to some energetic numbers, but as the club wound down, the music slowed.

Tristan moved behind me and held one arm across my front, his hand on the opposite hip like a seatbelt. I felt his erection pressed hard against my ass and I pressed back against him, leaning my head back onto his shoulder as his other hand came up to rest gently on my throat.

His hips were swaying, nestling his dick even deeper into the seam of my jeans. My heart raced and my cock seemed to be throbbing to the beat of the music. Tristan's tongue came out and toyed with the shell of my ear, finally grabbing my earlobe between his teeth. I reached a hand back to grab his ass and the other one over my shoulder to wrap around the back of his head.

I wanted him so badly. I wasn't sure if I could make it to my apartment before begging him to fuck me in public.

"Take me home before I shove your pants down and bend you over that stage," he growled in my ear.

Holy fuck.

When we reached the parking garage, our hands and mouths were all over each other. I started fumbling for his belt, but he grabbed my hands, gasping.

"*No.* No, baby. Home. Your place. I don't really want to get arrested even if you would make the best prison bitch ever."

"Fuck, you're a buzzkill," I panted, taking the keys he held out to me.

When we entered my apartment, hands and lips resumed their hungry attentions, shoes toed off, T-shirts shucked away, and we stumbled around trying to make it to a soft surface. I managed to get us to the bedroom and push Tristan down onto the bed.

I fumbled for my fly but then just stood there, staring. Tristan's eyes were glassy and his lips were red from kissing.

"You okay, baby?" he said in his smoky voice.

"Just looking at you there in my bed. It's strange... Nice. But weird, you know?"

"Like we've been in a bubble these past few days and now we're out in the real world?" he suggested.

"Exactly," I said, slipping off my jeans and stepping out of them before bending over to unfasten his.

"Blue, I want you to fuck me this time."

My hands froze on his zipper and I looked up. Gray eyes peered at me full of genuine desire.

"You sure?" I asked.

"Well, I guess I should ask first. Do you... I mean, do you do that? Do you top sometimes?" he asked. And I was reminded of just how new all this was to him.

"Yes, I have before. Not with Jeremy but with guys before him. I think it's always a good idea to try both so you know what you like, but are you sure you're ready for that? It's a big step," I said gently. "There's no rush to try everything right away."

"All I could think about in that club was giving myself up to you. Having you take charge and know what it feels like to have you inside of me like that. I want to feel you every possible way I can, Blue." He reached for my hand and pulled me down on top of him for a deep kiss.

His hips thrust up into mine and I felt how hard he was through his jeans. I reached down to strip them off.

"Let's take a quick shower to get the club stink off. Come on," I said, standing up and grabbing his hand.

"What? Right now? I'm hard as a fucking rock. You're going to give me—" I slapped a hand over his mouth.

"Don't you dare say Blue's Balls."

He laughed through my hand as he followed me to the bathroom.

As excruciating as it was to get naked and wet with Tristan without putting my mouth on him, I did it. He tried three times to go down on me and twice to get me to go down on him. Instead, I kept batting his hands away and promising he'd be grateful later. I washed his entire body carefully but quickly and followed with a wash of my own.

When we dried off with some towels and made our way back to the bed, Tristan was still grumbling about me being a cocktease.

I pushed him down on the bed, enjoying the sight of his muscles moving under his damp skin as he shifted to center himself on the bed. The dark hair leading from his navel to his groin got me every time. My dick was leaking by the time I stretched out over him and ran my tongue along his hard length. Tristan let out a groan and pushed lightly up against my mouth.

My tongue came out to lick his tip and my mouth cupped around the head of his cock. His length slid into my mouth and I coated it in saliva with my tongue as I pulled off it, tasting soap.

My mouth wandered down the crease of his thigh to find one of his balls and suck it into my mouth. His stomach muscles contracted and his voice turned gravelly as he cursed and called out my name.

I moved my tongue down to the base of his sac and then used my hands to push his legs farther apart. When I saw his pink hole, I felt giddy with anticipation. I'd bet big money he'd never gotten a rim job before.

My face moved in slowly, tongue tickling its way closer and closer until it finally found the tender skin of his entrance. He hissed and his muscles contracted while I continued my hot, wet attentions. My tongue circled and licked and explored until I heard him mumbling in disbelief at the sensations.

I leaned back up to take his cock into my mouth, enjoying the sight of precum dripping from the tip. And then I moved back down to his ass and pressed my tongue inside him, fucking him with my mouth.

"Mpfh, gahhh," he choked. "Baby, *baby*."

I leaned up to stick two fingers in his gasping mouth and he latched on to them instinctively, swirling his tongue around them and reminding me of the way it felt to have my dick in that hot mouth.

Moving back down the bed, I pressed a wet finger at his entrance and took his cock in my mouth again. I sucked and pressed and licked and fingered until he was writhing under me, begging for more.

I opened the lube and squeezed some onto my fingers before sliding two fingers in this time and stretching him. I started slowly, making sure not to overwhelm him more than I had already. When his movements turned antsy, I twisted and crooked a finger, searching for just the right spot to light him on fire.

"*Oh Jesus fuck!*" he cried before reaching to grab his cock and stroke.

"No, baby. No touching yet. Patience." I chuckled, pushing his hands away.

"Fuck you," he moaned.

"Mmmm, sounds good. Next time though. I'm having too much fun fucking you this time," I teased.

I quickly but carefully added a third lubed finger, knowing he was going to start feeling much more discomfort. I crawled up to whisper dirty shit into his ear to distract him and remind him to relax and breathe.

His face was flushed and his pupils were blown. Seeing him come undone by my touch was spectacular.

I finally couldn't take it anymore and suited up, covering the condom with lube and fingering his hole one last time. I rolled him onto his side and lay behind him, pushing one of his legs forward a little bit.

He was so drunk on lust at that moment I wasn't sure if he was still in the room with me. The blunt tip of my cock pressed at his entrance and I squeezed my eyes closed to try and control myself. All I wanted to do was shove in and hump the hell out of him.

Instead I went slowly, pushing as gently as I could but still firmly enough to breach the ring of muscle. I heard him wince and felt him clench. My words whispered straight into his ear.

"It's okay. It'll get better in a minute. Try to relax and push out against me. Just like that. That's good, baby, so good," I coaxed, entering him little by little as he pushed out against me. He felt unbelievable. Hot and tight like nothing I'd ever felt before. I tried to think of anything to stall the orgasm building inside me.

Finally I bottomed out and stayed still for a second, letting him breathe and calm down. His fingers were threaded through mine, stretched out on the bed in front of him.

"S'okay," he said. "Go."

I began to rock my hips back and forward in little thrusts, easing the way until I felt his body let go and relax. Then I pulled out almost all the way, Tristan whimpering at me pulling all the way out, before I thrust back into him. He screamed my name and begged for me to go again. So I did.

I thrust in and out of him, sweat dripping from my front onto his back. He tried pushing back onto me and we somehow ended up with him on all fours and me on top of him. His ass was in the air and his face was in the mattress, one arm stretched out in front of him reaching for the headboard, the other reaching down to stroke his cock.

"Oh god, Blue, god, please, fuck," Tris cried.

I don't know how I hadn't come yet. His body gripped me and his voice called to me. Finally, I reached around and gripped my hand over his on his cock, helping stroke him off as my own climax began to crest.

When he came, his body clamped around my cock and I screamed his name. My hand felt his hot come spilling out as my own shot into the condom. Warmth spread in waves throughout my body as my mind blanked out.

We stayed like that for a moment, heaving and sweaty, my front stuck to his back. I felt him begin to shake, and I freaked out.

"Tris, oh god. Are you okay?" I said, rolling off of him and trashing the condom before putting a hand on his back and leaning in to see if he was upset. That's when I realized he was laughing.

"What the fuck?" I asked. "You're laughing? Was I that bad?"

He rolled onto his back, making sure to avoid the wet spot beneath him. "Oh my god, Blue Marian. Why the fuck did I wait so long to do that? How did I spend so long without knowing what it felt like to have my prostate stroked by somebody's dick?"

I let out a breath. "So, it was good, huh? Now you know why gay men are so damned gay." I grinned. "And for the record, it wasn't just somebody's dick. It was the dick of dreams. Don't think just any dick would make you feel that way, because it wouldn't. Most dicks are broken. You should probably just stick with mine to be sure."

He smiled at me and said in a softer voice, "Dick of dreams, huh? Okay. I'll just stick with yours to be sure."

I blushed under that gray gaze.

36

TRISTAN

I cleaned myself up in the bathroom and returned to find Blue swapping out the blanket with the wet spot for a different one. He had grabbed us a couple of glasses of water and pointed to one for me on the nightstand.

While I drank, I looked around his bedroom. It was pretty plain and I remembered him telling me it was a temporary sublet. There was a bookshelf and I wandered over to check out the titles. Most everything was boxed up but there were a few items still on the shelf.

When I got closer, I saw a small metal figure of a jellyfish with intricate swirling tentacles. The jellyfish balanced on a thin stand so if you blew on it, it began to sway and the tentacles moved.

I reached up a finger but was afraid to touch it.

"He doesn't bite. You can pick it up if you want," Blue said from behind me.

I set my glass of water on a shelf and reached for the jellyfish, lifting it off the stand with my finger and thumb only.

Stepping toward the light of the bedside lamp, I studied it. I'd never seen anything like it. The dangling tentacles were made from regular metal objects like springs and chains and gears but the body was a smooth polished piece of wood, carved into the perfect shape to imply movement. The tentacles were connected to the wood with tiny metal pins and rings.

I raised my head up and met Blue's eyes. "Did you make this, Blue?"

He nodded and blushed.

"It's amazing. I've never seen anything like it. How in the world did you make something so tiny and intricate?"

"Concentration and the right tools. That's not the smallest thing I've made. I have a funky little bug dude, but it's packed up with most of my other things in storage at my parents' house. The jellyfish is my favorite."

I placed it back gently on the stand before turning around and gathering him into my arms. "You're really talented. I'd love to see some of the other things you've made."

"Most of them are packed away. I think I told you that Jeremy wasn't very supportive. I ended up getting defensive about my work to the point I didn't want anyone to see it. Once I move back in a few years, I'll be able to get some of it back out. Mom and Dad have a large metal sculpture of mine in their backyard. If I ever had space for one, that's the kind of piece I'd love to work on for myself."

I couldn't help but think of all the space I had at the vineyard. Workspace, studio space, exhibit space. Shaking my head but keeping my mouth closed, I led Blue back to bed and turned out the lights.

"Well, we definitely know Jeremy's an idiot," I said as we snuggled against each other in the dark. I could feel Blue's breathing slow down and wondered if he'd fallen asleep that fast. I felt my eyes droop.

"Oh shit." Blue laughed softly. "I totally forgot to tell you. Brad left."

"What? You're kidding," I said, perking up a little at the news. "How do you know?"

"When I went back into the poker room to tell the guys I was leaving, John told me Jeremy was back on the market. I think he was hoping I'd ditch you so you could go back to being straight. Like that's how gay works. Anyway, I didn't stick around to ask about the details, and then I forgot to tell you after you were done studying Art's box."

"Oh," I said while my mind began to race.

A few minutes later I felt Blue relax into the bed. All I could think about as I held him was whether Blue would ever consider going back to Jeremy if Jeremy wanted him. After all, it hadn't been Blue's choice to leave.

What if Jeremy had seen what he was missing now that he'd spent six months without Blue? What if he changed in an effort to get Blue back? How could I compete with three years of shared history between them? Jeremy was already in tight with Blue's family and the fact he kept trying to get Blue to talk to him probably meant he still wanted him. Fuck. I needed to stop worrying about shit I couldn't control.

It took me another hour to settle my brain. In the end, the only thing that worked was repeating to myself that Blue was there with me in that moment, wrapped up in my arms and only mine. That would have to do. For now.

Luckily we were able to sleep late, only rising when the sun made the room too warm. When my eyes opened, the first thing I saw was a pair of tiny freckles next to Blue's shoulder blade. I instinctively pressed a light kiss on them, memorizing the feel of his warm skin under my lips.

"Hey," he said with a gravelly voice, turning in my arms. He was fucking adorable. Sleepy, half-lidded eyes, hair sticking up on one side of his head, and lips looking completely fuckable.

"I'm in love with you," I blurted. My stomach dropped as soon as the words were out of my mouth. I was going to scare him off.

His eyes widened and then his face broke into a huge smile. "I know."

Now it was my turn for wide eyes. My mouth opened but I was unsure what to say. Blue chuckled.

"What do you mean you know?" I asked defensively.

"Because I can see it in your eyes when you look at me. And yesterday at the gas station I could tell you wanted to say it."

"I did. But I didn't want to say it when we were talking about Sheila. I meant what I said. I've never felt like this about anyone, Blue. It kind of scares me, you know?" I admitted.

"I know, baby. It scares me too," Blue said, leaning in to kiss me. "That's why I told you I loved you when I thought you were sleeping yesterday." His glittering eyes met mine and my heart stuttered.

"Wait, that was real? I thought I was dreaming that part."

Blue's hand came up to brush through my hair. "It was real. I love you, Tristan. It's scary because it happened so fast and so unexpectedly. But I can't stop thinking about you, wanting to touch you, wanting to be with you. You make me laugh. When I'm with you, I feel like the real me. Like the person I'm supposed to be, you know?"

My heart swelled at that. It was all too good to be true. "You are an amazing man, Blue. Smart and funny. Thoughtful and kind. Not to mention you have a killer ass."

He swatted my shoulder. "Fuck you." He laughed. "Apparently it's your ass now."

I grabbed it and squeezed. "Damned right it's my ass now," I growled before taking his mouth with mine again. We tumbled around in bed, naked limbs tangling, tongues tasting, hands caressing until I heard Blue's stomach grumble loudly.

"Your stomach sounds like a ticking time bomb. Let's find something to eat before you self-destruct."

37

BLUE

On the drive back to the vineyard I told Tristan more about my brothers. I didn't tell him about Jude's sexuality, but I did tell Tristan I was worried about Jude. He was lonely and exhausted. The life of a celebrity was narrowing in on him, creating a kind of solitude I couldn't comprehend.

Tristan reminded me Jude was lucky to live near a large family like ours. We were his safe place. Tristan was right. The only one of my siblings who didn't live in California was Jamie. Well... and soon-to-be me.

"What does Jamie do for a living?" Tristan asked as he changed lanes to pass a horse trailer. We were getting farther out of the metro area into the wine country.

"He's a wildlife veterinarian and consultant. He works in the national parks observing the animals, teaching rangers, assessing environmental challenges, and implementing conservation programs. Much of what he does is research through government grants. Right now he lives near Fairbanks, Alaska, in Denali."

"Wow, that sounds interesting. Have you been up there to visit him?" Tristan asked.

"I've been for a long weekend but didn't get to see very much.

We're hoping to do Denali as a family next summer if he's still there," I explained.

"And he's not married? Just Pete so far?" he asked.

"Right. Jamie was actually engaged to a guy but he fucked him over pretty badly. Left Jamie at the altar a few months ago. I'm sure he's still smarting from that. They dated on and off again starting in college or vet school, so it's been a bitch of a thing for him to get over. I'm secretly glad though. The guy was a douche."

He laughed. "Sounds like it. What happened?"

"Jamie is a serial monogamist. Turns out, Brian was not."

Tristan made a sound of disbelief. "Poor guy. And so both Jamie and Simone ended up in veterinary school?"

"Yes. My mom is a vet. We practically grew up at her clinic," I told him.

"Mmm, maybe that explains Piper's infatuation with you."

I smiled. "Maybe. Or maybe she's just trying to set us up. Whenever I'm not close enough to you, she nudges me in your direction."

"Smart girl," he said, reaching over and grabbing my hand. "So your parents have always been cool with you and Jamie being gay?"

"Totally. After I came out, Jamie went ahead and came out, not that we didn't already guess. Then my parents got all crazy about proving how much they supported us. They volunteered at an LGBTQ outreach program for abandoned teens. Mom and Dad took to it like ducks to water, and now we have three adopted brothers from the program. The only reason the guys aren't here yet is because Mom wouldn't let them skip classes." I laughed.

"Really? That's incredible. Tell me about them."

"Well, Mav has been with us the longest. He's twenty-five and in graduate school. He adores Mom and helps out in her clinic. Nice guy. Really sweet and good with the animals. Griffin is twenty-two and goes to UC Berkeley for journalism. He's talented but mouthy.

"Dante is twenty. He's the most guarded, even more so than Jude. He was abused and had a really rough life before coming to us. I was already out of the house by the time Mom and Dad took them in, so I didn't grow up with them. But they are definitely my brothers. Mom makes a big meal once every weekend, and we all make a point of getting together."

"That sounds incredible, Blue. So there are really nine of you kids. Your parents are generous."

"And levelheaded. I know. They've always been that way. Anyway, you'll get to meet those three knuckleheads either tonight or tomorrow," I said as I caught sight of the turnoff for the vineyard.

Tristan dropped me off at the lodge so I could check in with my family while he went to feed and pick up Piper.

Before reaching the front doors to the lodge, I saw Frank the bartender struggling to carry several cases of wine from the back of a trailer into the bar. I stopped to help him make several trips after he explained the kid who usually helped him was busy helping Stacey with something at the estate house. Afterward, he shook my hand with a sincere smile of thanks.

I made my way into the lobby and turned toward my room. Just before reaching my door, Jeremy came out of a nearby room and stopped short.

"Blue, where have you been? I've been looking for you since last night," he said.

"I drove to the city and spent the night at home. Sorry to hear about Brad," I said, trying to be polite.

He shrugged. "I understand why he bailed. Bringing him here without explaining first was a shitty thing to do."

"Sure was," I agreed, willing him to get on with it.

"Listen, Blue. Can we please talk for a few minutes? I need to clear the air about a few things. We could talk in your room?"

I looked at him like he had two heads. No way was I letting him into my hotel room.

"Please, Blue. Just a few minutes."

"Fine, but let's go talk in the lobby or out on the patio," I said, walking back toward the public areas of the lodge.

We found seats around a patio table and looked at each other. Neither one of us spoke at first, and I was suddenly aware of the lack of nerves in my stomach. I wasn't scared of being around him anymore.

I took a deep breath and waited, leaning back in the chair with my legs crossed. Finally he spoke.

"I fucked up, Blue," he said, eyes imploring.

My mouth stayed closed.

"Look, I'm really sorry. For everything. I really fucked up. It was stupid of me to let work come between us. I should have never handled it the way I did."

"You're right, Jeremy. You shouldn't have. I was just trying to do my job," I explained.

"I know that now. I do. Can you forgive me for being so selfish?" he asked, leaning forward in his seat.

I shrugged. "I'm not sure, honestly. I feel like it doesn't really matter anyway."

He frowned. "But it does matter. I want us to work this out. We can't build a life together unless you forgive me."

I couldn't help but bark out a laugh. "Jeremy, we're not building a life together. We're broken up, remember? Done. You dumped me and moved on. And now I have also."

"Pfft. You have not. You're hooking up with a straight guy to make me jealous. Everyone knows it. You can stop pretending now. It's okay. I forgive you for fucking around with him since I was fucking around too. We can just start fresh."

"You are batshit crazy if you think I'm starting anything with you," I snarled. "And I'm not pretending shit with Tristan. We really are together. Whether you want to believe it or not is your own business." I stood up to leave.

Jeremy looked at me with pity in his eyes. "Oh, honey. Is that what you think? Tristan's using you. John told everyone last night that Tristan was just fucking with you this week to get back at John for sleeping with his wife. The whole thing is a farce."

The blood drained from my face and I didn't know whether my heart was racing more out of anger at Jeremy or fear that what he said had any shred of truth to it.

Jeremy stood up and grabbed me by the arms. I needed to run but my legs were shaking. My hands came up to push him off me but he lurched forward, mouth coming down on mine.

"What the fuck are you doing?" I heard Tristan's deep voice thundering from behind me, quick footsteps approaching on stone.

I shoved Jeremy off and put a hand over my mouth, turning to Tristan with wide eyes, terrified of how the scene looked to him. "Tris, I…"

Tristan punched Jeremy square in the jaw. Jeremy stumbled back but caught himself before tripping over his chair. Tristan shook out his hand and looked at me with frantic eyes. Scared eyes, not accusatory ones. They raked over me, searching to make sure I was okay.

He grabbed me and pulled him into his chest, whispering into my ear, "You okay?"

I nodded and buried my face against his neck. Good god. He hadn't assumed the worst. He trusted me.

Either that or this was all part of the game. The one where Tristan pretended to be in a relationship with me to get back at John. While I didn't want to believe it, the part of me that had completely lost its self-confidence was still unsure.

It would make sense. This being just a game to him would explain why a tall, dark, and handsome vineyard owner would be in a relationship with a jaded, unsure-of-himself, fucking boring-in-bed guy like me.

Maybe Jeremy was right and this was all pretend after all.

38

TRISTAN

I considered myself to be a pretty laid-back guy up until I saw Jeremy kissing Blue on the patio. And then I understood for the first time in my life what it truly meant to be in a blind rage.

My vision dimmed until all I could see was that kiss. That presumptuous bastard. His boy toy bails and he puts the moves on Blue again? No fucking way.

I shouldn't have punched him. That was an overreaction, but I hadn't exactly been in control of myself just then. And the pain in my knuckles proved to be an appropriate punishment for the mistake.

Blue's body was pressed against mine and all I could think was *thank you, god*. How did I get lucky enough to meet him? And how the hell did I get lucky enough for him to choose me over men like Jeremy?

I saw Jeremy land his ass in the chair and rub his jaw, looking at me with hatred in his eyes while the man he loved found comfort in another man's arms. It sucked for him. I know it did. Because if I had been the one in that chair while Blue hugged another man, I'd lose my ever-loving shit.

Still holding on to Blue, I spoke to Jeremy. "I'm sorry, man. I shouldn't have hit you. Can I get you some ice or something?"

"Fuck you," he seethed. "At what point are you going to tell him this is all a big fucking act?"

"What are you talking about?" I asked, feeling Blue pull away so he could face Jeremy too.

"This bullshit about you two being together. It's all pretend. You made it up to piss off your brother. Admit it."

I laughed, expecting Blue to do the same but he didn't. He looked at the ground.

"Are you fucking kidding? I'm not even going to justify that with a response. Blue and I don't owe you any information about our relationship. You can think whatever you want. The only opinion here that matters to me is Blue's. Not John's, not my parents', and sure as shit not yours."

I turned to Blue, my heart broken at the defeated look on his face. "Can we please go somewhere else and talk?"

He nodded and began walking toward the lodge doors. Piper had been whining by his legs since I arrived. She went with him and I found them both loaded up in my vehicle in the lot.

We drove in silence to my cabin.

When we walked through the door, the silence between us was deafening.

"Do not tell me you believe his crap, Blue," I said in a voice that came out more angry than I intended.

Blue sighed and flopped down on the sofa, kicking off his shoes. "I don't. Not really. But it just reminds me that I'm fucked up."

"What do you mean by that?" I asked, sitting next to him.

"You're so confident, Tris. You walk out and see me kissing my ex and you don't assume the worst. You automatically trust I wouldn't do that to you," Blue explained.

"Right. So how does that make you fucked up? Are you saying I was wrong to trust you? That you wanted to kiss him?" *No. Please, no.*

"No! Jesus, no. I didn't want to kiss him. He lurched at me. I'm saying my breakup with him shattered my self-confidence. So when he told me you were using me, I doubted you instead of trusting you."

I blew out a breath and reached my hand out to turn his chin toward me. "That's okay, baby. It's completely understandable to lose your confidence after what you went through with him. And it takes time to get it back. You will though. Even if I have to tell you every day how amazing you are and how much I love you. Because you are and I do." I leaned forward to kiss him.

"How is that possible?" Blue asked, disbelieving.

"Before I met you, I thought love was a nice, steady flame based on companionship and shared history. I was so wrong, Blue. Love is a fucking inferno that ignites when you least expect it and lights you up inside. Now that I have it, I won't let it go out without a fight."

39

———

BLUE

Words I couldn't have imagined in a million years coming from someone a thousand times better than I could ever dream up.

I crawled onto his lap to straddle him, taking his face in my hands. Our noses almost touched and I looked right into those exotic gray eyes.

"How is it possible for me to be this loopy for someone after only a few days? Do I have cartoon hearts floating out of my eyes? Because I feel like I do."

And then I kissed him with as much love as I could possibly pour out of me and into him. His hands grasped my hips, thumbs finding their way under the hem of my shirt to caress my bare skin.

His hands slid higher up underneath my shirt, fingers ghosting over my abs and ribs to reach my chest. He gently tweaked a nipple, causing me to hiss and him to chuckle in response.

I moved my lips down his neck to his collarbone and over to his shoulder, stretching the fabric of his shirt. My teeth grazed his skin and then bit down, just enough to cause him to wince and shudder.

"I love you," I breathed into his ear.

A soft keening sound came from his throat and his eyes opened, revealing shimmering deep gray.

I slowly kissed my way around to his other ear and grabbed his earlobe with my teeth while I breathed again. "I love you."

When my lips returned to his I saw him close his eyes, causing tears to spill out. I drank them in, whispering to him about how beautiful he was, how sweet he was, and how loved I felt when I was with him. His hands shook where they rested on the skin of my back and he bent his head down to bury his face in my neck.

"I don't deserve you," he spoke against my skin, his low, smoky voice cracking.

"You're the best man I know, Tristan Alexander," I whispered.

"Baby, please. Hold me down and take me. I'm yours. *Please*." The last word was almost a sob, and I stood to lead him into the bedroom.

We made love face to face with Tristan on his back and me pressing into him from above. Our eyes locked and it was unlike anything I'd ever experienced in my life. My hands held his above his head, fingers entwined and pressing into the mattress as I stroked into his tight body.

Every muscle in my body was thrumming with desperate need to own him. My hips rolled in and out to the sounds of his moans and cries. He called my name and cursed at how good he felt and every sound he made only increased my desire to make him feel even better.

I leaned back and took his ankles in my hands, moving them together and to the side as I changed the angle of my thrusts into him. With his hands free, he began to jack himself just the way he liked it. He shouted as I hit his prostate over and over again, hot sparkles of pleasure building tight in my balls at the vision of my lover desperate and begging beneath me. His stretched hole sucked me in with every thrust; the sight of it nearly undid me.

"Oh god, Tristan, *god*," I cried out as the most intense orgasm of my life slammed into me, shooting straight from my balls in a shivering mass of heat and vibrations. My nerves went jangley and my breath froze in my chest for a moment before I remembered to breathe again.

White spurts painted Tristan's chest and abdomen as I felt his body tighten around me, milking me for all the pleasure left inside me. I finished with a few smaller strokes before letting myself lie gently on top of him, our skin sticking together with his fluid and our sweat.

As we lay together panting, I reveled in the feel of his happy trail brushing against my skin with each movement of his breathing. I leaned up to kiss him softly. Light tongue swipes and lip touches. He brought his hands up into my hair and tilted my head down to press a kiss to my forehead.

"Thank you," he whispered reverently.

I smiled at him and kissed him again before quickly withdrawing from him and making my way to the bathroom to clean up. He joined me and started a shower.

We didn't speak much as we slowly washed each other's bodies. The smell of Tristan's soap still made me swoon. He caught me sniffing the bar appreciatively and laughed. "You have a fetish I need to worry about?" he asked.

"Yes. I'm addicted to all things Tristan. Including his soap smell. Lather me up again and rub that shit in, will ya?" I winked.

So he did, paying special attention to my naughty bits.

"How's your hand," I asked when we finished getting dressed and sat down in the kitchen for a cold drink.

"Hurts. I acted like a Neanderthal. Serves me right."

I stood up to fix a baggie full of ice and brought it back to him. I held his hand in mine and then placed the ice bag on it.

"If it makes you feel any better, I appreciated your Neanderthal act just a little," I said with a grin.

"Oh yeah?" He quirked an eyebrow at me.

"Oh *yeah*." I smiled and took a sip of Diet Coke before remembering something.

"Hey, you were going to tell me why John calls you Alex. What's up with that?" I asked.

"He's an ass," Tristan said. "He heard a rumor that I'd kissed a boy in high school. It was total bullshit. I would have loved to kiss that kid, but I hadn't. Anyway, when the rumor went around, this asshole at school referred to me as Kristen. As if that was original. John went fucking ballistic. Railed at Mom and Dad for choosing such a gay name for their son. He came up with the plan for me to start going by Alex instead."

"Are you kidding? What did your parents say, or do I even want to know?" I asked, frustrated as hell he was related to such a homophobe.

"No surprise. Mom thought it was a good idea and Dad said I should at least consider it. No, thanks. I never did. John's the only one who's ever called me that. Now that I'm out, I should officially request he return to calling me by my gay name." He winked.

"Seriously. You should." I laughed.

LATER THAT AFTERNOON, I joined my parents and siblings for a family meeting. Mom and Dad had arranged to meet with all nine of us kids in the estate house dining room.

The first fifteen minutes were spent greeting Mav, Griff, and Dante, who had just arrived in Mav's car from the city. After we all settled down and were seated around a big table, Mom and Dad stood up to talk to us.

"We didn't arrange this meeting for any big scary reason, so just relax. You guys all know how rare it is for the eleven of us to be under the same roof. We just wanted to go over our holiday calendars for the upcoming year and try to get some visits planned. With Simone marrying, Jamie going back to Alaska, and Blue off to London in a couple of weeks, it's going to be hard to get all of us together," Mom began.

Dad cut in. "So let's pick two weeks next year where we agree to be together regardless of where it's going to be. That way we can all know well in advance and schedule other things around it, okay?"

We talked for the next half hour, trying to take into consideration college calendars, the vet clinic obligations, holidays, and anything else we needed to work around. We were already all going to be together at Christmas time.

We finally settled on the last week of June and the week of Thanksgiving. After that was settled, Mom and Dad tried to drum up interest in anyone who wanted to come visit London in the spring with them.

The thought of being in London suddenly made me feel like vomiting. It wasn't nerves about the move or excitement about the job. It was gut-wrenching wrongness at the idea of leaving Tristan right after I had found him.

Jude caught my eye and must have seen me start to panic or turn green. He quickly got up and asked me to step out into the hallway. When we got to the hallway, his bodyguard stood from his post leaning against the wall and looked worried.

"Bathroom?" Jude asked him. Wolfe pointed us in the right direction and followed us. When we got there, Jude wet some paper towels and handed them to me. I didn't notice Jude give a look to Wolfe, causing the man to leave us alone.

"Here, put these on your face and neck, Bee."

I did. My breathing was fast and I tried to slow it down.

Jude looked at me with those sad eyes. "Want to talk about it?"

"I love him," I said as if it was the worst thing ever. "Bells, Jude. All of the bells. And they're clanging so loud I can hardly think straight."

"Oh, Bee," he said, with a hand on my back.

"Right?" I exclaimed. "Why now? Why fucking now when I'm three days away from flying 5,000 miles away? It's so fucking unfair, Jude."

"You don't have to go. Couldn't you turn down the promotion and stay?" he asked.

"No. They've already hired my replacement. I trained her last week. And this promotion is the equivalent of one of the top spots in my profession. To be the creative director of the largest print media company in the world at the age of thirty-two? It's unheard of. How do you walk away from that? You don't. And you surely don't for someone you've known for, like, ten minutes. It's ridiculous."

Jude kept rubbing my back as I leaned over with my hands on my knees. "I didn't realize your promotion was that big of a deal, Bee. That's amazing. Why didn't you tell us how huge it was?"

"Because it was too good to be true. The chance to guide the vision of that many publications? I didn't really believe it was happening until they threw me the going away party the other day and my office was packed up. Right before I came here, my editor handed me my new business cards. It just hit me all at once. But then I got here and everything with Jeremy and Tristan happened. And it got lost in the shuffle, you know?"

"Then it sounds like you want to go. For the job," Jude said softly.

"I do. I did. I don't know... I think I'm going to be sick," I said, lunging into a stall and throwing up. I knelt on the cool tiles and felt the usual snot and tears reaction I had when I puked. Jude handed me more wet paper towels.

"You don't have to stay with me, Jude. Go tell everyone I'm just having stomach problems or something, okay?"

"I don't want to leave you here alone. They'll figure it out or they'll come looking for us," Jude said, trying to get me to stand up. I resisted him, preferring to stay on the bathroom floor rather than try to stand on shaky legs.

Jude wasn't happy with that so he pulled out his secret weapon. "Stand up and let me take you back to your room, or I'll have Wolfe do it for me."

Fuck.

"Fine. I'm coming," I relented, pushing myself up and rinsing my mouth in the sink.

Wolfe was waiting for us in the hallway again and walked with us back to the lodge. I thanked them both before going into my hotel room, changing into pajama bottoms, and brushing my teeth. Jude came back in to give me a bottle of Gatorade and some headache pills. Then I slipped between the crisp, cool sheets of the bed and let myself drift off, not realizing the pain pills were the kind that knocked you out.

40

TRISTAN

I hadn't heard from Blue in a few hours. Since he was supposed to be spending time with his family, I didn't want to bother him. Keller had called to update me about Art. He had deteriorated. Pneumonia on top of the lung cancer was weakening his heart. I told him that I would arrange to fly out on Sunday night so I could be there for him and Uncle Henry.

I had dinner with my parents to update them on what was going on with Keller and Art and Henry. It wasn't until after dinner with my parents that I started to wonder why I hadn't at least gotten a text from Blue letting me know what he was up to.

My texts to him weren't answered and I finally started to worry when I saw most of his family hanging out by the fire pit in the estate house courtyard. They were having pizza they must have called in, and someone had procured some coolers of beer for them. I was happy to see the Marian clan feeling at home on the estate. The only thing missing was Blue.

I approached Simone and asked after him. She said he hadn't been feeling well after a family meeting and had gone back to his room several hours before.

Maybe he was napping. I walked back to the lodge and

approached his room. Jude's bodyguard sat in a chair outside Blue's room.

"Hi, Wolfe. I heard he's sick," I asked, reaching for the doorknob. Wolfe stood up and stopped my hand.

"He's sleeping," he said in his quiet voice. "Don't go in there."

"I'll be quiet. I won't wake him up," I promised as I reached again.

Wolfe grabbed my wrist gently but firmly. "Mr. Alexander, I can't let you in there. I'm sorry."

"Like hell you can't let me in there. Let go of me," I said, starting to get annoyed.

"Just hold on and calm down. Let me get Jude," Wolfe said, pulling out his phone.

I gritted my teeth and stood there like an idiot, waiting to see what Jude was going to say.

He came out of his room and approached me. "Tristan, he's sick. Please let him sleep. I'll tell you when he wakes up, I promise."

"Fine, Jude. But I'm going in there to sit with him while he sleeps. Jesus, what's with the watchdog?" I said, jerking my thumb at Wolfe.

"I asked him not to let anyone in," Jude said.

"What's wrong with Blue?" I asked, starting to get a little worried. "Does he need a doctor?"

"No, nothing like that. He got stressed out and it made him sick. Let him sleep. Maybe he'll think more clearly after he wakes up."

"Shit, Jude. What the hell happened in that family meeting?" I asked.

"Everyone was talking about visiting him in London and he freaked out."

"He's stressed about the move?" I asked like an idiot.

Jude looked at me.

"What?" I asked. "What am I missing?"

"He's stressed about leaving you, Tristan. But he has to go. This job is a big fucking deal. Did you know he's going to be the global creative director for Universal Print Media?"

"The whole corporation?" I asked incredulously.

"Yes. He'll be the most influential print media designer in the world. It's a much bigger deal than any of us knew."

"Why didn't he say anything?" I asked, still dumbfounded.

"He said it was too good to be true. It didn't really sink in until they sent him off on Monday with his new business cards. And then he met you."

The reality of his conflict hit me like a cartoon anvil to the head. "Fuck," I muttered.

"Yeah," Jude agreed.

I squatted down, sitting on my heels in the hallway with my head in my hands.

Jude squatted down in front of me. "Tristan. You can't ask him to stay."

I looked up at his soft brown eyes. "I wasn't going to. Not that I don't want him to stay because, god, I've never wanted anything more. But if I asked him to stay and he did, he'd end up resenting me. That's not fair to either one of us."

"I'm sorry," Jude said in his quiet way. "You're a good man and he deserves you. I wish I could help figure out a way to make it work for you two."

"Thanks, Jude. He's the good one though. The best. And don't think for a minute that I'm going to give him up just because he's moving to London," I said defiantly.

Jude's face broke into a grin that reached his eyes. "Good. I was hoping you'd feel that way."

"Now, can I please go in there and just be with him? I'll stand in the corner if I have to."

He laughed and stood up, pulling me up by the hand. "Sure, go ahead."

Jude and his bodyguard disappeared, and I used my master key to open the door. Blue was asleep, curled up in a ball under the duvet. His strawberry-blond hair was messed up and his face looked pale. But he appeared at peace in his sleep. I put the chain on the door to keep everyone else out and slipped off all my clothes except my boxers. Then I walked around the bed to slide under the duvet behind him and wrap myself around his warm body.

When I awoke a couple of hours later, Blue had turned and was facing me, a finger lightly tracing the planes of my face.

"Hi," I said with a sleepy smile.

"Hi. How'd you end up here?"

"Came looking for you," I answered, relishing the feel of his legs tangled in mine.

"I wasn't feeling well," Blue began tentatively.

"So I heard," I said, leaning in to kiss his forehead.

"And?" he asked.

"And what, baby?" I said, rubbing his nose lightly with mine.

"Aren't you going to ask me more questions?" he asked.

"Oh, right," I said. "What time is it?"

Blue looked at me like I was crazy. "How the hell would I know?"

"Hmm. Okay. It's late. Probably doesn't matter what time. You hungry?"

"Did Jude talk to you?" he asked, clearly unhappy with the direction of our conversation.

"About what?" I asked breezily.

"Me."

I looked at him with an eyebrow raised. "What about you?"

"Fuck," he muttered, flipping around to face away from me.

"You hungry? I could go for some food," I said again.

"Fine. Yes, I'm hungry. Fuck," he said in a clipped tone before standing up and looking for clothes to put on.

"You get cranky when you're hungry, don't you?" I asked innocently.

All I heard were grumbling noises muffled by the shirt being pulled over his head.

I grabbed my phone from the nightstand. "Too late to order food. I can fix you some pasta at my house. Does that work?"

"Fine," he said as he threw on his running shoes.

We exited the room and made our way back to my cabin. I had

been secretly hoping we'd run into some people in the lobby since Blue had forgotten to straighten his hair in his anger at me.

I whistled during the drive to my place and when we got into the cabin, Blue's top finally blew.

"Jesus fuck, I love you and I don't want to move to London! There. I said it. I know Jude told you. Now what do I do?" he blurted.

I couldn't help it. I laughed.

"What the fuck is wrong with you, Tristan? You're a fucking asshole. I'm having a major life crisis and you're laughing at me? Jesus. Maybe I misjudged you and you're really an insensitive ass that I can just fuck and leave. Please, god, let that be the case."

My legs ate up the distance between us in three long strides. I took him into my arms in a fierce, possessive embrace. "I wanted you to tell me yourself," I admitted.

"Well, then, I fucking hope you're happy now," he grumbled.

"I'm not. I'm miserable. My heart is broken and it's taking everything I have not to get down on my knees and beg you to stay. If you had any idea how close I've been to sobbing into your neck for the next seventy-two hours, you'd probably puke again. I love you, and I'm terrified of losing you."

Blue let out an enormous breath before buying his face into my neck. "Good. Then we can be miserable assholes together. Is this what they mean when they say misery loves company? Because this shit sucks, but it's better somehow. With you."

After holding him like that for a few minutes, I pulled away. "We are going to figure it out. But right now I have to fix us something to eat before I literally die."

I fixed a tomato basil pasta dish that was quick and easy. When we sat down to eat, I could see Blue was deep in thought.

"I have an idea," I began.

41

BLUE

Tristan continued, "I'll book a flight to come see you in two weeks. We'll spend a long weekend together in London brainstorming longer-term solutions. I can show you some of my favorite London haunts from my jet-setting days. Meanwhile, knowing we'll be seeing each other in just two weeks will make it much easier to say goodbye on Sunday. What do you think?"

"Hmm," I thought. "You might be onto something. It would help us put off the big talk and just enjoy the rest of the wedding weekend."

"Exactly. And if we decide to do this plan, we agree not to stress anymore until at least Sunday at midnight. No discussions, no tears, no puking. Just fun, and… you know… banging." Tristan looked at me with clear platinum eyes and a sexy grin.

"Slut," I accused.

"Fine," Tristan said breezily. "No sex. Just platonic, enjoyable friendship this weekend. Sounds pleasant."

"Like hell it does," I growled. "I didn't say I didn't love a good slut."

"Is it a deal?" Tristan asked.

"Can I still cry and whine until your plane ticket is booked?" I asked hopefully.

"Absolutely," he said, fetching his laptop from his bedroom. "You have approximately five minutes."

He went online to book a ticket while I pretended to wring my handkerchief and fret and swoon over his impending absence. He really ought to invest in a fainting couch.

Finally, Tristan held up one finger dramatically over the keyboard. "Any last laments before I push the button?"

"*This fucking sucks*," I yelled. Then I shook out my shoulders and stretched my head from side to side. "Okay. Go for it, champ."

He pressed the button and then asked for my email address to forward the travel confirmation to my account.

Then he stood and hugged me. His scruffy cheek brushed against my ear until I could feel his soft lips against my lobe. "Let's bang," he said in a mischievous voice, lips moving against my skin. I shivered and pulled back with a wolfish grin.

"First one to get naked wins a blow job," I called out as I ran for the bedroom, Tristan hot on my heels.

After both of us earned blow jobs just for participating, we took showers and then went at it again. This time Tristan learned the art of rimming under the tutelage of a dedicated master. Ahem.

Because of the long nap earlier in the evening, we stayed up really late watching *Talladega Nights* and eating ice cream straight from the carton. When morning came, I relished the feeling of Tristan's muscular frame encasing me in its warmth. He was the best damned cuddler in the world, and I loved the sensation of being safe and snug in his bed.

Eventually, Piper jumped up onto the bed, obviously bored with our lazy asses. She licked my face before starting in on Tristan's.

"Bleck, agh, gross." Tristan thrashed under the wet tongue of the wrong lover in his bed. "Off!"

"Aww, that poor baby. All she wanted was a wittle ol' French kiss to start her day off right. You're a meanie," I accused.

Tristan pounced on me, shoving his tongue in my ear and pressing blunt fingertips into the spots between my ribs that he knew damned well were ticklish.

"Now you see how it feels," he sexy-growled at me.

I laughed under the ticklish onslaught. "Yes, but I actually like it."

Tristan went full throttle, tickling me, wrestling with me, and French kissing me until my laughter turned to desperate begging.

"Fuck me, you gorgeous bastard," I gasped. "Fucking teasing me with that tongue. Agh, *god*, right like *that*."

In mere moments, his fingers were lubed and fucking me, curling and twisting and scissoring me into a lather. I wanted more and begged him for more. "Fuck me, dammit. Want to feel you. Stop playing arou... AHH!" I nearly choked on my tongue when he thrust his dick inside me and immediately slid his finger in beside it. Holy fucking hell.

"*Oh god, oh god, Tris*," I babbled. Felt so damned good.

"Feel me, baby?" he teased. "You sure?"

"Gnuh," I said. "Mphf."

He pulled his signature make-Blue-crazy move on top of everything else and leaned his motherfucking lips against my ear while he thrust in and out of me, pushing me to the edge of the cliff.

"Are you gonna let go, baby?" that smoky voice teased. "That's it. Come for me, beautiful."

Every nerve ending in my body exploded as those words went straight to my balls and lit the fuse. My climax was like the finale of the fireworks show with more explosions coming one after the other until you think it's done but it's not. My ass pulled Tristan's climax out of him and squeezed him over and over until he was spent.

As we gasped and tried to recover, I laughed. Every time I had sex with Tristan Alexander, I felt like I won the orgasm sweepstakes.

"Care to share?" he asked from his spot plastered to my side, head resting on my shoulder.

"I'm trying to figure out what it says about me if the best orgasms I ever got were from a straight guy."

He nudged me with his elbow. "Shut up."

"For real. Maybe it's true what Jeremy said. Maybe I'm so vanilla in bed that I'm easily impressed." I was joking but Tristan didn't see it that way.

"You are anything but vanilla in bed, Blue. Seriously. He was just chucking insults at you to be mean. If he likes crazier shit in bed than the things you do, then he can find someone more compatible elsewhere. Meanwhile, if this is what vanilla sex is like, then sign me up for vanilla for life. Because that shit is delicious."

"Thank you for saying that. But I was truly joking. Out of curiosity though, do you think British boys like vanilla?" I asked with a straight face.

Tristan sat up in bed with a storm front blowing across his face.

"Whoa, whoa," I said, laughing. "Kidding. Only kidding. Down, Cujo."

"Not funny," he said, still wearing his angry eyes.

"Oh, I don't know. Your reaction made it kinda funny." I chuckled.

"We didn't talk about it because I thought it went without saying it. But just to be clear, I'll say it. No fucking anyone but me. Got it?" he said in his corporate attorney voice.

"You're kinda hot when you're bossy," I teased.

"Are we clear, baby?" he said in a softer voice. "Tell me no one else is going to touch you but me."

My heart stuck in my throat.

"Blue?" he asked, in a whisper now.

"Clear." I swallowed. "No question. Same goes for you."

He nodded, his concerned brow finally smoothing and a tentative smile coming out. "Don't make me tattoo your ass before sending you off. Because I'll do it. Big ol' tramp stamp in Comic Sans that says 'Tristan Wuz Here' with an arrow pointing down."

I snorted. "Oh my god, that's heinous. I don't know where to even begin. Comic Sans? Surely you jest. Do you know who you're talking to?"

"Not only that, but I'll bribe the tattoo artist extra to make sure it's a little off center and the word 'here' is spelled h-e-a-r just for good measure."

"Fuck you. Now I'm going to develop a tic just thinking about it."

We showered and made our way to the lodge. The day was

gorgeous, blue sky and warm sun. It was Friday, the day of the rehearsal dinner.

Most of my family was gathered around the breakfast setup in the lobby. Wedding guests sat at tables around the food and on the back patio.

Tristan poured us some coffee while I filled up a couple of plates with muffins, yogurt, and fruit. When I saw John and Simone get up to start greeting friends and family members at their tables, we took their spots at a table with my parents.

My mom reached over and squeezed my hand. "How are you feeling, sweetheart?"

"Much better." I smiled. "Jude drugged me into a stupor, and I slept it off."

"I'm worried about that boy, Bee. Any idea what's going on with him these days?" she said with a furrowed brow.

"He's wiped out from the tour and just needs to get home and recover. Make sure you force him out of his house for family dinners, though. Because I have a feeling's he's going to try and hibernate."

My dad chimed in. "Don't worry, son. We will. He overdoes it and needs to realize he's not as young as he was when all this started."

"Dad, he's twenty-eight. Hardly on death's door." I chuckled, scooting over to make room for Aunt Tilly's arrival.

"What he needs is a partner," Mom said. "Someone to take care of him and love on him."

I found her choice of the word "partner" curious. Moms always seemed to know more than they let on.

Aunt Tilly said, "Maybe he just needs to get laid. A good fuck ought to fix him right up. Works for me anyway," she said with a shrug.

Tristan spit out his coffee and I shot him a look. His eyes were bugged out and he looked at all of us like we were crazy. We were, but we didn't look it.

"What?" I asked him innocently. "Don't tell me you aren't used to her by now. And Granny is ten times worse."

He wiped his face with a napkin. "I keep forgetting, that's all. And

I haven't had my coffee yet. At this rate, I'll never get enough down to make a difference."

My dad gave Tristan an understanding smile. "Tristan, tell us more about yourself. What do you like to do when you're not running the vineyard?"

"I do agility training with Piper. The man who manages the estate's animals helps me. We have an agility course set up in a ring behind the horse barn. I'm also learning falconry. Still in the early days of that, though."

Mom's eyes widened. "Falconry? That sounds interesting. What got you into that?"

"Falcons are being used as organic pest control in agriculture. They scare away starlings and other smaller birds who want to eat the grapes. We also use dogs to rid the vineyard of smaller pests like rabbits. Our estate has two golden retrievers trained to work around the trellises and three peregrine falcons," he explained.

I turned to him, grabbing his hand. "I think I've read about that somewhere. Don't some vineyards even introduce bobcats for pest control?"

"Yes." He laughed. "But not in the States. Can you imagine? Not the best way to make friends with your neighbors."

"I guess not," I agreed, imagining the complaints about cats and small dogs going missing from backyards.

My nieces had come up to give Mom and Dad good morning kisses and Dad told them what Tristan said about agility and falconry.

Hazel's eyes lit up. She loved animals and had spent twenty minutes discussing ladybugs with Tristan the first time she met him. "Uncle Tristan, after breakfast will you show us what Piper can do?"

We all sat there staring at her.

Uncle Tristan.

42

TRISTAN

Out of the mouths of babes.

When she called me Uncle Tristan it sounded so natural. So normal. It occurred to me that kids pick up on small cues and accept them. Blue held my hand at the breakfast table. The girls had seen us together all week, touching each other casually and speaking to each other as partners.

"Sure, ladybug. I'll even let you girls give Piper some treats if she does a good job with her tricks," I promised.

The girls scampered off squealing with excitement. They were most likely going to go tell every other kid they'd met about the agility show that was happening after breakfast.

Blue's mom looked at me with a smile. "Do you have any idea what you just signed on for?"

"A full morning of finally making Piper earn her keep?" I joked.

"Every child at this resort is going to come watch you put on a show." She laughed.

"That's okay. My poor dog has been neglected this week. She's been so bored; she's even taken to following Blue around." I winked at the gorgeous man sitting next to me.

"What can I say, I'm irresistible." He smirked.

"No shit," I said under my breath. Unfortunately it wasn't soft enough to escape Tilly's notice.

"Gag me with a spoon," Tilly griped. "Tristan, you got any hot uncles coming this weekend?"

"No, ma'am. Just the plain ones."

"Ah, well, introduce me anyway. Beggars can't be choosers."

THE REST of the morning was busy but fun. We gathered everyone who was interested in the agility demonstration and led them to the course behind the barn. I put Piper through her paces and she was in heaven.

John's college buddies had brought their children, and there ended up being about ten kids who pretended to be agility dogs when Piper was finished. They jumped and climbed their way through the course with me as their leader.

Everyone went their own ways for lunch and I ended up taking Blue and his brothers Jamie and Jude a few miles away to a sandwich shop I liked. Wolfe joined us and stayed as unobtrusive as usual. He was so attentive to Jude that it seemed to relax Blue. Maybe he realized Jude had someone in his life looking out for him, even if that someone was on the payroll.

When we sat down at the cafe's outdoor tables, I asked Jamie about his work in Denali. What I really wanted to know was how his heart was faring after being jilted by his asshole fiancé a few months before. Blue was worried about him but was too nervous to ask himself.

Jamie said he'd gotten a large grant approved for his work with Dall sheep herds and another for a project involving some kind of owls that needed nesting boxes in the park. While we were talking, his phone chimed with a message alert. He read it quickly and rolled his eyes, letting out an exasperated huff.

"Sorry about that. I'm expecting an email with travel info for a stop off at Mount Rainier on my way home from here. They have a baby beaver they need help with. The mom died and the kit is having trouble. I have a beaver family in Denali with a kit the same age. They're hoping I can transport theirs to Denali and see if my beaver mom will take the kit on as a foster."

"Will it work?" Jude asked.

"Don't know. But when I got the call from Rainier this morning, they made it sound like I'm this kit's only hope. We'll give it a try. The beaver family I've been observing in Denali is pretty healthy and confident around me. So I'm hoping it works out."

"So that wasn't them on the email?" Blue asked, taking a sip of my soda. I swatted his hand away and told him to go get his own.

"No. That was some jackass nature photographer who keeps trying to arrange to come shadow me and take photos of me with the wildlife. He's been at it for a month now," Jamie explained. "It's bordering on harassment."

I looked around at the others, wondering what I was missing. "Why don't you want him to take the photographs?" I asked.

Before Jamie could respond, Blue chimed in. "Jamie is considered the wildlife whisperer. People are always hounding him like he's the second coming of Christ when it comes to wild animals in parks. He doesn't like people to see him interact with the animals."

"Shut up," Jamie scoffed. "The problem is that what I do is dangerous. So whenever someone publishes a photograph of me interacting with animals, it gives people a false sense of security. They think the animals aren't as dangerous as they thought because there's Dr. Marian, touching one."

Jude added, "A photo came out a couple of years ago showing Jamie cradling a grizzly bear cub. A tourist had lucked into the shot while on vacation in Yellowstone. The guy was able to sell it for big bucks to the media. When it was published, it was insanely popular because it was so rare."

"And adorable," Blue added.

"And adorable," Jude agreed. "But only a month later, a child tried approaching a bear cub at a campground in Yosemite. The mama bear attacked."

"Oh god," I said. "Did the kid...? Was the kid...?"

Now it was Jamie's turn to speak up. "The boy survived, but he will always have an enormous scar on his face and shoulder. It should have never happened."

"But surely everyone knows that even when a wildlife vet is interacting with animals, it's because they've had extensive training?" I asked.

"Not if they see photos of it in the mainstream media. Maybe it would be different if this had been published in a scientific magazine. But it was all over the media as a 'cute' moment. Not the medical rescue it actually was," Jamie explained.

"Now I understand, Jamie. I'm sorry. That must have been awful for you." I could see the pain on his face as he remembered it.

"Not as awful as it was for that young boy," he said.

Now it was Wolfe's turn to interject. "Look at the bright side. That kid will forever be able to tell people about the time he got into a fight with an angry grizzly bear and won. Lucky shit. Every man's dream."

We all laughed and agreed.

When we returned to the estate, most everyone gathered on the patio behind the lodge and Jude brought out his guitar. Simone hadn't stopped hounding him, and for that, we were all grateful.

Jude sat on the wide stone steps leading down to the lawn and played as many songs as people requested. I sat in the grass a few feet away, legs stretched out and leaning back on my hands. Blue's head rested in my lap and at one point I thought he dozed off. Pete's girls tried throwing a frisbee for Piper, but they could never get a good toss.

I felt the rumble of Blue's voice vibrate against my leg and realized he wasn't sleeping but humming and singing along under his breath.

"Go up there and sing with him," I leaned down to whisper. "You know you want to, and it would make your mom and Simone happy."

He turned on my lap until he faced my stomach. "You sure it's not you who wants me to?"

"That too," I admitted. "Show me what you got, lover boy."

He wrapped an arm around my waist for a squeeze before pushing himself up to stand. After joining Jude on the steps, he joined in for the end of "I Fall to Pieces" by Patsy Cline. Jude was right, Blue's voice was good. Like, dick-hardeningly good. When they finished, Jude handed Blue his guitar.

And then that fucking man put his fingers to work and sang the next song straight into my soul.

43

BLUE

Jude handed me the guitar, insisting I play something. One of my favorite songs to play once I got a little better on the guitar as a teen was "Friday I'm in Love" by The Cure.

I started out with the acoustic intro and saw Tristan's surprise that I could even play the guitar. My fingers felt tender on the strings but my muscle memory kicked in. I'd played that song a thousand times over the years. Never did I imagine I'd feel its lyrics so keenly.

When I began to sing, I had to look away from Tristan for the first two stanzas to keep from losing my shit.

When I finally looked back over at him, his eyes were shining and his goddamned dimple was out in full force. That fucker. My fingers missed a chord, making me laugh and stumble to catch up.

I looked over and winked at Simone, who had her hands clasped together in front of her mouth. John stood next to her with his arm around her shoulder. My parents had stopped chatting and were watching intently, my mom's gaze traveling between Tristan and me. I felt Jude's hand land on my upper back and when I got to the final repeat, he joined in and gestured with his free hand for anyone else to join in. By the time the final line came, everyone yelled it out in celebration for John and Simone.

But Tristan's eyes were locked with mine as we joined the others in yelling it out with whoops of celebration. *It's Friday I'm in love.*

Before it was time to shower and dress for the rehearsal, I found time to return to the piece of wood I was carving. Tristan was off double-checking things around the estate, and I enjoyed the same quiet bench in the trees behind the lodge where I had carved the first time.

The wedding rehearsal went by quickly that evening under a huge tent on the property, the mood was light and happy as we headed over to a nearby vineyard for the sit-down rehearsal dinner.

The large wine cellar was decorated beautifully. Colorful spring flowers spilled out of fat glass jars. Fresh greenery was woven with cream-colored ribbons interspersed with thick pillar candles and tiny votives. Crystal wineglasses and sparkling china sat waiting at each place setting, and servers stood around the edges of the room ready to help everyone to their seats.

I noticed Jeremy sitting with his parents, who must have arrived earlier that day. Other than a polite smile from them when they walked in, they seemed to be ignoring me. It made me wonder what he had told them about me and our breakup. I really didn't care much, honestly.

Aunt Tilly walked in with Granny and Irene, laughing and probably close to being shitfaced already if their flushed faces were any indication. After several minutes of mingling, I began to look for the place card with my name on it, knowing my parents would have never put me next to anyone I knew well. They believed in spreading out the Marian love to make sure everyone felt included.

I was surprised to see my card next to Tristan's on one side and Jude's on another. As I looked up to try and catch my mom's eye, I saw Aunt Tilly give me a wink. That sneaky devil. After blowing her a kiss and watching as she nearly knocked over a chair pretending to catch the kiss, I took my seat.

A minute later I felt stubble graze my ear. "This seat taken?" a familiar smoky voice purred beside me. I smelled Tristan's soap.

"Yes," I answered. "My boyfriend is sitting here. He's kind of intimidating so you'd better not fuck with him."

"Boyfriend, huh?" he rumbled against my ear. I shuddered, trying to maintain my composure.

I nodded and swallowed. "Yup. Although, I think he prefers the word 'partner,'" I teased.

His deep laugh bubbled out as he lowered himself into his seat. "Not going to ever let me live that down are you?"

"Nope."

"Well then, I'll have to come up with something else we can call each other," he said, giving me a pointed look.

Before I had a chance to overanalyze that exchange, some other people joined our table and began to introduce themselves. Jude showed up a little late and looked... recently fucked. What the hell was that about? I asked him about it, but he told me I was seeing things through fuck-colored glasses.

The dinner was lovely. Good food, excellent wine, funny and loving toasts to the bride and groom. Simone was beautiful in a pale yellow dress. John sat next to her with an arm wrapped around her shoulder. I noticed him squeeze her upper arm attentively when she got particularly emotional. It was a subtle reminder he must love her. I could only hope it was enough for them to build a successful marriage together.

My brother Pete gave a toast that included some funny and meaningful stories from our childhood, and I got a little tearful. Tristan reached for my hand and held it tightly after pulling a tiny pack of tissues from his pocket and sliding them over to me. I looked up at him in silent thanks, and he leaned over to whisper in my ear, "Love you."

God, that man was so fucking nice.

After the dinner ended, all the people our age dragged our tipsy asses to the bar at the lodge. Frank was on duty, pouring generously after a nod from Tristan.

The space was crowded and I was a little disappointed not to get the same stools at the bar where Tristan and I first met. But my disappointment was short lived when Tristan found an empty chair at a table and pulled me onto his lap. Music played, people laughed, and the mood was contagious. Simone and John seemed to be loving the opportunity to catch up with their closest friends and college buddies.

My brothers were giving each other shit and buying each other drinks. At one point I saw Jude laugh so hard beer shot out of his nose. Wolfe stood against the wall behind him and looked at him like Jude hung the moon. Even quiet Dante was laughing and joking with the rest of us. He wasn't twenty-one yet so he had ordered soda. None of us would have cared if he'd ordered a beer, but I got the feeling he either didn't want to drink or didn't want to make things weird for Tristan, who knew how old he was.

When I took a break to go to the men's room, Jeremy found me. I sighed and shot him a look. He held both hands up, palms outward.

"I just wanted to say I'm really sorry," he said. "I was completely out of line. All of it. The breakup and the presumption that you'd want me back."

"Thank you," I said wearily.

"That's all. Maybe one day down the road we can be friends again. I'm sorry I fucked that up for us."

"Me too," I said. "I hope you can patch things up with Brad. He seems like a nice guy."

"We'll see. And I can see that what you and Tristan have isn't what I thought. The way he looks at you... it's... it's the real deal, I think."

I let out a big breath and couldn't top my face from breaking into a goofy grin. "Yeah. It is."

"But London. What are you going to do?" he asked.

I thought about that and felt the familiar pang of sadness and fear. Then I remembered my deal with Tristan and I smiled. "I'm going to go to the bathroom. And then I'm going to go back into that bar and celebrate with my family. That's what I'm going to do."

44

TRISTAN

I was listening to Ginger tell drunken stories about being a parent when I felt my phone vibrate in my pocket and took it out to see a text. It was from Blue.

Blue: This is a nice bathroom. You should come in here and sex it up with me.

Tristan: You're texting me from the bathroom?

Blue: Sexting.

Tristan: Dude, you're drunk. And we both probably have whiskey dick.

Blue: Not me, I'm hard right now just thinking about fucking you in this bathroom.

Tristan: Is that true?

Blue: No. I'm sitting on the floor and I'm too drunk to stand up. Come get me?

Tristan: Is this another ploy to get me to come in there for sex?

Blue: Yes, is it working?

Tristan: It would be if I wasn't too drunk to figure out where the bathroom is.

Blue: If I come back to the bar, I'll drink more and then sex will be a distant memory.

Tristan: Come back and we'll switch to water together.

Blue: Promise?

Tristan: Would I lie to you?

When Blue wandered back in with a silly grin on his face, I waited until he was almost to our table when I shouted, "Frank! Two red-headed sluts, please!"

Blue burst out laughing and sat back down on my lap, smacking my lips with a wet kiss.

"You asshole," he said with a grin on his face. "I knew you were lying."

"Can't help it. Wanted to see you get drunk," I snickered. "Plus, if we can't make it back to my place, we can just sleep here in one of the rooms. I know the owner."

"Babe, I have a room here already, remember?" Blue said.

"Oh right. Much better. But don't make me use that ass-torture chair," I said.

Silence all around us.

I looked up into a table full of big eyes. "What?" I asked.

Jude smirked. "Care to tell us what kind of sex chair you and Blue have in that hotel room?"

Blue burst out laughing, setting off his siblings. My face turned beet red. "It's a stupid French chair thing," I spluttered. "Not a sex thing."

"Oh my god," Blue said, giggling. "You should see your face right now."

"Shut up. You all have dirty minds," I accused.

"Says the guy with the ass-torture device." Jamie giggled, smacking Pete and causing him to fall into Ginger. "Wait, I dated a guy that had one of those, but it was the swing version."

Ginger piped up, "Honey, we should look into one of those things. Maybe we can attach it to the girls' playground in the backyard and... you know. Do it French style." More giggling.

Someone brought over our shots and I handed one to Blue. We clinked and threw them back. Because god knew we needed more alcohol like a fucking hole in the head. Which we were sure to also have the following morning.

The party finally broke up and I somehow convinced my shit-faced Blue to walk back to the cabin with me instead of staying in the lodge. When the cool air of the outdoors hit my face, I looked up to the sky. Stars sprinkled overhead, and I pointed them out to Blue.

As he tilted his head back, he stumbled. I reached out to grab him, and he swung around to kiss me. My lips tingled as I drank in the alcohol taste of his tongue. His hands squeezed my ass and I felt my drunk-ass dick try desperately to stir to life. Blue dropped a hand to my crotch and began to stroke.

"Mmmm, baby," I mumbled against his lips. "Wait. Not home yet."

I began walking even though there was a beautiful man attached to my face. He shuffled backward and finally had to remove himself from my front when he realized I was determined to get to our final destination.

We held hands and wandered down the last part of the dirt lane to my front porch. When I reached out to unlock the door I heard

Blue say, "Home sweet home," and it sounded pretty damned good coming out of his mouth.

Piper greeted us enthusiastically, and I made sure there was food in her bowl before collapsing on the sofa.

Blue was wandering around in circles as if he couldn't remember where he wanted to go.

"You were looking for water," I reminded him.

"Oh right," he mumbled before going to the fridge.

He came over to where I was sitting. He was empty handed.

"Water?" I repeated.

"Oh right," he mumbled before returning to the fridge.

I couldn't help but chuckle. When he appeared in front of me again empty handed, I hooted with laughter.

"What?" he asked, seeming perplexed.

"Sweetheart, you were going to get some water."

"Oh right," he said and turned around. I grabbed his wrist.

"No," I said. "I'll get it. You sit."

"What? I can get it. Just tell me what you want," he said.

"You, on the sofa," I answered, shoving myself up again and moving toward the fridge.

"So bossy," he muttered as I opened the door and looked inside the fridge.

Huh. If only I could remember what I was supposed to be getting. Oh well.

I returned to the sofa and saw Blue staring off into space. When he saw me he looked up with an adorable grin on his face. "Did you get it?"

"Get what?" I asked.

"Water."

Fuck.

I sat down on the sofa and shrugged. "We're all out."

Blue straddled my lap and began kissing me. His hands were holding my face and I could smell the cologne he'd been wearing that night. So sexy.

"You drive me fucking crazy, Blue Marian," I said between kisses. "That song. That song you sang for me." I shivered.

Blue pulled back to look at me. "You liked it?" Saucy grin.

"More than you'll ever know," I admitted. "Your voice is like liquid sex. I could listen to you sing to me for the rest of my life and never get sick of hearing it."

"Want me to sing you another song?" Blue teased with waggling eyebrows.

"Hell yes."

Blue stood up and pushed the coffee table out of the way. I stared at the way his suit trousers draped over his tight, round ass when he bent over to push the table across the floor. Mmm.

He came back to stand in the middle of the space between my spot on the sofa and the television. And then he began to sing Marvin Gaye's "Let's Get It On" while he performed the sexiest drunken strip-tease ever.

Sleeve cuff buttons came undone before he slowly twisted each shirt button down his chest. He pulled the fabric apart, showing his tight abs and pecs, dotted with those hardened nipples begging for my mouth.

The shirt floated to the floor as he reached for the buckle of his belt, sliding it slowly open while he sang to me and moved his hips.

It was the hottest fucking thing on earth.

When he finished pulling his belt open, he slid it out of the loops and let it fall to the floor. His nimble fingers moved to the button of his trousers and he rotated his hips while I drooled in anticipation. He turned around and raised his arms over his head, shaking his ass slowly in time to the song, the muscles of his back moving under his skin and lighting me on fire.

He leaned forward, placing his hands on his knees and rocking his hips, teasing me with that fine fucking ass.

When he turned back to face me, still singing, he opened his fly and let the fabric fall open, exposing tight red briefs. My cock was taunting me with false promises. I palmed my dick and moaned.

I began to unbutton my own shirt while I watched him. He danced for me with his pants hanging open, his semi-swollen cock trying to escape the small briefs. When he peeled back his trousers farther to let them drop to the floor, he turned around again to show me his backside.

Holyfuckingshit they weren't briefs. It was a tight red jockstrap, allowing his gorgeous, fuckable ass to move freely in all its glory.

I was up and moving before he had a chance to take another breath. I tackled him to the floor and mauled him, all lips and hands. He was busy laughing so it was like trying to kiss a moving target.

"You like?" he asked through his laughter.

"*Jesus fuck* you had those on all night?" I panted. "While you were sitting next to me at the rehearsal dinner and then sitting on my lap in the bar? You had those little things on *all night*?"

"Just for you, baby." He laughed. "Glad you like."

"Get on my bed on your hands and knees. I'm going to fuck you until I pass out. And keep on the jock." I growled, knowing full well it was never going to work. We were both way too drunk.

He saluted me and made his way to the bedroom, detouring to the fridge to get some bottles of water. Oh right. Water.

When I finished turning out the lights and checking the door lock, Blue walked back out of my bedroom toward me.

"What do you need, baby?" I asked him.

"Something to drink," he said.

"Gatorade or juice?" I asked.

"No. Just water. You said we were out of water. I thought I'd look for some in the fridge."

I walked up and pulled him into my arms. "I think there are two bottles in the bedroom," I told him with a smile before walking him into the room and pulling back the covers.

We forgot to drink the water even though the bottles were right where Blue had left them on the nightstand. Instead, I stripped him out of the jock and helped him get into bed. I may or may not have copped some major feels in the process of removing the red jockstrap. I took off my own clothes and snuggled in behind him.

"Sorry I fucked up the fucking," he mumbled.

I laughed. "You didn't. I'm pretty sure the vats of alcohol we both drank fucked up the fucking. We'll just have to make up for it after some sleep. Now rest up. Big day tomorrow."

"I love you, Tris," he said, squeezing my hand.

"Love you too, baby. I had so much fun with you tonight."

45

BLUE

The day of the wedding began with an excruciating throb in my head and a piercing blindness in my eyeballs. What the fuck had I done last night?

I was immediately suffocated by toxic morning breath and complained to my stinky bed partner.

"Did you eat a skunk last night?"

"Hmpf?" Tristan mumbled.

"Your breath is disgusting," I chastised.

"Baby," he yawned, "you're breathing against my lower back. You can't possibly smell my breath from there. Plus, I took a shower and brushed my teeth about an hour ago."

"Oh fuck. That's my breath. It's bouncing off your skin and attacking me. So aggressive," I whined. Why was I face to face with his lower back? "Did I eat a skunk last night?"

Tristan swiveled around in bed so I was facing his gorgeous happy cock instead of his stinky breath reflector unit. "Well, hello there, handsome," I said to one of my favorite things. Tristan's hips reflexively thrust up toward me.

I looked up at Tristan's gray eyes. "I'd suck you off but then I'd actually die from fatal contact with my own hangover breath. It's pretty much a public health hazard at this point."

"Tell me about it," he said, wrinkling his nose.

"Fuck you," I grumbled, rolling out of bed. "It wouldn't be this bad if you hadn't made me suck down that red-headed slut last night," I called back over my shoulder on my way to the bathroom. "Why am I so damned thirsty? Were we not smart enough to drink any—?"

"Say the word 'water' one time, jackass. I dare you," he said.

AFTER A COUPLE of cups of coffee and a simple but greasy breakfast, Tristan and I walked to the lodge. People were already up and finished with their breakfast with plans to enjoy the beautiful day before it was time to dress for photos and the ceremony.

I knew that Tristan wanted to double-check everything for the ceremony and reception since Keller was no longer on site to manage it. On his way to the estate house, I had him take me by the tool room to pick up some detailing tools for my carving project.

After I found what I wanted, Tristan headed to his office while I headed back to the lodge. I sat on the patio with Piper and got to work on my project. Jude came out with a notebook, scribbling song notes and ideas for lyrics while I carved.

The simple downtime together was a treat. I couldn't remember how long it had been since we'd just hung out in easy silence for longer than a half hour. Jude seemed more relaxed than he was the first day here, and I hoped he would continue on that trajectory after returning home. I resented the fact he was finally going to be home for a while right as I was leaving.

Mom and Simone had gone with several of the other ladies to have massages and salon treatments. Dad came wandering out with a book and joined us on the patio. He helped Jude brainstorm song ideas until it turned into a competition for who could come up with the corniest, most stereotypical country music titles ever.

Dad texted Jamie and Pete to see if they wanted to come hang out with us, while my phone pinged with a text from Tristan.

Tristan: Hey gorgeous.

Blue: Hey yourself.

Tristan: What are you up to?

Blue: Hanging out in my favorite spot with some of my favorite people and my favorite dog. Something is missing though.

Tristan: Let me guess... water?

Blue: Ha-fucking-ha. You get me sloshed then make fun of the result? See if I let you get me drunk ever again.

Tristan: Sweetheart, I'm getting you drunk tonight. No doubt. That was so fun it must be repeated.

Blue: That's going to be hard since I've sworn off alcohol.

Tristan: La-la-la, I am not listening to you.

Blue: Where are you? Why aren't you here? I'm in the mood for a little nookie.

Tristan: Only if you're wearing a certain undergarment.

Blue: Oh, never mind then.

Tristan: Damn.

Blue: I neglected to put on any undergarments today.

Tristan: Be there in three minutes.

I couldn't help but laugh. Jamie gave me hell about the schmoopy face I was making into my phone.

"Man, that's so unfair. Why couldn't I have been the one to meet the gorgeous vineyard owner and have a week-long fuck fest?"

My dad cleared his throat and tried not to look uncomfortable at the idea of his son, any of us really, having anything to do with fucking.

Jamie continued unfazed. "Do you have any idea how hard it is to meet gay men in Denali, Alaska? It's impossible. There's one gay guy who works with me in the park. It's like he thinks because we're the only two gay men in a fifty-mile radius, we're meant to be together. He's totally not my type," Jamie complained.

"What type is he?" Jude asked.

"The marrying type." Jamie shuddered.

We all looked at him. "So are you," I countered. "Have you forgotten the almost-wedding we all attended earlier this year?"

Jamie shot me the bird. "That's exactly why I'm not the marrying type anymore. No, thanks. I can't imagine ever trusting someone enough again to go through all that. Plus, this guy is too... sweet. Like, not good sweet. Boring sweet."

Jamie's phone pinged and he growled at it.

"What the hell is that all about?" I asked.

"It's this fucking photographer who keeps trying to get me to agree to a photo shoot in Denali. He's so damned arrogant. Won't take no for an answer and now he's just plain fucking with me by texting me jokes. Listen to this." He read from his phone. "'Why are mountains so funny?'"

Jude chuckled. "I've heard this one. Because they're hill areas."

"Yup. Oh hey, there's Tristan," Jamie said.

I looked up and saw his long legs striding across the lawn from the side yard. He must have sprinted. I placed my carving inside the bag I'd found to collect the shavings. Once the bag was wrapped up, I tucked it under my arm and stood up.

I heard Pete snicker. "Speaking of fuck fest…"

"Shut the hell up. If you'd been more sober last night, maybe you would have noticed just how drunk I was and realize that I'm fighting a massive hangover right now. What I want more than anything is a nap that actually includes sleep," I lied.

Jamie and Pete both snorted. "Right," Jamie said. "Do you see the look on Tristan's face? He's thinking of a different kind of nap."

I shot them the bird again and met Tristan by the double doors to the lodge lobby. My brothers were right. The look on Tristan's face was completely predatory.

I leaned in to whisper. "Do you mind wiping that look off your face until we're in private?"

"What look?" he whispered back.

"The look that says 'I want to lick come off your chin,'" I said helpfully.

"Oh, that look. But what if I do? Want to lick come off your chin, I mean." He smirked.

I blushed as I caught sight of Tristan's mom in the lobby. She didn't see us, and I let out a breath when we were safely inside my hotel room.

"Think she'll ever be okay with me?" I asked.

"Yes," he answered without elaborating. He was already undressing me and I didn't want to interrupt such important work.

Tristan began kissing me while he undid the button on my shorts. My hands roamed under the back of his shirt and I could feel his shoulder blades moving under my hands. He smelled amazing as usual and I was sniffing him like a glue addict.

Tristan's phone rang and he ignored it, continuing to lower the fly of my shorts carefully since he knew I was commando. My small hairs were grateful for his caution and my cock stood up to thank him for his attention.

As soon as the fly was down, Tristan's large hand grasped me and I moaned into his mouth as he stroked me.

"Fuck that feels good. I want your mouth on me," I breathed.

Tristan pushed my shorts down and knelt on the floor in front of me. His phone rang again.

"Dammit. Fuck," I complained. "Don't they know this is the worst possible time for a—*oh god yes.*" The tip of my cock rammed the back of Tristan's throat as he took me down. My legs began to buckle as I felt his hot, wet mouth surrounding me. "*Fuck, Tris. Fuck that feels good.*"

Tristan's hands clasped my bare ass and I felt him squeeze and hold me up at the same time. His phone pinged with incoming texts. Someone was clearly trying to reach him.

"Ignore the phone," he growled. "Concentrate on what I'm getting ready to do to your tight little hole."

"Oh god," I whimpered, finally sinking to the floor. Tristan stood up and lifted me, shoving me onto the bed and crawling over me. He reached for the lube and condoms in the bedside drawer and unfastened his pants.

"Want to fuck you so bad," he panted as he opened the lube. "See you fall apart while I'm inside of you."

I closed my eyes and tilted my head back as I grabbed my cock to stroke it. I couldn't think. My head was dizzy with naked desire. Desire to be completely taken, penetrated, owned by this man. I wanted him completely. At that moment I would have let him do absolutely anything to my body if it would give him pleasure.

Slick fingers entered me and I cried out, feeling my body clench around him. He stroked until he found just the right angle and watched as I began to buck in response to the stimulation of my prostate. It felt amazing and somehow Tristan knew how to take me to the edge but not over it.

His mouth began to travel along the edge of my jaw as his two fingers fucked me. His lips and tongue trailed down my throat to the dip of my collarbone and down to one nipple. As he latched on to that nipple with a hard suck, he thrust a third finger inside me, slamming his free hand over my mouth as I screamed his name.

46

TRISTAN

Blue's moans turned to small whimpers of need. I shucked off my clothes as quickly as I could and rolled on the condom. After coating it with lube, I climbed back onto that exquisite man and slid home.

As I moved in and out of his body, my mouth worshipped his until I could barely catch my breath. I pulled my face back and locked eyes with him. His blue eyes were so bright and beautiful. I felt like I could see his entire soul in his eyes during that moment, and I felt certain he could see mine too.

I reached down to stroke his hard cock as I continued to thrust in and out, our eyes still connected. As his orgasm began to hit, he threw his head back and opened his mouth in a silent scream. Hot streams shot over his belly; my hand stroked him through his climax until my own hit.

Just as waves of pleasure crashed over me, I heard banging on Blue's door.

I plunged once more inside Blue as I felt my body convulse and empty. The banging continued on the door, and I heard the voice of my father.

"Open the goddamned door, Tristan! I need your help out here," he yelled.

I scrambled off Blue, chucking the condom in the bathroom trash and grabbing towels to do a quick cleanup.

"Hang on, Dad. Let me put on my shoes," I called out. I threw a towel at Blue and raced to get my clothes on. What the hell could be so important?

Blue wiped up his stomach and looked at me in a daze. "What's going on?"

"How the hell should I know?" I whispered as I grabbed my shoes. "But if he's the one who's been calling and texting, something must be up."

Blue stood up to get dressed as I slipped out of the door and joined my father in the hallway. I tried smoothing my hair down as I looked at him for answers.

"What's going on?" I asked.

"Your goddamned wife is here making trouble," he spat.

"What? Sheila is here? Where?" I said incredulously. "And why does everyone insist on calling her my wife instead of my ex-wife?"

"She's in John's room, and I think she's drunk. She's making crazy claims and seems to think John shouldn't marry Simone. Come on. We need to get her out of here," Dad said.

Just then, Blue came out of the room and joined us. I explained, "Apparently Sheila is here harassing John."

"I'm coming with you," he said.

Dad looked at Blue and narrowed his eyes. "We don't need you to come with us. Tristan can handle his wife. We'll get this under control before Simone comes back and gets upset."

"EX-wife," I corrected again. "But Blue, Dad's right. Why don't you stay here?"

"Forget it, Tris. If there is shit going on between Sheila and John, I want to know. It's my sister's wedding day for god's sake."

The three of us made our way to John's suite and I could see the door was propped open with the chain. When we entered, my mom stood against the wall, her face pale and her hands over her mouth. Sheila was in the process of slapping John hard across the face.

I raced across the room to grab her, but before I got close, John launched himself at Sheila, cupping her face and kissing her.

The four of us spectators froze in place as the scene played out in front of us. John and Sheila kissed as if they were alone and making up for years of lost time. Hands grasped each other's clothes, hips met, and sounds of longing slid out of them.

Oh god, no. Those fucking idiots.

My mouth dropped open and blood rushed in my ears. Mom wailed. Dad screamed John's name. And Blue looked at me with complete horror and devastation before turning around to bolt.

Before Blue made it to the doorway, Simone walked in laughing at something she was telling her mom. When she entered the room, she looked up to find us all standing there. Blue, pale and stricken, Mom still wailing, Dad still yelling, and John and Sheila still locked in a tight embrace, clutching each other's clothes for dear life.

It was every bride's nightmare. And there Simone stood, hair in a fancy bridal updo, nails freshly painted, and the beginnings of heartbreak slamming through her entire body.

Blue grabbed her and turned her, pushing her out of the room along with his mother. I snapped out of my stupor and lunged to close and lock the door behind him before turning on my brother.

"What the *fuck* are you doing?" I roared. "Are you really that heartless that you could do this to Simone on your wedding day?"

John seemed to awaken from a daze. "I didn't mean… I mean… I… I need to go talk to her. Explain. I'll explain everything."

"How?" I raged. "How the hell are you going to explain kissing another woman on your fucking wedding day? Huh? Tell me."

Sheila shot daggers at me. "Tristan, calm down."

I swiveled my head to look at my ex-wife. "How could you? It's one thing to sleep with my brother while you and I were married but quite another to come here and ruin his wedding day. Explain yourself."

My parents both gasped at the news of John and Shiela's affair.

Sheila ignored them. "I'm sorry, Tristan. But I couldn't let him marry her without telling him I love him."

"Are you fucking insane? If he loved you, why didn't he pick you instead of Simone? Let it go. He obviously doesn't want you," I yelled, hoping like hell I was right.

"He picked Simone because he was terrified of losing you and his family if he picked me," Sheila said. And fuck if I didn't see the truth of it in John's face.

"Oh god." I groaned, rubbing my face with both hands. "You stupid bastard."

John looked crushed. "Tristan, I screwed up. I'm so sorry."

I was so angry, I wanted to choke him until his limp body gave up the fight. My entire body was shaking with rage and heartbreak for Simone. If only I'd done something, or warned her. Blue was right. We should have warned her.

Oh god. Blue. He was going to blame me. He was going to hate me.

Before I could lose my shit and go completely berserk, I strode out the door to find him. Before I got ten paces, my phone started ringing again. Assuming it was Blue, I answered.

It was Keller. Art had passed away and Uncle Henry was inconsolable. He needed me.

I raced back to my cabin and threw clothes together in a suitcase before loading up to head for the airport. I called Stacey to ask her to look after Piper. As I drove out of the vineyard, I did my best to avoid looking at the wedding tent set up on the lawn behind the estate house. Flowers and ribbon decorated the area and wooden folding chairs were tied with big swaths of fabric that blew gently in the breeze. What the hell was John going to tell all the people who had come for the wedding. What the hell was he going to tell Simone?

I tried calling Blue but he wasn't answering his phone. When I got to the airport I had to race to catch the next flight out. Stacey was scrambling to deal with the cancellation of the wedding and I had to talk her through it until the flight attendant forced me to turn off my phone. I sent one more quick text to Blue before powering down.

Tristan: I don't know what other words to say except I'm sorry. I'm so sorry. And I love you.

I didn't expect him to respond right away if he was driving. It wouldn't have surprised me if he waited until that evening to text me back. But when I hadn't heard back from him by the time I fell asleep that night, dread had already made a poisonous nest inside my gut.

My heart was begging me to call him, but my brain insisted on giving him some space.

BLUE

Simone swung from angry to sad to disbelieving to angry again practically with every blink of her eye. I couldn't blame her. Who would have imagined that glorious week of anticipation and celebration ending like this?

By the time we got to my parents' house, she was exhausted from crying. Mom forced her to take a sleeping pill and then put her to bed in Simone's old room before joining me in the kitchen for some coffee. When we sat down with our mugs at the table, she asked me some more questions about John and Sheila.

"What did Tristan say about all this? He must be very upset," Mom said.

"We didn't have a chance to discuss it. You saw me herd you guys out of the room, and I haven't talked to him since." I studied the mug in my hands and furrowed my brows.

"Well, you should call him. I can't imagine how it made him feel to see his brother kissing his ex-wife," Mom continued.

"Mom, he knew. He knew John had slept with Sheila while Tristan was married to her. He caught them in bed together. And he didn't warn Simone off. And then when I found out about it a couple of days ago, I didn't warn her off either. I should have. We both should have," I ranted, telling her about meeting Sheila and then confronting John earlier in the week.

My mom looked at me with sympathy in her eyes. "Honey, do you think Simone would have just accepted your warning and broken it off with John? Have you met Simone?" She smiled.

"Maybe if she'd known, she could have been aware of his continued attraction to Sheila."

"Maybe. But she didn't. And now she does. What happens between her and John is between her and John. I know that's hard. I know you boys think of her as your baby girl. But she'll be okay. She'll come out of this stronger than ever. And maybe she'll get luckier in love next time. We never liked John anyway. So I see this as fate intervening at the last moment."

I sighed. "You're right. But I still don't think I can forgive Tristan."

"Forgive Tristan for what?" she asked.

"For talking me out of telling Simone about John and Sheila," I told her.

"But didn't you confront John yourself?" Mom asked.

"Yes."

"Did Tristan want you to confront John?"

"No," I admitted.

"But you did it anyway," she said.

"Yes. I thought that was the right thing to do."

Mom looked at me in that know-it-all way that moms have. "So, what you're saying is that if you thought talking to Simone was the right thing to do, you would have done it, even if Tristan told you not to?"

Fuck mothers and their motherly logic.

"Talk to him, honey. Call him and tell him you aren't going to let John and Simone's issues come between the two of you."

"What's the point, Mom? I'm leaving the day after tomorrow. Maybe I should let him go. It's not fair to ask him to get into a relationship with someone who lives 5,000 miles away. How could things ever work between us now that his own brother has broken my sister's heart?"

"Pfft. Give Simone more credit than that, Bee. And give Tristan more credit than that. It's awfully funny to hear you describe getting into a relationship as if it's a choice. Seems to me, that ship has sailed. The question now is, are you going to enjoy the ride or jump off before it's even out of the harbor?"

I shrugged and got up to wash out my mug in the sink. "I don't know, Mom."

"Well, honey. Why don't you sleep on it?"

"Do you want me to stay here tonight?" I asked her.

"No, we'll be okay. Why don't you go on home. I'm sure you have packing to finish up."

"Okay. Love you," I said before kissing her on the cheek and taking off.

Walking in to my almost empty apartment was depressing as hell. The only thing that made it worse was seeing two water glasses in the bedroom, Tristan's and mine. I walked over and grabbed them, quickly taking them to the kitchen sink to wash them before thinking too hard about it.

I pulled out my phone and saw that it was dead, so I found my charger in my hastily packed suitcase and plugged it in. The bag with my half-carved wood and Tristan's antique chip carving knife stuck out of the top of the suitcase.

I turned on the television and found a Doris Day movie marathon. My mom had made me watch these movies when I was a kid, and I loved Doris Day. Settling on the sofa with an empty trash can between my legs, I began carving to keep my hands busy so I wouldn't break down and call Tristan before I'd had a chance to think things through.

While I carved I thought about my new job and the goals I had for the company. Despite the incredible opportunity being offered to me, I still felt jaded about the industry. Did I really think I would have the latitude to create the looks I wanted to for the magazines?

I thought about the question Tristan had asked when we first met. What got my creative juices flowing? Sculpture. Carving, welding, making things with my hands and raw materials. What about graphic design?

My favorite kind of graphic design was when I had free reign over what I was designing. With magazines and corporate ads, there were regulations and standards that needed to be met. The times I loved graphic design the most were when I helped a friend out with a small business logo or did charity design work for the animal shelter.

Then my mind wandered to what I wanted from my life. What was I looking for in England? Prestige in my industry? Recognition? A fresh start with new friends and new possibilities?

I definitely looked forward to traveling around Europe when I had time off, but when I pictured those trips, they seemed awfully lonely. Wouldn't they be way more fun with Tristan?

What if Tristan could move to London with me? Assuming he could get Keller to run the vineyard in his absence, I imagined what Tristan would want to do for a living in England. Get back into international law? But he hated it. No, he would never want to leave the outdoors on the vineyard and return to a big city. Hell, even I wasn't looking forward to that part of the move. I enjoyed London as a tourist, but the idea of moving to another big city wasn't thrilling at this stage of my life. And the cost of renting studio space in London? Forget it. Couldn't even fathom it.

When I had finally carved until my hands cramped and what-if'd until my head ached, I stripped and got into bed. And fuck if I didn't smell Tristan on the sheets.

48

TRISTAN

Maybe I could move to London to be with Blue. I could get Keller to take over the vineyard for a few years while Blue and I started a new life together in England. What would I do while Blue was proving himself in his new job, though? He was probably going to be working his ass off and putting in excruciating hours at that level. And I'd be stuck in some London flat waiting for him to come home.

Why wasn't there a good answer? Wasn't it enough that two people found each other and wanted to be together?

I forced myself not to text him again that night. I had spoken to my parents and learned that John and Sheila were actually going to try to be together. It made me feel sick. I wondered how Simone was doing.

And of course I wondered how Blue was doing. I didn't even know where he was. I was alone in a hotel room far away from him, and I realized I wouldn't get back in time to see him before he left for London.

The sound of my phone buzzing woke me up just before 10 a.m. My heart lurched, assuming it was Blue. I grabbed it to read the text.

Blue: Hi. I'm sorry too. I love you too.

**Tristan: Oh thank god, baby. I was worried. How are you? How is
Simone today?**

**Blue: I'm okay. Don't know yet about Simone. I'm on my way to my
parents' in a few minutes. How are things there?**

Tristan: I'm in Florida. Art died yesterday.

My phone rang and I immediately accepted the call.

"Hey, babe." The sound of his voice on the other line was
heavenly.

"Hey," I replied.

"I'm so sorry about Art. What happened? Why so soon?"

"I don't have many of the details but with the cancer and pneumonia, I think he just wore out. My parents are flying out today.
Uncle Henry is beside himself, as you can imagine," I said.

"Do you want me to come down there? When's the funeral?" Blue
asked.

"No. You can't come down here, Blue. You've got a different flight
to catch tomorrow. I don't even know yet when the funeral will be. I'm
heading back over there in a few minutes to help make
arrangements."

"Call me tonight?" he asked.

"Sure thing. Hey, Blue?"

"Yeah?"

"I..." My throat felt tight. "I mean, I..." I couldn't figure out what
words to use to describe this longing I felt. It was like love and loss
and frustration all rolled in to one giant shit ball.

"I know," Blue said in a quiet voice. "I'll talk to you tonight, okay?"

"Yeah, okay."

The day was spent making funeral arrangements and trying to
keep Uncle Henry from flying apart.

When I finally got back to my hotel room late that night, I showered and got in bed. I tried calling Blue but there was no answer. It

was probably just as well. My head was killing me and I was exhausted. I fell asleep quickly and slept soundly.

In the morning I saw I had missed a text from Blue explaining he'd taken Simone to see a movie and had his phone off. It was still too early to call him, so I dressed and met my parents for breakfast in the hotel restaurant.

We spent the day at Art and Henry's, going through Art's things and helping Uncle Henry deal with more details. It was so obvious once we were at the house that Henry and Art had been partners. I felt like a complete idiot for not having known, and I was overcome with grief for what Henry must have been going through.

If I felt the way I did about Blue after only a measly week, I couldn't imagine what Art and Henry had together after fifty years and what it would feel like to lose it.

Around lunchtime, Blue called. It was 9 a.m. in California and he would be leaving for the airport in a few hours.

"Sorry I missed your call last night," Blue said as I stepped into the backyard in search of privacy.

"It's okay. How's Simone?"

"Bitter and sarcastic. But Mom reminded me that everything happens for a reason so maybe this means she'll find someone better suited for her in the long run."

"I hope so. John's an idiot," I griped.

"No shit. How are you with all of this? I didn't think to ask."

"What do you mean? I'm pissed. I'm sad for Simone."

Blue sighed. "No, I mean John and Sheila. Together. How does that make you feel?"

"So angry. Not because of Sheila and me, but for Simone. She wasted two years of her life with him. Two years she could have been with someone who truly loved and respected her. She deserved better than that."

"I agree. But if John and Simone hadn't planned their wedding, you and I would have never met," Blue said.

Silence while I let that sink in.

"Well, fuck. I'm not quite selfless enough to wish for that when you put it that way," I admitted.

Blue laughed, the sound like nectar. "Me neither. Couple of selfish bastards, aren't we?"

I laughed and agreed.

"How's Henry holding up?" he asked.

"It's so sad, Blue. They were so clearly a couple. I can't imagine what Henry's going through right now. The whole thing makes me so sad. They were together but weren't able to share it with everyone. And now Henry is grieving the loss of his partner while Keller's mom is acting like she's Art's only family.

"I've always thought about how many years they spent working their asses off at the vineyard only to have it never really thrive. But shit. I think it finally dawned on me that they didn't care about being the best winemakers. The vineyard was their way to be together. It wasn't about the achievement. It was about them building a life together that made them both happy," I explained.

Blue agreed. "They had their own little slice of heaven and were able to live and work together. Hopefully Henry will hold those memories close. Does he have people in Florida to keep an eye on him when you all return home?"

"I think so, but Keller is making sure. I think I'll ask Henry if he might want to move back to the vineyard. Just so he knows that's an option. I'd love to have him, and the apartment upstairs at the estate house is still vacant since they moved out," I thought out loud.

"That sounds like a great idea, Tris," Blue agreed.

"Are you all packed up?" I asked gently.

"Yes. I said goodbye to everyone last night at my parents' house and the car is coming to take me to the airport in two hours."

"Good," I said, trying to be normal despite the tightness in my throat. "You're going to have a busy week hitting the ground running before you've had a chance to adjust to the eight-hour time difference. You're not going to know your days from nights."

"Maybe that's a good thing," he said. "Make these two weeks go by faster. If I'm either working or sleeping I won't have as much time for moping."

I smiled. "Well, maybe you can set aside a little time for Skyping. I'll make it worth your while."

"Is that right? Hmmm, I might be able to pencil you in for a few late-night sessions. Let's see… if it's 10 p.m. my time in London, and I'm in bed missing your sexy-ass body, it will be 2 p.m. your time in Napa and you can give me a live sex show from your office computer in the estate house. Kinky."

"I can always take my lunch break at the cabin. Unless you want Keller to walk in. Not sure how well that would go over."

Blue made gagging noises. "Eww, gross. No Skype threesomes. I'm not good at sharing."

I laughed. "Me neither."

"I'm assuming you're not in a nice private hotel room naked right now, correct?" he asked.

"Correct. I'm at Henry's house, standing in the backyard."

"Damn. Well, then I'd better let you go before this goes down the dirty path."

I reluctantly agreed, but my stomach began twisting in knots at the thought that I was getting ready to say goodbye to Blue before he got on a plane to England.

"I miss you," I said.

"And I love the fuck out of you. Take good care of yourself for the next two weeks, okay? Rest up and carbo-load. You're going to need stamina for your visit."

"You take care of yourself too, baby. And let me know when you get there safely. I'm going to hang up really quickly before I lose my shit, okay?" I asked.

He disconnected before I could and I exhaled a shaky breath.

49

BLUE

When I got to London, I barely had time to settle in to my temporary executive accommodations before I was inundated with work. Emails, meeting requests, and layout approvals all waited on my new desk first thing Tuesday morning. I met more people than I could remember names, and I worked straight through until after 9 p.m. every day that week.

The work was familiar, it was just more. More magazines, more staff, and more stress. Besides the additional workload, the biggest change was working on magazines besides the ones in the fitness industry. Now I was in charge of fashion magazines, teen magazines, home magazines, and anything else you could think of. Each one had their own creative director who reported to me, and I spent the first week meeting with most of them to get the lay of the land.

When Tristan and I spoke and texted, I kept it light. He got through Art's funeral and made it back to the vineyard. When he got home, there was a package waiting there from me. It said to call me before opening so he Skyped me Friday night to open it with me.

Seeing his beautiful face on the screen was enough to make my eyes sting. I couldn't wait to see that face in person in just one more week.

"Hey you," I said, smiling big.

When he saw my image come up on his screen, his smile went into big fat dimple mode. The best ever.

"Hey, sexy boyfriend. TGIF," he said. "How was work today?"

"Busy and interesting. What about you?"

"Definitely busy. I wasn't thinking with my brain when I booked that ticket to England. It's almost harvest time. I wish you could be here to see it in a couple of weeks. I'll have to send you some pictures."

"That sounds like a lot of work. Do you need to change the trip?" I asked.

His face darkened. "No fucking way, but," he sighed, "yeah, maybe."

I laughed, trying to cover up the squeeze in my chest. "Okay, just think about it. We'll figure it out. Did you get the package I sent you?"

He lifted it up for me to see. "Right here."

"You can open it now," I told him.

Tristan ripped into the package and took out the little item I'd finished carving for him. It was a small likeness of Piper leaping to catch a frisbee. It was carved with one back leg still on the ground so I could include a base to keep the statue upright.

Tristan's face lit up in wonder as he examined it. Then he looked into the camera. "Baby, oh my god, this is incredible. I love it!"

I smiled. "Good, I'm happy with how it turned out."

He kept looking at it and smiling, noticing small details like one floppy ear and the one area of fur on her back that stuck up in a cowlick.

"Blue, thank you," he said, holding the carving reverently.

"Okay, enough about that. It looks like you're in your cabin. Are you for sure alone?"

He looked at me with a side-eye of suspicion. "Yes, why?"

I stood up and began to strip, noticing his eyes widen until I was sure his eyeballs were going to fall right out.

When he realized what I was doing, he smirked. "What, no song this time? It's awfully quiet."

"Watchu want? 'Hot In Herre' by Nelly?" I teased.

"I'm not picky, but listening to you sing is a guaranteed hard-on for me."

"Baby," I said, pulling my shirt off and moving my hands down my chest and abs to my belt. "Are you telling me you don't have a hard-on already?"

He stood up and all I could see was the tent pole in his pants. He began unbuttoning and unzipping, and I forgot what I was saying.

Before I got to see the goodies, he leaned his head down to peer at me sideways. "You first," he said with a grin.

I finished undoing my pants and let them drop. I was wearing the black version of the little red jock that had excited him so much previously.

Tristan groaned. "Why are you five fucking thousand miles away right now? You're killing me."

I turned around and wiggled my ass for him before grinning into the camera again.

"Tell me you didn't wear those to work," he growled.

"I didn't wear them to work," I lied.

"Liar."

"Okay, fine. But I wore them to work so every time I remembered I had them on, I'd think of you and showing them to you tonight."

"Good answer. Show them to me again."

"Nope, your turn."

Tristan didn't make it back to the office that afternoon.

The following day, on Saturday, I forced myself out into the city to enjoy the beautiful September day. A walk through Hyde Park, lunch at a busy pub, and some retail therapy on Oxford Street had brightened my mood until Tristan called to tell me he'd have to change the trip afterall.

"Blue, I can't find any way around it. Keller is still tied up in Florida and the grapes are ready to be harvested. There is no one else here I trust enough to take charge," he said. I could hear the disappointment in his voice.

"I understand, Tris. We'll just postpone it a few weeks. Change the ticket to when you think you'll be able to make it and let me know, okay?" I tried so hard to project calm when really I wanted to scream at him for buying a damned vineyard in the first place. I knew how ridiculous that was, but I was feeling raw with missing him.

The following week was a complete bitch. I didn't meet the CEO until Tuesday morning because he had been in Dubai for a conference. When we finally did sit down, I shared with him some of my ideas for small changes in a few of the underperforming publications.

He seemed supportive of my ideas but as the week progressed, I realized he was a pro at making you think he was supporting you but really he was manipulating you around to his way of thinking. It was truly masterful.

Add to that frustration was Tristan's and my inability to connect. When I was free, he was out in the fields or sleeping. When he was free, I was in meetings or sleeping. I began to feel untethered by the inevitable pulling apart of a relationship that was too new to bear the strain of long distance.

During a meeting during my third week in London, the CEO told me about the new focus of one of the teen boy magazines to be more masculine. More outdoors, more sports, and less "girly shite." I balked at his input and asked him why he wanted to make the shift.

"What's the point in having both girl and boy magazines if they're each going to have the same things in them? As long as we include fashion and emotional content in the boy ones, and sports and science in the girl ones, they might as well be the same fuckin' mags. As far as I'm concerned, if a boy wants to read about girly shit and take mood quizzes, he can very well buy the girl magazine."

I sat there trying not to gape at his ignorance. Was he seriously intending to make the girl magazine more vapid and the boy one less human?

"With all due respect, won't that contribute to the gender stereotypes the younger generations are trying to fight against?" I argued.

"Blue, don't honestly tell me you care more about our readers than our advertisers. You know what percentage of our income comes from paid subscribers? Very little. Do you know how much comes from gendered ads? Boatloads. It's not about the readers; it's about who gives us the money," he said.

And that was when I returned to my office and typed up my resignation letter. I gave them a standard two weeks' notice.

Understandably, the CEO was beyond livid. The only reason he allowed me to work out my final weeks was to help put some issues to bed in time to make print deadlines.

I kept the information about my resignation a secret from everyone at home, including Tristan. I wanted to talk to him about it in person to make sure that he didn't feel pressure because of my spontaneous decision.

50

TRISTAN

The weeks without Blue were brutal. The harvest took up all of my time and energy and by the time I stumbled back to my cabin each night, it was the middle of the night in London.

When I woke up each morning and tried to call Blue, he was inevitably unavailable in a meeting. It was never urgent enough for me to justify interrupting him, but by the end of that second week, my nerves were shot from not being able to hear his voice or see his image on my laptop screen.

During the second weekend, we finally connected. Things between us were awkward and strained. It was like we needed some time to find our rhythm again. I didn't like the feeling. Maybe if I could touch him, it would be different.

"Baby, I'm coming to London in three weeks," I told him. "The harvest should be done and Keller will be back."

"Thank god," Blue sighed. "I'm horny as shit."

I barked out a laugh. "Is that all I'm good for?"

His grin widened on the screen. "Nah, you make a mean butternut squash soup too."

I shot him the bird. "Just for that, I'm not getting naked for you today."

The hurt look on his face just made me laugh harder.

"Kidding. But really, I can't get naked today. My parents are on their way over to take me to lunch," I explained.

"Fuck," Blue said. "So, three weeks, huh?"

"Yep, three weeks."

There was an awkward moment heavy with unspoken words. We just stared at each other across the miles.

"I miss you, Tristan," Blue finally said.

I let out a big sigh. "Yeah. Me too, Bee."

The following week we had the same missed connections, but this time they began to feel normal. It was unnerving that I expected not to be able to talk to him each day, and the feeling began to crawl all over me until I couldn't stand it anymore. I had to go to him. No more waiting around for the situation at the vineyard to be just right.

It was a Saturday when I decided just to head to the airport and catch a flight to London. I packed my bag and made arrangements for Keller to watch Piper. He had just returned a few days before from Florida, and I apologized for throwing him directly into the fire of managing everything as soon as he got back.

My nerves were jangling with anticipation. Would Blue be mad at me for showing up unannounced? Did he have plans? Would he even be around? I'd gotten his address from his mom and asked her not to tell him my plans. She sounded thrilled that I was doing something "so romantic." I wanted to tell her it wasn't romantic so much as desperate.

Before I left for the airport, I was honestly in a foul mood. I'd already waited four weeks to see Blue, and I just wanted to feel his arms around me. I kept daydreaming about arriving at his London flat and spending the rest of the day and night naked in his arms.

After taking a last look around the cabin to make sure I hadn't forgotten anything, I heard a knock at the door.

"Yeah? Who is it?" I called, grabbing my keys from the kitchen counter.

"Strip-O-Gram."

The familiar voice of Blue Marian was too good to be true. I opened the door and stared at the man on my front porch. My man. Here. In California.

"What?" I cried, launching for his face. "What are you doing here?" I kissed him like crazy before giving him a chance to answer me. I could feel him smiling beneath my lips.

I pulled him in for a tight hug, and he instinctively put his face in my neck. Oh god, that felt amazing. Like home. The only home I ever wanted.

His lips were soft on my neck and I relished the familiar scent of him. I wanted to cry with relief, but I was too happy.

"What are you doing here?" I repeated, pulling back just enough to look at his face.

"I had to see you," Blue said with a grin. "And, as much as I'd like to jump your bones right now, I'd feel way better if I could take a quick shower first," he told me.

"Can I take one with you?" I teased, as if the answer would ever be no.

"Ohdeargod yes please." We attacked each other, undressing and kissing and stumbling to the bathroom. My hands were all over his skin and his did the same to me.

After we got into the shower and the warm spray was rinsing the airplane stink off of him, Blue immediately dropped to his knees and took my cock in his mouth. I braced my hands on the tile wall and let out a moan of appreciation.

"Fuck, I missed that mouth," I said, reaching down to stroke the side of his face. He smiled around my dick and continued sucking for all he was worth.

It didn't take long before I was gasping for breath and crying out his name as my come shot down this throat. After I recovered my wits, I reached down and pulled him up into a kiss before turning him around to face the spray and slicking up his hard-on with soap. I jacked him slowly at first, using one arm across his chest to hold him to me.

Blue's hand came back to grab my hip and the other reached

behind him to the back of my head. It reminded me of how we'd danced once, and the memory traveled to my worn-out balls.

I stroked and pulled him and cupped and tugged until his hips were moving in the same rhythm. Then I bent him forward to brace his hands on the shower while I lowered myself and spread his cheeks. My mouth found his rim and licked around it, enjoying the sounds of his curses and stuttered breaths.

"*Tristan*," he cried. "*Tristan*."

"I'm right here baby. I've got you."

I sucked and probed with my mouth until he was whimpering and begging. I loved it when he got that way.

Soapy fingers replaced my tongue inside of him and I reached around to jack him at the same time. His hips bucked forward to fuck one of my hands and then backwards to fuck the other. It was so damned hot.

I leaned my face over his shoulder and brushed my lips against his ear. "That's it, gorgeous. So beautiful when you let go."

He came with a scream and a clench as white streams landed on the shower floor and my hand.

After he recovered his breathing, I washed him gently and washed myself before wrapping him up in a big towel and finding one for myself.

We dried off and collapsed in bed, immediately rolling toward each other to entangle our limbs together.

I kissed his forehead and closed my eyes, content to drift off for a few minutes with this sweet man in my arms.

"I quit my job."

My eyes flew open and I nearly knocked Blue over when I scrambled up to sit against the headboard.

"You what?" I exclaimed.

His face was a mixture of excitement and nerves. "I quit my job. I'm home for good."

It was too good to be true. I was dreaming.

"Wait," I said, shaking my head. "That can't be right. You said work this week was really good."

"It was really good because it was my last week."

"I don't understand," I said. "What are you going to do?"

"Well," Blue said. "That kind of depends on you."

My heart slammed even harder in my chest.

"Anything baby, you name it. Whatever you want to do, we'll figure out a way. But you need to be sure. I don't want you to regret it or resent me later for this, Blue."

"I won't. The job wasn't for me. It wasn't really what I wanted to do. I want to sculpt. And in the meantime, I can do freelance graphic design from anywhere to make some money."

"Blue, I can support you. Move in with me. Come stay with me at the vineyard and sculpt here. I already started converting one of the barns into a welding studio for you," I admitted.

His face lit up. "Really? You did that for me?"

I nodded enthusiastically, and he laughed.

"Cocky motherfucker aren't you? Were you so sure I'd end up here one day?" Blue asked.

"I was hopeful," I grinned.

Blue climbed onto my lap and put his hands on my face. "I would love to move in with you if you're sure."

"I've never been more sure of anything in my entire life, Blue Marian." I said before kissing him deeply.

EPILOGUE - BLUE

It was Christmas Eve and we had invited all our closest family for a sit-down dinner at the vineyard. The main dining room in the estate house was decorated for the holiday and the staff had set out beautiful china rimmed in gold and red for the occasion. Glass lanterns dotted the room and reflected off of the big windows lining two walls. The vineyard Christmas tree was fat and happy in one corner with twinkling lights sparkling off the ornaments.

The wine flowed and I looked around at all the happy faces enjoying the evening. Everyone was staying a couple of nights in the lodge and having a big Christmas morning breakfast and present exchange the following day. I hoped it was the first of many Marian-Alexander holidays together at the vineyard.

Noticeably missing was Tristan's brother, John, but I suspected he had stayed away out of respect for my family. Simone was there along with all of my brothers, including Jamie, who had flown in to be with the family over Christmas. One of the desserts being served that night was an eggnog version of baked Alaska in his honor.

I caught Tristan's eye from across the room as he visited his parents' table. He smiled and winked at me and my heart nearly exploded. Those twinkling eyes reached right into my chest and squeezed my heart every fucking time.

I had transitioned into my new life on the vineyard with relative ease. Freelance graphic design jobs were coming in faster than I could handle, and we had talked about hiring more staff and building offices somewhere on the property for the design business since my small office next to Tristan's in the estate house was too small for even an assistant.

After only a few days of being back from England, I'd tackled the welding studio Tristan had started in one of the barns. I set everything up the way I wanted it and began working on some large-scale projects I'd been dreaming about for years. Because of the scale of the projects and having to build back up my confidence, my progress was slower than I'd hoped. Tristan kept having to remind me to enjoy the process and stop worrying about the end result.

Piper had officially shifted her allegiance and considered me her personal property. Her days were spent by my side and she particularly loved lounging in the sun in the open doorway to my studio when I was sculpting. Tristan didn't seem to mind. He said it was nice knowing I was being watched over, and he couldn't blame the girl for her obsession with me. However, he drew the line at her sleeping with me in our bed.

When it seemed like everyone had finished their dinner, Tristan clinked a spoon on his water glass to gather everyone's attention.

"We are going to have dessert and coffee in the cellar by candlelight since it's a special night. If you don't know the way, just follow Keller to the stairs and Blue and I will join everyone in a minute."

After the room cleared, I walked up to Tristan and put my arms around him.

"You weren't hoping for a quickie in your office before joining them, were you?" I teased. "Because I'm totally on board with that."

He laughed. "This morning's flip-fuck wasn't good enough to tide you over till later?"

"Mmm, it was good. Don't get me wrong. But you look pretty hot when you use the lord-of-the-manor voice to get everyone to do your bidding." I leaned in to kiss him, running my tongue along his lower lip before latching on with a gentle clamp of my teeth.

He pulled back and put on his serious face. "Then you'd better do my bidding, boy."

I laughed and headed for the staircase to the cellar after swatting his tight, perfect ass.

He was right behind me when we entered the candlelit room to see all our friends and family standing there staring at us expectantly with champagne glasses at the ready. I turned to look at Tristan with a questioning glance, and then that motherfucker got down on one knee.

My hand came up to my mouth and I felt myself blush to the tips of my ears. No way. *No fucking way.*

Tristan held my hand in his and used his other one to gesture above us at the small antique bells strung all around the room.

"Baby, you told me that when someone found the right person, they would know it by the thousand tiny bells ringing. Mine started ringing last summer when you told me I was a damned fine kisser for a straight guy." Laughs broke out around the room. "You are the sweetest, most loving man I know. Every day with you is an adventure full of laughter and exploration. I want to spend the rest of my life showing you how grateful I am to know you and love you. Will you please marry me so I can finally call you my husband?"

Tears streamed down my face as he smiled up at me, his own eyes brimming.

"Do you promise to still refer to me as your partner every once in a while just for fun?" I asked.

"No, absolutely not. Now answer my fucking question, beautiful." He laughed.

I nodded enthusiastically and launched myself at him, nearly knocking him over as everyone broke out in cheers and clinked champagne glasses. We kissed as Tristan struggled to stand up under the onslaught. After the kiss, I buried my face in his neck and he brushed his stubble against my ear.

"Love you so much," he whispered into my ear.

I pulled my head back and looked up at him. "I will love you for the rest of my life, Tristan Alexander."

Later that night when we were back at the cabin undressing each other, I unbuttoned Tristan's dress shirt and burst out laughing when I saw the T-shirt he had under it. Instead of a plain white undershirt, he had put on my Katy Perry parody T-shirt.

I kissed a boy and I liked it.

~

Up next is Taming Teddy! *Follow Jamie Marian to Alaska where he meets a moody wildlife photographer.*

Want to find out what happened to Brad (Jeremy's date) and Keller (Tristan's co-worker)? Be sure to check out Made Marian Shorts, *a short story collection featuring some of your favorite Made Marian side characters!*

LETTER FROM LUCY

Dear Reader,

Thank you for reading my debut novel, *Borrowing Blue*. Blue and Tristan continue to hold a special place in my heart, and I can't wait for you to read about the rest of the Marian family.

In the next book, Blue's brother has to deal with a bossy wildlife photographer named Teddy in the wilds of Alaska. *Taming Teddy* and the rest of the Made Marian books are out now! All Lucy Lennox novels can be read on their own but are more fun as a series.

Please take a moment to write a review of this book on the site where you found it as well as Goodreads. Reviews can make all of the difference in helping a book show up in book searches.

Feel free to stop by www.LucyLennox.com and drop me a line or visit me on social media. To see inspiration photographs for all of my novels, visit my Pinterest boards.

Finally, I have a fantastic reader group on Facebook. Come join us for exclusive content, early cover reveals, hot pics, and a whole lotta fun. Lucy's Lair can be found on Facebook.

Happy reading!

Lucy

ABOUT THE AUTHOR

Lucy Lennox is a mother of three sarcastic kids. Born and raised in the southeast, she now resides outside of Atlanta finally putting good use to that English Lit degree.

Lucy enjoys naps, pizza, and procrastinating. She is married to someone who is better at math than romance but who makes her laugh every single day and is the best dancer in the history of ever.

She stays up way too late each night reading M/M romance because that shit is hot.

For more information and to stay updated about future releases, please sign up for Lucy's author newsletter here.

Connect with Lucy on social media:
www.LucyLennox.com
Lucy@LucyLennox.com

WANT MORE?

Join Lucy's Lair
Get Lucy's New Release Alerts
Like Lucy on Facebook
Follow Lucy on BookBub
Follow Lucy on Amazon
Follow Lucy on Instagram
Follow Lucy on Pinterest

Other books by Lucy:
Made Marian Series
Forever Wilde Series
Aster Valley Series
Twist of Fate Series with Sloane Kennedy
After Oscar Series with Molly Maddox
Licking Thicket Series with May Archer
Virgin Flyer
Say You'll Be Nine

Visit Lucy's website at www.LucyLennox.com for a comprehensive list of titles, audio samples, freebies, suggested reading order, and more!

www.ingramcontent.com/pod-product-compliance
Lightning Source LLC
Chambersburg PA
CBHW061319190726
48288CB00002B/579

9 781954 857001